Game of Cones

Cynthia Baxter

KENSINGTON BOOKS
www.kensingtonbooks.com

KENSINGTON BOOKS are published by

Kensington Publishing Corp.
119 West 40th Street
New York, NY 10018

All Kensington titles, imprints and distributed lines are available at special quantity discounts for bulk purchases for sales promotion, premiums, fund-raising, educational or institutional use.

Special book excerpts or customized printings can also be created to fit specific needs. For details, write or phone the office of the Kensington Special Sales Manager: Kensington Publishing Corp., 119 West 40th Street, New York, NY, 10018. Attn. Special Sales Department. Phone: 1-800-221-2647.

Library of Congress Card Catalogue Number: 2020939479

Kensington and the K logo Reg. U.S. Pat. & TM Off.

ISBN-13: 978-1-4967-2682-7
ISBN-10: 1-4967-2682-0
First Kensington Hardcover Edition: December 2020

ISBN-13: 978-1-4967-2684-1 (ebook)
ISBN-10: 1-4967-2684-7 (ebook)

10 9 8 7 6 5 4 3 2 1

Printed in the United States of America

Game of
Cones

Chapter 1

In August 1850, the women's magazine *Godey's Lady's Book* said that a party without ice cream would be like "breakfast without bread or a dinner without a roast."

—*Everybody Loves Ice Cream: The Whole Scoop on America's Favorite Treat by Shannon Jackson Arnold*

"This isn't exactly my idea of a romantic getaway," Jake mumbled, peering out the rain-splattered window of my truck.

I leaned closer to the steering wheel, struggling to focus on the curving road ahead of me. Given the sheeting rain, the ominously dark afternoon sky, the *Wizard of Oz*–style wind, and the thick mist that was threatening to turn into serious fog, I had to agree that this certainly wasn't what either of us had expected.

The idea of spending a long weekend at the Mohawk Mountain Resort, an old-fashioned lakeside hideaway nestled in the Catskill Mountains just thirty miles away from our hometown, had sounded positively idyllic when I'd first gotten an email from the resort's general manager a few months earlier. Growing up in the Hudson Valley, I had heard plenty about the historic hotel that had been a popular retreat since the mid-1800s. Yet I'd never actually had a chance to stay at the sprawling resort, enjoying its unique style of rustic luxury and pretending that I was living in another era.

True, when I was a teenager I'd hiked around the 30,000-acre property a few times. I had had the pleasure of tromping through the woods and across clearings and over ridges, making my way along trails with colorful names like Pine Needle Walk and Mountain Vista Ridge and Rocky Road—a name which these days, as an ice cream empress, I found especially endearing.

But that was just the grounds that surrounded Mohawk. The glorious stone and wood building that constituted the actual resort, perched high atop a mountain as if it was the preserve's centerpiece, had merely served as a distant backdrop during my day trips. After all, while the outdoor area was open to the public, the 250-room hotel and its reported Old World luxury had been reserved for guests only. And those aforementioned guests were required to have some pretty impressive credit card limits in order to bask in its splendors.

So when I'd unexpectedly received an invitation from the hotel's general manager, Merle Moody, I had literally whooped with joy. In fact, I had decided to say yes even before I'd read her entire email.

In her note, she had explained that Mohawk frequently conducted theme weekends as a way of attracting visitors during the off-season. Past theme weekends had ranged from jazz workshops to yoga-and-meditation retreats to storytelling marathons. She told me that she was getting in touch with me because she knew I had an ice cream emporium, the Lickety Splits Ice Cream Shoppe, located nearby. In mid-November, she was interested in having Mohawk host a weekend of lectures, demonstrations, and hands-on workshops built around the theme of ice cream. Payment would be minimal, but the gig would give me a chance to combine work and play in a scenic spot.

The general manager went on to say she wanted to call this theme weekend We All Scream for Ice Cream. She hoped I'd offer classes on topics like Making Exotic Ice Cream Flavors at Home and Thirty-Three Toppings to Make Your Ice Cream Sensational. Ms. Moody noted that mid-November was a particularly slow time, so she was anxious to offer something exceptionally upbeat.

I wasn't surprised that business at the resort was sluggish at this time of the year. My ice cream shop had also been experiencing a dramatic slowdown. And all I had to do was look out the window to understand why.

"Think of it this way," I told Jake as we chugged along in my red pickup truck. "You and I will be tucked away inside a cozy mountain retreat, sipping hot chocolate and eating ice cream in front of a roaring fireplace. We won't care at all about the storm raging outside."

"I was hoping to do some hiking," Jake said. As I glanced over at him, I saw that he was squinting as he gazed out the window. I got the impression he was wondering if somehow he could will the rain away. "And according to the website you can go canoeing on the lake. They have rowboats and paddleboats and kayaks, too. And paddle boarding, which is something I always thought would be great to try, since you actually stand up as you skim the surface of the water. Then there's swimming in the lake. And fishing, of course . . ."

He let out a deep sigh. I knew exactly what that sigh meant: That given the storm raging all around us, none of those options was going to be even close to feasible.

Even though I was already pretty bummed out over the weather being so horrid, Jake's dismay over the way it was ruining our plans was making me feel even worse. While his purpose in tagging along was supposedly to serve as my "assistant" over the course of the weekend, there was a lot more behind my decision to bring him with me.

He and I had recently rekindled our old romance, one that had started when we were back in high school. While our relationship had been rudely interrupted by fifteen years of having no contact whatsoever, fate seemed to have brought us together once again. The two of us were still feeling our way, trying to decide whether or not we could make a go of it now that we had been given another chance.

My sense was that Jake had few doubts about the two of us being a couple once again. In fact, he had been the one who'd pushed for it. Not long after he and I had accidentally run into each other after our long separation, he had made it clear that he'd be happy to pick up where we'd left off. And I had finally agreed that our relationship deserved another chance.

Now that we were actually back in that relationship, however, I continued to wrestle with uncertainty about whether or not I had made the right choice. I thought I had forgiven him for the painful and abrupt way our high school romance had ended. But deep down, I still wasn't 100 percent convinced.

But there was more to it. I wasn't sure about whether or not I even *wanted* to become involved with anyone at this stage of my life. I was working long, exhausting hours as I struggled to get my own business off the ground. Lickety Splits was still brand-new, having opened only six months earlier. Running a retail store that specialized in homemade gourmet ice cream was a huge change from working at a public relations firm in New York City. And while I loved being my own boss, the demands of running my fledgling enterprise practically single-handedly were turning out to be a lot more daunting than I'd ever dreamed.

There had been plenty of other huge changes in my life,

too. After a decade and a half of being pretty much on my own, I was back in my hometown, Wolfert's Roost, living under my grandmother's roof. While this was the house that I'd pretty much grown up in, a wonderful Victorian that I truly loved, being back there was still a major adjustment. Cohabitating with my grandmother as an adult, rather than as a child, gave me delightful companionship but less independence. And because I'd moved back so I could help Grams as she aged, it also meant that I'd taken on more responsibility.

Then there was the fact that suddenly I was also looking after my eighteen-year-old niece, Emma, who had moved in with Grams and me unexpectedly. She was lively and strong and very much her own person, but it was still my job to serve as a sort of mother figure to her.

I'm not saying that I was unhappy about my new situation. It was just, well, *different*—not to mention demanding, complicated, absorbing, taxing, and at times absolutely exhausting. And the idea of adding Jake Pratt into the mix sometimes struck me as one challenge too many.

But as I drove along, I reminded myself that this wasn't the best time to be thinking about my ambivalence about my relationship with the man sitting beside me.

"The weather can't be this bad the whole time we're there, can it?" I said.

I had just turned off the main road onto a considerably narrower one. It was marked by a rather crude wooden sign with the hand-painted words MOHAWK MOUNTAIN RESORT and a big arrow. But I already knew the answer to my own question. I'd been checking the ten-day forecast all week. Not only was rain predicted for the entire weekend ahead. The torrential rain, fog, and wind that already surrounded us had been labeled a nor'easter, a serious storm that's almost as bad as a hurricane.

As if to answer the question I'd just asked, at that very moment a tree branch flew into the windshield with a loud bang, making me jump. Instantly my heart leaped into high gear as adrenaline coursed through my body.

"Whoa!" Jake cried. "This is going from bad to worse! Hey, you don't suppose they'll cancel the workshop, do you?"

I shook my head, meanwhile making sure to keep my eyes glued to the road ahead. By this point I was pretty sure the mist could officially be called fog. That was because I could only see about ten feet in front of me.

"I got an email from Merle Moody early this morning," I told him. "You remember me mentioning her, don't you? She's the general manager of the resort and the person I've been in contact with all along. She said that Mohawk hasn't ever shut down, or even cancelled a program, since the day it first opened in 1868 as a simple tavern with four guest rooms."

"It was nice of her to check in with you," Jake commented.

"Actually," I said, "from the tone of her email, I got the feeling she wasn't trying to reassure me as much as she was making it clear that I'd better not be thinking of cancelling."

Or maybe I was just being too sensitive, I thought. The wording of the general manager's email had struck me as crisp. Cold, even. But I told myself that the feeling I got, that she was ordering me to show up rather than simply being matter-of-fact, was probably related more to my own apprehensions about the weekend ahead than anything else.

Jake and I were both silent as we continued up a road that was quickly becoming steeper, narrower, and more twisting. We were already surrounded by a dense growth of trees, mighty maples and white-barked birches and towering evergreens so dense that they practically formed a barricade. The fog was growing thicker with every turn in the road. Yet even through the hovering mist's dense grayness, I could make out signs printed with warnings about deer, and then wild turkeys, crossing the road.

"Funny, I don't recall this road being so scary," I finally remarked, hoping I wouldn't encounter any wildlife along the way. "Then again, the last time I was here was when I was about sixteen. Willow and I drove up on a Saturday in October. I was so excited to be spending the entire day with my best friend! It was positively thrilling that the two of us were going off on an adventure all by ourselves.

"I remember that the air was brisk and the leaves were absolutely gorgeous," I went on, feeling as if I was actually going back in time. "They were blazing with color, bright red and orange and gold . . . It was one of those perfect autumn days that make you glad you live in the Hudson Valley. Willow and I spent the whole day hiking and taking pictures. I also remember that we brought along a fabulous picnic lunch that Grams had packed up for us. She made the best chicken salad, with walnuts and grapes and celery. And she'd baked tiny chocolate chip cookies that were so much fun to eat . . ."

"That sounds really nice," Jake commented. From his wistful tone, I got the feeling that the rest of that sentence, best left unspoken, was something along the lines of, "unlike now."

We drove on, my teeth clenched so hard that my jaw started to ache as I slowly veered around one treacherous turn after another. At least there were no deer or wild turkeys flinging themselves into the road. Unlike us, they were apparently much too smart to venture outside on a day like today.

Jake and I traveled higher and higher up into the mountains, with clouds of fog still drifting past. At times we could see just how perilous the road was, while at other times we could scarcely see what was in front of us at all. Frankly, I didn't know which was worse.

And then the fog suddenly cleared. In the distance I could

see the resort's expansive main building looming up ahead of us like a mirage.

In all the photographs I'd seen, as well as in my own memory, Mohawk had seemed like paradise. The hotel, with its jaw-dropping backdrop of mountains and forests and a gigantic lake, had looked palatial. The resort was huge, a jumble of half a dozen different wings and extensions jutting off the original wood-and-stone building that stood at the center. The newer parts were painted a muted shade of apple green that blended in with the natural setting. As for the oldest section, it remained dark brown, with the same rough-hewn wooden shingles and craggy gray stone walls it had always had. The wooden porch that lined the original building, overlooking the lake and the mountains beyond, had been duplicated in the newer sections as well, creating a cohesive look to what might otherwise appear a bit chaotic.

In the photographs, the lake was invariably sparkling in the bright midday sun. Happy guests in canoes and rowboats cheerfully waved to each other. Other guests, also smiling, strolled along the trails, looking as if there was no place else in the entire world they would rather be.

Today, however, Mohawk reminded me of a haunted house. Hill House, perhaps, the eerie mansion that was featured in the classic black-and-white horror film *The Haunting*. That's the movie in which the actress Julie Harris sees throbbing walls with eyes and hears children crying until she's driven to near insanity, rushing out onto a road where she's accidentally run over by—

Stop! I told myself. *There's nothing the least bit creepy about the Mohawk Mountain Resort! It's a luxurious, historic hotel with a fine reputation and a top chef and a fireplace in every room. And you're going to enjoy every single minute you're there.*

Three seconds later, I heard a tremendous boom and felt the earth shake.

"What was that?" I shrieked, stomping down on the brake and bringing my truck to a complete stop with a jolt.

Jake had already turned around in his seat, trying to see out the back window. "It sounds like it was behind us," he said, "but I can't see anything from here. I'll have to get out."

"Don't get out!" I cried. I had visions of never seeing him again. I figured that like Julie Harris, he'd meet up with some terrible fate, perhaps one that involved evil deer or malicious wild turkeys.

"I'll just take a quick look around." He had already opened the door and was climbing out of the truck, pulling up his hood in a feeble attempt at protecting himself from the pelting rain.

A few seconds later, he was back, hurling himself into the truck and splattering me with so much water that I might as well have gone outside with him. His light brown hair was soaked. So were his shirt, his pants, and from the looks of things, everything else he had on as well.

"A tree fell," he announced grumpily.

"Is *that* all," I replied, relieved.

"You don't understand," he said. "A *big* tree. A *really* big tree. With a thick trunk. Like a five-foot-wide trunk. And it fell right across the road."

I'd barely had a chance to digest his words before he turned to me and explained, "From the looks of things, nobody's getting in or out of here for a very long time."

"You mean we're *stuck* up here?" I cried. Suddenly, the idea of spending a few days in a lovely but remote mountain resort struck me as terrifying. I tried to remind myself that nothing much had changed, that this had been the plan all along. But somehow, having no choice in the matter put a very different cast on the situation.

"Maybe it's not that bad," Jake said. "If a work crew came in here with some electric saws, they could probably clear the road. If they worked on it for a while, anyway."

I tried to believe him. But I definitely got the feeling that he was just trying to make me feel better.

I started driving again, my heart even heavier than before as we continued on our way. Whatever enthusiasm about the weekend ahead that had lingered even after the horrendous weather had put such a damper on things—pun entirely intended—had by now fizzled out completely.

As the big house got closer, I wondered how many people would manage to make it up the mountain for the theme weekend.

Jake must have been thinking the same thing. "Even if they have to cancel the ice cream workshops," he said with forced cheerfulness, "we can still have that romantic getaway we've been planning."

I looked over at him and forced myself to smile. "Candlelit dinners, cuddling in front of a roaring fire . . . yes, we certainly can."

I tried to hold on to that thought as I drove into the circular driveway in front of Mohawk, the uneven cobblestones that paved it making for a strangely bumpy ride.

While the scale of the building was truly grand, the façade was anything but. The rough-hewn wooden shingles were faded and in some spots missing. As for the front porch, up close it looked pretty dilapidated, as if a serious gust of wind could knock it over. The windows that ran along the front as far as I could see were dark, almost like eyes that were staring out at us dully. On a dreary day like this one, I would have expected the entire place to be lit up in an attempt at making it look at least a little bit inviting. Yet it almost looked as if no one else was here.

The main entrance, an imposing wooden front door, was marked only by a small sign. I pulled my truck up in front of it, expecting a bellman to appear. Jake and I were going to need some serious help to unload. It wasn't our suitcases that were the problem. It was all the paraphernalia I'd brought along for the workshops I'd be leading. My demonstrations on how to make ice cream and all kinds of assorted related concoctions, for example, required multitudes of bowls, spoons, machinery, and of course lots of ingredients. But as we sat in the truck, staring at the front door, we still didn't spot any signs of life.

Jake and I exchanged nervous looks.

"Should I honk?" I asked, my voice cracking.

Before he had a chance to answer, the big wooden door opened. Slowly. In fact, the only reason I even noticed it was opening at all was because of a dim light that was on inside, a striking contrast to the grim gloominess all around us.

But rather than a perky bellman leaping out, a thin, slightly stooped woman eased her way through the door. She stood on the porch for a few seconds, studying the two of us as we continued sitting in the cab of my red truck.

My first impression of her was that she was stern. The serious expression on her face was a good match to her simple gray dress, navy-blue cardigan, and practical black shoes. Somehow she managed to emanate an air of gloom, as if she was a member of the Addams Family. She reminded me of someone, but I couldn't quite place who that was.

Jake and I climbed out of the truck, each of us grabbing one of our suitcases.

"You must be Katherine McKay," the woman called to me from the porch. It almost sounded like an accusation.

"That's me," I replied. "But please call me Kate. And you must be Merle."

"Mrs. Moody," she corrected me sharply. "I prefer to be addressed as Mrs. Moody."

It was then it clicked. I finally figured out who she reminded me of: creepy Mrs. Danvers from the Daphne du Maurier classic novel *Rebecca*. Somber, disapproving, and as cold as the icy rain that was dripping down the back of my neck.

Jake and I exchanged another look. *Oh boy*, it said.

"This is Jake Pratt," I said once we'd hauled our bags up onto the porch. "Jake is my assistant. I mentioned in my emails that he'd be coming along to help me out this weekend."

Mrs. Moody looked at each one of us appraisingly, then stuck her chin in the air and sniffed. "I've assigned you separate rooms," she said, making it clear that there'd be no hanky-panky on her watch.

"That's fine," Jake said. "Exactly what we expected."

I grabbed an oversized tote bag packed with sprinkles, hot fudge sauce, and other ice cream–related goodies and headed up the front stairs. As soon as I walked inside the building, I was struck by the smell of oldness. Not a bad smell, exactly, but one that immediately told you that you were in a place that had been around for a while. Partly mustiness, partly dustiness. And partly the smell of the knotty wood that lined many of the walls and the damp wool of the thick, well-worn Oriental carpets that covered the lobby and stretched along the endless corridors branching off it.

The furniture contributed to the feeling that I'd just been transported back in time at least a century: big, heavy-looking chairs upholstered in dark red velvet, wooden tables with ornately carved legs, sagging couches in front of brick fireplaces. On the walls were portraits of somber-looking individuals, glowering at us. I wondered if they were Mrs. Moody's ancestors.

In addition to the usual features of a hotel lobby, a half dozen wooden display cases were scattered around. Laid out inside them, under glass, were what appeared to be historical artifacts.

In one display case, I saw several items that reflected the

area's Native American heritage. I spotted an assortment of stone arrowheads, a few pieces of pottery, and a single beaded moccasin that could have been a few decades old or a few hundred.

The Hudson Valley's Dutch settlers were also represented. In a different display case I saw a black hat with a floppy brim, a long-stemmed clay pipe, and a wrinkled pair of knee-length breeches.

"Wow, this place looks like a museum," Jake observed.

Mrs. Moody's chest puffed up with pride. Yet I still didn't see even a trace of a smile. "Here at Mohawk, we feel that the region's history is very important," she said, sounding mildly annoyed. "After all, the Mohawk Mountain Resort is very much a part of that history."

Jake gestured toward the breeches in the Dutch display case. "What's up with the short pants?"

"I'm sure you know that the Dutch were the original settlers of New York and the Hudson Valley," she replied. "Of course that changed in 1664, when the British took possession of the area. But those 'short pants,' as you call them, are what's known as knickerbockers. The word 'knickerbocker' comes from the pen name the great writer Washington Irving used when he published his book *History of New York* in the early 1800s. One of his friends was named Herman Knickerbocker. I suppose he thought it was catchy. Eventually the word Knickerbocker came to refer to members of New York's aristocracy."

"So that's where the New York Knicks got their name!" Jake commented.

In response to Mrs. Moody's confused look, he added, "The basketball team?"

"Yes, of course," she said unconvincingly. The woman clearly wasn't a sports fan. "And in the early 1900s, the name 'knickerbocker' was applied to the short pants that were fashionable, after the Dutch version of men's pants from a few hundred years earlier. The name was eventually abbreviated to 'knickers.'"

"Interesting," I mumbled. But my attention had already turned to another display in the resort's little museum. Standing in a corner was a mannequin with straight black hair. The male figure was dressed in a full-length tan coat that looked like it was made of animal skin. The garment was elaborately decorated with fringe and hand-painted with bright red and blue designs that ran along the hem and the collar. The man wore moccasins and a pair of leggings, also made from skins.

In one hand, he carried a bow and arrow. In the other, he held a weapon that looked like a tomahawk with a handle as long as a spear. And hanging from a beaded belt was a knife that was encased in a leather holder.

"This guy looks a little scary," I commented, walking over to the mannequin to get a better look.

"He represents the Lenape tribe, who lived in this area," Mrs. Moody said. "The Mohawks, the namesake of our resort, actually lived west of the Hudson Valley." With a wan smile, she added, "Perhaps the resort's founder thought 'Mohawk' was easier to remember than 'Lenape.'"

"Are all these things authentic?" I asked, leaning forward to get a better look at the serious-looking weapons.

"As far as we know," Mrs. Moody replied, coming over and standing beside me. "It's certain that the weapons are genuine. Our founder was an avid collector of Native American artifacts. He had a particular interest in weaponry.

"The bow was fashioned from wood," she explained, pointing, "while the arrowhead is made of stone. Those date back thousands of years. The knife, however, would reflect more recent developments. It wasn't until the Europeans came that the natives began using metal. This one is made of iron."

"He sure doesn't look like anyone I'd want to tangle with," Jake commented.

"Me either," I muttered under my breath.

I turned away, realizing that at the moment I had more pressing problems to deal with. Like hauling in all the supplies I'd brought for the weekend.

Mrs. Moody watched in silence, wearing what I'd already learned was her signature frown, as Jake and I made multiple trips back and forth to the truck, unloading all the things I'd brought for my workshops and depositing them in the lobby. Some of them were pretty heavy, especially the three-gallon tubs of freshly made ice cream that I'd made earlier that day and packed in individual nests of dry ice. By that point I wasn't the least bit surprised that she made no move to help. I was irritated, certainly. But not surprised.

"You certainly brought a lot of baggage," Mrs. Moody finally said. "I suppose I should have asked Tarleton to help."

"Tarleton?" I repeated. "Who's he?"

"The bellman," she replied.

Y'think? I thought angrily. *You mean there's actually someone on staff whose job it is to haul suitcases down the endless hallways?*

"Then again, it never occurred to me that you'd bring so many things for such a short stay," Mrs. Moody added.

"It's for the workshops," I said, hating that I sounded so defensive. I handed her one of the ice-encrusted tubs of ice cream—Cappuccino Crunch, one of my all-time favorites, and said, "I brought some of my ice cream so the workshop participants can try some of my unusual flavors. Hopefully Tarleton or someone else can get them into a freezer as quickly as possible." I hesitated, then added, "We *are* still holding the workshops, aren't we?"

"As I said in my emails," Mrs. Moody said crisply, "Mohawk has never closed or even cancelled a workshop since it first opened—"

"In 1868," I said. "Yes, I'm aware of that. But you may not know that a huge tree fell across the access road a few minutes ago. It came down right behind us as we were driving up."

Mrs. Moody narrowed her eyes and peered at me suspiciously. I got the feeling that she held me personally responsible for the tree falling.

"It's completely blocking the road," Jake added. "I don't see how anyone else will be able to get here."

Or get out, I thought.

"That's most unfortunate," Mrs. Moody said with a frown. "And it's not only workshop attendance that will be affected. The entire staff is gone for the afternoon, aside from Tarleton and me. It's Mohawk's custom to give everyone a few hours off every Friday afternoon since weekends are always our busiest time. The calm before the storm, for lack of a better expression." Her frown deepened. "I'm afraid we're going to be a bit shorthanded until this tree business gets cleared up."

I was amazed by how quickly this situation was going from bad to worse.

"Fortunately, a few of the workshop participants have already arrived," Mrs. Moody continued. "At least we'll be able to carry on as planned."

With a staff of two, I thought miserably. *One of whom is a bellman who doesn't seem to feel the need to carry out any bellman-related activities.*

"I'll have Tarleton put the supplies for the workshops in the Great Room," Mrs. Moody went on, back to being all briskness and efficiency. "But for now I'll see you to your rooms."

I assumed she meant both Jake and me until she turned

to him and said, "You wait here. I'll take Miss McKay to her room first. Yours is located in a different section of the building."

From the chagrined look he cast me, I could tell that he was thinking exactly what I was thinking, which was, *What have we gotten ourselves into?*

While Jake waited near the front desk, I followed my hostess down a long carpeted corridor, past a seemingly endless row of closed doors. We went up a flight of grand but creaky wooden stairs, then continued down another long corridor.

My room was at the very end.

"I specially picked this room for you," Mrs. Moody said as she turned the big metal key in the lock. "I thought you'd appreciate the privacy. It also has an excellent view of the lake."

As we walked inside, I had to admit that the room was lovely. It instantly sent me back in time a good century and a half, but in a good way. The modest-sized space was decorated with pale blue flowered wallpaper. Hanging on the walls were framed black-and-white photos of the lake in different seasons, all of them taken on sunny days. There was a fireplace opposite the comfy-looking four-poster bed, which was covered in a cream-colored chenille bedspread. The wooden nightstand on spindly carved legs, the rickety rocking chair, and the tiny, only minimally useful desk, all looked like antiques.

Hand-crocheted doilies covered tables and the mantel, oval-shaped dark blue rag rugs were scattered over a wooden floor, and cream-colored lace curtains framed the double windows that did, indeed, look over the lake. Peering outside, I saw that the rain continued to come down in sheets and the wind whipped around the branches of even the biggest trees along the shore. That is, what I could see of it through the fog that had settled over it like a giant cloud.

"The room is charming," I told Mrs. Moody sincerely as I took the metal room key she handed me.

I smiled at her, but her expression remained as stony as ever.

"I think you'll find that it's very well-appointed," she added. "There are personal care products in the bathroom, and in the closet there's an iron and an ironing board. We've also supplied a laundry bag that you'll find there, since we offer guests laundry service. We usually have a six-hour turnaround, but given what's going on right now with our staffing . . ."

"It sounds as if you've thought of everything," I commented. "I'm sure I'll be very comfortable here."

She nodded curtly. "Then if there are no other questions . . ."

"Actually, I do have a question," I told her. "Is there a password? For WiFi, I mean?"

"There's no internet service in the rooms," she replied. "WiFi is only available in the common areas like the lobby and the sitting rooms branching off it. And there's virtually no cell phone service up here in the mountains. I'm afraid that if you're one of those people who's addicted to your phone, you're going to have a rough time." She offered me a small smile that seemed just a tad triumphant. "However, there are pay phones in the lobby if it becomes necessary for you to make contact with the outside world."

"I see," I said, trying not to look disappointed. Always the optimist, I reminded myself that taking a little break from technology, at least some of the time I was here, might not be such a bad thing.

"If you don't have any more questions, I'll leave you to settle in," Mrs. Moody said crisply. "Dinner is at seven. You'll get a chance to meet the workshop participants who've managed to make it here. After that, you can set up in the Great Room for tonight's introductory lecture."

And then she was gone, closing the door silently behind her. I took a deep breath, immediately noticing how much more pleasant the room felt now that Mrs. Moody was no longer in it.

I opened the suitcase I'd lugged to my room without any help from the elusive Tarleton. I was just taking out my blue and white striped zippered pouch with my toothbrush and other personal items, when I heard a loud creak outside my door. It was definitely the aged floorboards, a sign that someone was standing outside. Or at least walking by.

I wondered if it was Jake. It was possible that he'd come to find me. Or perhaps he had magically talked Mrs. Moody into giving him a room near mine. I went over to the door and opened it.

No one was there. At least, that was my first impression. But as I glanced to the right, I saw a shadow where the hallway took a turn. At least I thought I did. But when I looked harder, I didn't see a thing.

I must be imagining things, I thought. *It's all because of that creepy Mrs. Moody.*

I looked to the left. Nothing there, either.

But when I turned my head to the right once again, I jumped about ten feet in the air. A large man was suddenly looming in front of me. He was at least six feet tall, with a bulky build. His hair was cut very short and he had ears that stuck out a little too far. He wore his gray polyester pants pulled up almost to his armpits, covering up much of the red plaid flannel shirt he was wearing.

He stood there awkwardly for what seemed like a very long time, just staring at me.

"I'm Tarleton," he finally said. "Welcome to Mohawk."

He spoke woodenly, as if he'd been instructed to say those words without really understanding them. I certainly didn't *feel* welcome.

"Uh, thank you," I said. "I'm glad to be here."

When he didn't say anything more, or appear to be in the least bit inclined to, I added, "I think Mrs. Moody needs help moving some of the things I brought for the weekend into the Great Room. Then there's the ice cream. It's packed in dry ice, but it should still be put into a freezer right away."

He continued to stare at me.

"Let me know if I can help you with anything," he said in the same robot-like voice.

"I will," I replied, meanwhile thinking, *That's* obviously not going to happen. I wondered how any of the workshop supplies I'd brought were ever going to make it to the various spots in which they belonged.

I forced myself to smile at Tarleton. "Thank you," I said, for no particular reason other than to signal that we were done here.

I retreated back into my room, this time locking the door. With the double lock. And the chain. I took a few deep breaths, then reminded myself how much I'd been looking forward to this weekend.

I resumed unpacking, arranging some of my clothes in the drawers of the heavy wooden dresser and hanging up the rest. As I did, I was once again struck by how delightful my room was. I noticed a few details that hadn't registered before: an old-fashioned alarm clock on the night table, a ceramic pitcher of ice water on a tray along with a crystal glass, and a needlepoint pillow on a wooden rocking chair that reminded me of my grandmother's expert needlework.

I could finally feel myself relaxing. The storm raging outside really did make my surroundings feel all the more cozy, as if I was snuggled up in my own little hideaway.

Of course, the one thing that was missing was Jake. Even though we had a busy weekend ahead of us, I was committed to finding a way to do some of that cuddling we'd been planning on.

For now, however, I was anxious to track him down so the two of us could get a good look at the rest of Mohawk. I wanted to check out the room in which I'd be conducting my workshops, find out where the dining room was, and identify the best fireplaces and most comfortable couches for that aforementioned cuddling.

Even though Mrs. Moody was apparently Mohawk's unofficial ghoul in residence, that didn't mean I couldn't make this a truly fabulous weekend. And even though it hadn't exactly started out in the smoothest way, hopefully the rest of it would go by without a single hitch.

Chapter 2

"With the ban on alcohol aboard ships in 1914, the US Navy sought to offset the loss of alcohol at sea and found that ice cream was popular among the sailors. It was so popular that the Navy borrowed a refrigerated concrete barge from the Army Transportation Corps in 1945 to serve as a floating ice cream parlor. At a cost of $1 million, the barge was towed around the Pacific to provide ice cream to ships smaller than a destroyer that lacked ice cream making facilities."

—https://news.usni.org/2015/01/30/unique-ships-u-s-navy

Finding my way back to the lobby wasn't easy. As I walked through the endless hallways, all of them pretty much identical, I wished I'd left myself a trail. I also found myself keeping a wary eye out for Tarleton. I didn't want him leaping out at me from any doorways or sneaking up on me from behind.

Fortunately, great minds think alike. As I neared the lobby, I spotted Jake hovering near the front desk as if he was waiting for me. When I grew closer, I saw that he was scanning a rack of brochures about local sights throughout the Hudson Valley, like wineries and outdoor sculpture gardens and historic homes.

"This is quite a place!" he greeted me. He was wearing such a big grin that I was immediately struck by what a good decision it had been to bring him along.

As soon as we began strolling around, I saw that he was absolutely right. Despite the slight feeling of decay that permeated the place, Mohawk was turning out to be just as grand as I'd imagined it would be.

Just beyond the lobby, separated by two sets of double doors, was the tremendous Great Room. It was well named, since the space was large enough to serve as a ballroom, should anyone suddenly get an overwhelming urge to do the waltz. It had polished wooden floors, white walls with light-colored wooden wainscoting that covered the bottom half, and a few chandeliers that were almost as big as compact cars.

But it was the row of huge windows running along the back wall that made the Great Room truly spectacular. They overlooked the lake, just as my room did. But the glass panes were so big that they also afforded a view of the mountains and woods and craggy stone cliffs that was so dramatic and so beautiful that it literally made me gasp.

"This is where I'll be leading the workshops," I told Jake. Glancing around, I added, "I'd better set up in a corner, probably over by the windows. Otherwise, we're going to feel like field mice in the middle of a pasture the size of Rhode Island."

"Good idea," he said. "Besides, the view is stupendous. Everyone can enjoy it while they're learning about how to make the best food in the world even better." Peering outside, he added, "Of course, it'll be much *more* stupendous if this rain and fog ever give up and go home."

We retraced our steps back to the lobby, then headed off to our right. As we walked down the long corridor that stretched off in that direction, our footsteps were muted by the same thick Oriental carpeting that padded the corridors leading to my room. We passed a small gift shop, a TV room that compensated for the resort's policy of no televisions in the guest rooms, and a lounge with a somewhat dated computer. It was one of Mohawk's few nods to the twenty-first century.

At the end of the hallway we found the dining room. That, too, was on a grand scale. The walls of the cavernous octagon-shaped space were paneled in the same light-colored wood that helped give the other rooms their woodsy, old-fashioned feeling. I had already dubbed it Rustic Elegance.

The centerpiece of the dining room was the huge stone fireplace that went halfway up to the ridiculously high ceiling. And since the room jutted out to the side of the building, it had walls of windows on three sides. Even though it was already dark outside, I knew that in the morning it would afford truly magnificent views of both the lake and the mountains that stretched out in the other direction. That is, if the fog ever cleared.

At least two dozen tables filled the space, each one decorated with a dark green linen tablecloth and matching cloth napkins. In the center of each table was a colorful arrangement of branches festooned with brightly colored autumn leaves. Jutting out of the middle were tall, graceful candles. The tables were set with complete sets of silverware, gleaming white china, and simple yet elegant crystal glasses. I found the juxtaposition of the wood and the stone walls and the sophisticated details that were superimposed over it completely consistent with the resort's ambiance.

Jake and I wandered back to the lobby. Branching off in the other direction was a series of three small sitting rooms, each one with a fireplace of its own. The rooms were all outfitted with overstuffed chairs, comfortable love seats, and a few shelves with board games and hardcover books. They even had charming names, carved into irregularly shaped wooden plaques hanging over the doorways: the Mountainview Room, the Maple Tree Room, and the Lakeside Room.

"This place is great," Jake said breathlessly as we studied the games of Clue and Monopoly stacked up on the shelf of the last room. Turning to me, he added, "Thanks for bringing me here, Kate."

"My pleasure," I said.

And then he leaned over and gave me a sweet, gentle kiss.

When I heard someone clearing their throat, I jumped. Instinctively I turned. Standing in the doorway right behind us was Mrs. Moody.

"I just thought I'd remind you that dinner is at seven," she said curtly. "I'm sure all the workshop participants who've made it here will be anxious to meet you, so it would be a good idea to get there on time."

I couldn't believe that I was thirty-three years old, yet still felt guilty about having been caught kissing my boyfriend.

"Of course," I told her. I glanced at Jake, who looked as if he was doing everything he could to keep from laughing.

"We'd better go back to our separate rooms, then," he said earnestly. "It looks like it's time to dress for dinner."

When I went back to my room, I realized that I already felt at home in it. Somehow, it had immediately become my little retreat from—well, from whatever demands were going to be put on me this weekend. After all, I was just beginning to realize that while I'd been looking at my time at Mohawk as a nice little getaway with Jake, Mrs. Moody, my employer for the next few days, had her own agenda. And I was committed to following it.

But I still intended to make the most of it.

Keeping an eye on the time, I went into the bathroom. It had the same old-fashioned feeling as the rest of the place.

The walls were covered with lemon-yellow and white flow-ered wallpaper, while the tiles, the sink, and the magnificent claw-foot bathtub were all sparkling white. I brushed my hair and put on some blush, mascara, and lip gloss. Next, I smeared on some of the almond-scented body lotion I found next to the sink.

Then, anxious to present a positive image to the other guests, I wriggled out of the jeans and sweater I'd been wear-ing. Instead, I slipped on the dressy outfit I'd brought along in case the weekend offered a chance to dress up. It consisted of a pastel-colored flowered dress with a flowing skirt that swirled around my knees when I walked and a pair of pink ballet flats. After putting on a thin silver necklace and a fa-vorite pair of dangly earrings, I was ready to sweep into that elegant dining room in style.

By that point, it was nearly seven o'clock. I retraced my steps, going back into the lobby and down the long hallway jutting off it.

Once I reached the dining room, my first impression was that it looked a little lonely. Only one of the tables was occu-pied. Jake sat at it all alone, looking uncomfortable.

He smiled at me warily as I joined him.

"So far, this experience is making me wish I'd never seen *The Shining*," he said, grimacing. "This building is fantastic, but I'm beginning to think that we're the only people in it be-sides Mrs. Moody."

"You obviously haven't yet had the pleasure of meeting Tarleton," I replied. "But Mrs. Moody did say that we'd be meeting the workshop participants who've already made it here at dinner. Which implies that contrary to appearances, there really are other people who arrived before The Great Tree Disaster.

"I'm just hoping the delightful Mrs. Moody doesn't consider dining with the guests one of the duties of her job," I added. "Or the hired help, which is how she seems to view us."

Suddenly Jake cried, "Look! Signs of life!"

I turned and saw that there was indeed another living soul on the premises. A woman hovered in the doorway, studying us shyly as if trying to decide if she dared to interrupt us.

"Please join us!" I called to her. "Are you here for the We All Scream for Ice Cream workshops?"

A look of relief crossed her face. As she came over to us, she smiled hesitantly, saying, "And here I'd been thinking I was the only guest who'd made it!"

"We're not actually guests," I said. "We're the people who are conducting the ice cream workshops."

As she neared our table, I was able to see that this seemingly timid woman was in her mid to late forties. Her dark brown hair, slightly streaked with gray, was pulled back into a low ponytail. She wasn't particularly tall, perhaps five-foot-four, and her torso was unusually rectangular, due to her thick waist. Like Mrs. Moody, her choice of outfit veered slightly onto the dowdy side: a crisp white long-sleeved blouse with a Peter Pan collar, a navy-blue skirt, and black flats that were fairly well-worn. Half falling off her shoulder was a floppy, oversized black purse. Still, as she took the seat opposite mine, I saw that she had accessorized with a pair of starfish-shaped clip-on earrings and a heart necklace. She had also put on a touch of mascara, a sweep of blush, and a pale pink lipstick that didn't quite mesh with her skin tones.

"I'm Kate McKay," I said. "And this is my assistant—and friend—Jake Pratt."

"I'm so happy to meet both of you!" she gushed, the shyness she had exhibited earlier seeming to vanish. "I'm Frances Schneffer, but everyone calls me Franny. I can't tell you how thrilled I am to be here! Imagine, an entire weekend dedicated to ice cream! It's as if a childhood fantasy of mine has actually come true. And have you ever seen such a beautiful place in your life? I feel like I'm living in a fairy tale!"

I was taken aback by her enthusiasm. But because it was accompanied by real warmth, it struck me as genuine.

I made a mental note not to be so quick to make judgments about people I didn't even know.

Just then I noticed that Tarleton was making a beeline in our direction from the kitchen, clutching a basket of rolls with both hands. He was holding on to them so tightly and keeping his eyes fixed on them so intensely that you'd have thought he was carrying toxic waste. Being a waiter clearly wasn't part of his usual job duties.

As he set them down on the table, he breathed an audible sigh of relief. I saw that balanced on top were three small dishes containing disks of butter the size of silver dollars. Each one was embossed with the word MOHAWK and a simplified image of the building.

"This is Tarleton, everyone," I said. "Tarleton, this is Jake and this is Franny."

They both smiled and said hello. In response, Tarleton nodded once, his cheeks turning bright red. Then he abruptly turned and scurried back to the kitchen.

"I'm starving," Franny announced breathlessly, reaching for the rolls. "I came all the way from Minnesota and I've been up since four a.m."

The basket, I saw, contained two varieties: fluffy dinner rolls and dense seeded rolls. She took one of each.

"Coming here for this ice cream weekend was expensive, of course," she went on. "Not only the sky-high rates here at Mohawk, but also the plane fare. But my forty-eighth birthday is next week, and I said to myself, 'Franny, if you don't treat yourself to the better things in life now, when will you?' Besides, I had so much vacation time built up from the library where I work that I had to start using some of it or else I'd lose it. I mean, I'm head clerk and everything, and I practically run the front desk, but I figured they could manage without me for a few days. Anyway, I decided to splurge. And, well, here I am!"

Her eyes, a pale shade of gray, were gleaming. "But you two live nearby, right? I read all about your ice cream store, the Lickety Splits Ice Cream Shoppe, in the flyer. That's such a cute name! And it's right here in the Hudson Valley, isn't it? A town called Wolfert's Roost?"

I said that both Jake and I did indeed live in the area. I also gave her a brief overview of my personal history, especially the part about how opening my own ice cream shop had been the realization of my own lifelong dream.

Then Jake explained that he ran the local organic dairy and was one of my suppliers. He also mentioned that he and I had known each other since high school. Of course, what he didn't say was that he and I had been the Romeo and Juliet of our class during our junior and senior years. At least that was the case until prom night, which was supposed to be one of the most memorable experiences of high school but instead turned out to be a complete disaster. He didn't say anything about the fifteen-year silence between us that followed, either, or the fact that only a few weeks earlier, after the two of us had reconnected following my return to Wolfert's Roost, he and I had decided to give being a couple another try.

"Running an organic dairy sure sounds like a lot of work!" Franny exclaimed as she helped herself to a third roll. "Mmm, these are so good! I usually try to watch my carbs, but this is such a special weekend for me. I decided to just say no to all the rules I usually live by."

"Jake is also starting a second business," I told her, not even trying to mask my pride. "He's about to open a high-end farm stand not too far from here. It's called Jake's Hudson Harvest."

He nodded. "And it will feature Lickety Splits ice cream,

made by this culinary genius." Proudly, he added, "The ice cream we sell will be in addition to local produce and of course organic dairy products. But we'll also have home-baked pies and other baked goods, locally made crafts like wreaths made of dried flowers that Kate's grandmother is making for us—"

"Gee, it sounds amazing!" Franny exclaimed. "If they ever clear the road, I might be able to find the time to go see it."

"The farm stand hasn't opened yet," Jake and I replied in unison. Then he added, "But at this point, we're merely putting on the finishing touches. I hope to launch it in a couple of weeks, right after Thanksgiving."

Franny nodded. "Just in time for Christmas," she said. "I bet you'll sell plenty of those handmade wreaths, not to mention tons of the homemade pies!"

Jake was about to respond, probably with some comment along the lines of *I sure hope so!* when the sound of loud, shrill laughter caused us all to jerk our heads up.

A man and a woman had just sauntered into the dining room. The woman appeared to find something hysterically funny. Her piercing laughter seemed painfully out of place in a serene setting like Mohawk.

It wasn't only her loud laugh that came across like fingernails screeching across a blackboard. Her hair, her jewelry, and her outfit were also at odds with the low-key style of our surroundings.

Somehow, everything she wore managed to scream Money. The tailoring on her white wool jacket was so sharp that she reminded me of a four-star general. The gleaming gold buttons certainly added to that effect. Her simple dark skirt, which also looked like wool, looked as if it had been cut to fit her curves precisely. Her shiny black, ridiculously high heels had the bright red soles that told the world they were Christian Louboutins. Like anyone who's the least bit interested in fashion, I knew that the prices for that particular designer's footwear started in the multi-hundreds. Her haircut was so impeccable that not a single hair dared to misbehave.

As for the man beside her, I couldn't help wondering if she saw him as just one more fashion accessory. He was extremely handsome, with punctuated cheekbones, a square jaw, and eyelids that drooped just enough to make him look coolly indifferent. It was the kind of face that had made men like George Clooney and Brad Pitt household names. Even though it was November, he sported a tan. It looked about as natural as his sparkling white teeth. As for his hairstyle, it had no doubt taken half a tub of gel to perfect. The expensive-looking suit he wore was complemented with a gold bar–shaped tie tack and gold cufflinks the size of marbles.

The two of them looked as if they were going to be dining at the casino in Monte Carlo or the Hotel George V in Paris rather than in the funky wood-paneled dining room at the Mohawk Mountain Resort.

Remember your pledge to stop judging people based on their appearance, I reminded myself. *By the end of the weekend, these two will probably have become your best friends.*

As soon as the couple spotted us, they headed over in our direction.

"We got here just in time!" the woman exclaimed as she and her escort sat down in side-by-side chairs. "I'm sure you heard about that big tree that fell across the road. I was just checking the weather report online. The entire Hudson Valley has come to a virtual standstill. From the looks of things, no one's getting in or out of here for days!"

"Do you two live around here?" Jake asked.

"Heavens, no," the man replied. "We both live in the city."

"Do you mean New York City?" Franny asked, wide-eyed.

"Of course," he said, sounding a bit irritated about the need to explain. "I live on the Upper West Side, while Bethany is across the park, on the Upper East Side."

"Are you here for the ice cream workshops?" I asked.

"Not only is that why we came this weekend," the woman replied. "I'm absolutely thrilled to be here! I love ice cream, and anything and everything that's connected to it.

"As a matter of fact, I've been writing about coming to this weekend here at Mohawk on Facebook and on Instagram and of course on my blog. I've been tweeting about it, too." Glancing around, she said, "I'm surprised there aren't more people who came up here for it."

"No doubt the storm is responsible," Jake commented.

"True," she said. "That must be it. After all, I would have thought that this event having my stamp of approval would have been a huge draw. I'm really big on social media and I have a tremendous following. All I have to do is mention something and half the world is clamoring for it."

"By the way, I'm Jake Pratt," Jake interjected.

"And I'm Kate McKay," I added, picking up on his cue. "I'm leading the ice cream workshops this weekend. Jake is my assistant."

"I'm so happy to meet you!" the woman gushed. "I'm Bethany La Montaine. And this is my adorable boyfriend, Gordon Bradley."

"Pleased to meet you," I said. "It's funny—every time I buy makeup, which I admit isn't very often these days, I buy a brand that's called La Montaine. I don't suppose you're related . . ."

Bethany was beaming. "That's my family's company!" she exclaimed. "My mother, Gloria La Montaine, started it back in the 1980s. And I've been working there ever since I graduated from college."

"And today it's a five-hundred-million-dollar firm," Gordon said, sounding proud. "Granted, it's not as big as some of its competitors like L'Oréal and Estée Lauder, or even Revlon and Avon, which are considerably smaller. But that's because it's still very much a family firm."

"True," Bethany noted. "And my mother runs that place like a mom-and-pop business. She makes sure that she knows as much as she possibly can about everything that goes on there."

"What fun!" I said. "Working in the cosmetics industry must be very glamorous."

"I'll say!" Franny exclaimed. "It must be amazing! I'd love to hear all about what it's like. That is, if you're willing to tell us."

"To be perfectly honest, I was hoping not to talk about work this weekend," Bethany said. Reaching over and giving Gordon's shoulder a squeeze, she added, "This is supposed to be a romantic getaway for the two of us. Something we haven't had in ages."

I wasn't about to admit that Jake and I had the same thing in mind, just in case Mrs. Moody was lurking under the table or inside the sugar bowl.

"In that case," Jake said, "let's talk about . . . how about food?"

"One of my favorite subjects," I commented.

"I read online that the chef here is supposed to be really something," Jake continued. Ruefully, he added, "But given the circumstances, it looks as if we won't be able to experience his genius firsthand. It's really a shame, since he studied at some fancy cooking school in France and became head chef at a top restaurant in Paris called Le Parapluie Bleu, which means *The Blue Umbrella* . . ."

"I absolutely *adore* Le Parapluie Bleu!" Bethany gushed. "The last time Gordon and I were there—when was that, sweetie, in April? Or was it in May?—we had the most fabulous coq au vin of my entire life. Now I know what you're all thinking: that coq au vin is *so* nineteen eighties. But I'm telling you, the chef put *such* a distinctive twist on it. I don't know what secret ingredients he sneaked in there, but the results were absolutely *magnifique*." Her eyes were bright as she glanced around the table and asked, "Do you all love Le Parapluie Bleu as much as I do?"

An awkward silence followed. Anxious to break it, I said, "I've been to Paris twice, but I've never eaten at that particular restaurant."

"And I've never been to Paris at all," Franny said meekly.

"Me either," Jake said. Smiling warmly at Franny, he added, "I guess that gives both of us something to look forward to, doesn't it?"

While Jake had done an excellent job of smoothing things over, it was still a relief that someone else had just joined our group. We had been so involved in getting through the last two minutes that we didn't actually notice until the newcomer pulled out the empty chair between Jake and Gordon.

This guest was easily the youngest of our group. I estimated that she was in her mid-twenties. She was probably just a bit taller than five feet, with a slender build. Her dead-straight, jet-black hair was precision cut, her thick bangs as straight as a ruler and her bob perfectly aligned with her narrow chin. Her skin was the color of porcelain, and her dark eyes had just enough of an almond shape to give her an exotic look.

Not only was this young woman pretty, thin, and poised; she was also stylishly dressed in a draped wine-colored top studded with bling, silk black-and-white striped pants, and short black boots.

"Welcome!" Franny said brightly. "We're all so glad to meet another brave guest who managed to make it here despite the storm!"

"I got here a couple of hours ago," the newcomer explained. "But I got so involved with some work stuff that I totally lost track of the time. I run a web-based retail business, so I pretty much work twenty-four-seven."

As if to illustrate her point, as soon as she sat down she reached into her floppy black leather purse and pulled out a cell phone. Its cover, I noticed, was pale pink and, like the top she was wearing, studded with shiny rhinestones.

"Oops, I forgot," she said. Grimacing, she added, "There's no cell phone service up here in the mountains. And the only place you can get an internet connection is in the lobby." With a sigh of defeat, she tucked her cell phone back into her purse.

It was only then that I noticed that Bethany's entire demeanor had completely changed. She sat as if she was frozen, just staring, meanwhile blinking nervously as she seemed to be searching for something to say.

"Yoko?" she finally managed to utter. "Is that you? Is that really you?"

"It's me, all right," the newcomer said, sticking her chin up a little further. "I bet you never expected to see me again."

"Well—n-n-no," Bethany replied. "I mean, not in a place like this." She blinked a few more times, then managed to regain some of her composure. "And what a delight it is to have run into you like this! Goodness, it's been how many years?"

The new arrival laughed coldly. "Not that many, actually. In fact, it seems like only yesterday."

The distinct chill in the air put us all on edge. The tension between the two women reminded me of two power-hungry alpha males who were simply waiting for just the right moment to strike.

So it was a great relief when a voice at the far end of the room boomed, "This must be the gathering of ice cream lovers!"

Bethany wasn't the only one who was clearly relieved that someone else had suddenly appeared in the doorway. The new arrival strode into the dining room confidently, flashing all of us a smile that showed off his even, gleaming white teeth.

The gentleman was in his late sixties or possibly his early seventies, a tall, portly fellow who exuded confidence and charm. He had clearly pulled out all the stops when it came to dressing for this evening's dinner, donning an expensive-looking suit and a brightly colored flowered necktie. His hair was almost as black and straight as Yoko's. And while his facial features were pleasant—dark brown eyes, a straight nose—it was his thick black eyebrows that dominated.

"Good evening to all of you!" he said as he headed toward us. "I hope I am not interrupting, although I suppose that is inevitable since I am obviously one of the last ones to join this little group."

He's British, I observed, already charmed by his accent. I knew enough about different English accents to recognize his as decidedly upper-class.

"Please allow me to introduce myself—" He stopped abruptly and a slow smile crept over his face. "Somehow, every time I say that phrase, I cannot help also hearing Mick Jagger singing 'Sympathy for the Devil.'"

"Are you also 'a man of wealth and taste'?" Jake interjected. Turning to the rest of us, he added, "For those of you who aren't Rolling Stones fans, those are the lyrics at the beginning of the song."

Still smiling impishly, the British gentleman continued, "All that aside, my name is Naveen Sharma."

"Given your lovely accent, it sounds as if you hail from distant shores," Franny said gaily. "London, if I may venture a guess?"

I was startled by her tone. I wasn't positive, but I was pretty sure she was flirting.

"London, indeed," Naveen replied. "Are you familiar with that fine city?"

Franny shook her head. "Unfortunately, no. I haven't traveled much. Actually, I haven't traveled at all. At least, not yet. Seeing the world is one of the top items on my to-do list. But I read all the time, and I especially adore books that are set in Great Britain. Agatha Christie, Ian McEwan, Ruth Rendell, P. D. James . . ."

"I adored *Bridget Jones's Diary*," Bethany interjected.

"I loved that book," I agreed.

"Oh, I didn't read the book," Bethany said. "I saw the movie. Is that Hugh Grant cute or what?"

"He's definitely cute, at least for such an old guy," Yoko interjected. "At last, something Bethany and I can agree on!"

I could sense that the tension in the room was about to get thick again. So I was greatly relieved when Franny turned to Yoko and chirped, "Yoko is such a pretty name. Is it . . . foreign?"

"It's Japanese," Yoko replied. This was clearly a question she'd answered before. "My mother is Japanese and my father is Scottish, which is where my last name, Wallace, comes from." Glancing around the room, she added, "Haven't they brought out the wine list yet?"

"I'm sure Tarleton will be back shortly," I volunteered.

As if on cue, he reappeared at that very moment. But not with a wine list. Instead, speaking in a monotone and refraining from making eye contact, he read the evening's choices off a sheet of paper he clutched in his hand. It was limited, consisting of two appetizers and two main courses. And the offerings themselves were simple, most likely the result of some quick improvisation on Mrs. Moody's part. As we ordered, Tarleton scribbled down notes, his forehead furrowed and his mouth drawn into a thin straight line.

As soon as our makeshift waiter headed back to the kitchen, Franny turned to Naveen and said, "Naveen is an unusual name, the same way Yoko is. Don't tell me: Indian?"

"You have an excellent knowledge of names," Naveen said in his lilting accent, which was distinctively British but also tinged with the occasional Indian inflection. "My parents moved my family to England from Mumbai when I was just a child."

"What an interesting group!" Franny cried. "And from the looks of things, we're the only ones who made it to Mohawk for the We All Scream for Ice Cream weekend before the big tree fell."

"Yes, we are the lucky ones," Naveen said. With a teasing half smile, he added, "A least, I *think* we are the lucky ones!"

"I'm sure we can still have a wonderful weekend," I said. "Even though we're a smaller group than we were supposed to be, we've got all the elements we need. Enthusiastic participants, for one thing."

"And, of course, a highly qualified instructor," Jake added. "If anyone knows ice cream, it's Kate."

"I brought everything we'll need to make our own ice cream," I said. "All kinds of ingredients, equipment like ice cream makers . . . and I'm sure Mohawk has a nice big freezer for us to keep our creations in. We'll be making so much ice cream that there's bound to be plenty of leftovers.

"I also brought some of the more interesting ice cream flavors I sell at my shop," I added. "I thought we could try some tonight, for dessert. I brought Honey Lavender, which I've been selling for quite a while. Cappuccino Crunch, too, which is my all-time favorite. But I also brought a couple of new, experimental flavors, just to give everyone an idea of what you can actually do with ice cream. Flavors that think outside the box—or as I like to think of it, outside the carton. I brought Meyer Lemon ice cream that's laced with raspberry balsamic vinegar. It's an amazing combination of sweet, sour, and tart. I also brought a flavor I just tried for the first time that's in honor of Elvis Presley. Apparently the King loved the combination of peanut butter and bananas, so I created—"

Suddenly the lights flickered. And then, a few seconds later, they went out completely, leaving all of us surrounded by complete darkness.

Chapter 3

"Vanilla ice cream was introduced to the United States when Thomas Jefferson discovered the flavor in France and brought the recipe to the United States . . . During the 1780s, he wrote his own recipe for vanilla ice cream. The recipe is housed at the Library of Congress."

—*https://en.wikipedia.org/wiki/Vanilla_ice_cream*

Franny immediately let out a scream.

The sound nearly made Gordon jump out of his seat. "Must you?" he griped.

"The loss of electricity is probably nothing more than a power outage caused by the storm," Naveen said, his tone soothing.

Franny whimpered.

"Don't you have power outages wherever it is you come from?" Gordon muttered.

"We have them all the time!" Franny replied. "But that doesn't mean I *like* them!"

"And having one in this particular place, at this particular time, isn't exactly ideal," Jake noted. "I don't blame Franny for freaking out a little."

I appreciated his inclination to protect Franny, especially given Gordon's nastiness.

"What do you suppose happened?" Franny cried, as if it wasn't already obvious.

"Probably another tree went down," Jake replied. "But this time, it fell over some wires."

"Hopefully, a resort hotel of this size is equipped to deal with incidents like this," Naveen observed. "I expect that it has a generator."

"I sure hope so," Bethany said, her lower lip jutting out in a pout. "The last thing I want is for the weekend to be ruined because of this stupid storm."

I had been thinking the exact same thing. More specifically, that I didn't want all the ice cream I'd brought to be ruined because of the stupid storm.

But I was inclined to agree with Naveen. My precious ice cream wasn't the only thing that was being stored in Mohawk's freezer. There was undoubtedly plenty of valuable food stashed in there, ingredients that the French-trained chef had planned to use to whip up wonderful meals.

Gordon reached across the table and grabbed the tall white candle that stood in the middle of the autumn leaf centerpiece. He pulled a silver cigarette lighter out of his pocket and with the flick of his finger we suddenly had light. Naveen, following his lead, went from table to table, retrieving enough candles that we could each have our own.

"This could actually turn out to be kind of fun," Franny said, giggling as she accepted a candle from Naveen. "Like we're camping out or something."

"Right," Gordon said dryly. "Camping out in a fancy hotel with a nightly rate that's almost as much as the monthly payment on my Porsche."

As soon as we'd managed to get all the candles lit and had finished making "kumbayah" jokes, Tarleton reappeared. This time, he was bearing two large platters of food. It wasn't what we had ordered, but instead was probably whatever

Mrs. Moody had managed to get onto plates while surrounded by near darkness.

Even so, I was hungry enough that I was cheered by the arrival of cheeses, meats, bread, and assorted condiments and side dishes. The others seemed to feel the same way, too.

We had just dug in when a face suddenly materialized next to the table, practically glowing in the candlelight. I felt as if I'd stepped into a vampire movie.

But this wasn't a vampire. At least, as far as I knew. Then again, the possibility that Merle Moody was indeed a vampire wasn't totally out of the question.

"I am sorry for this inconvenience," she said. "Given our location up here in the mountains, we do lose power from time to time. But I can assure you that the situation is only temporary."

"How temporary?" Gordon asked crossly.

"Mohawk is equipped with an excellent generator," Mrs. Moody replied. Her mouth drooped downward as she added, "Unfortunately, it's a rather *old* generator."

"Great," Yoko said with a sigh. "Which means it's going to be impossible to recharge our electronics once they die."

At first I was irritated by her obvious attachment to cell phones and computers. But I quickly realized that I, too, was dependent enough on both that I was undoubtedly going to find being without electricity as much of a hardship as she was. Especially since I had spent hours putting together a PowerPoint presentation with photos of gasp-worthy ice cream concoctions that I planned to show at one of my workshops.

Then there was the fact that without a way to communicate with the outside world, we'd all be even more isolated than we already were.

For no logical reason, that thought made me shiver. I had

to remind myself that at least the resort had a landline. Which I hoped would work even under these conditions.

"So does this 'old generator' actually work?" Bethany asked, sounding at least as annoyed as her beau.

"It does," Mrs. Moody replied. "It just takes a little . . . cajoling."

"Great," Gordon mumbled. "Just great."

"But I'll get Tarleton working on it," Mrs. Moody added.

Oh, that's reassuring, I thought, realizing I was just as cynical as Gordon and Bethany.

The mood in the room had plummeted dramatically in the past ten minutes. Even so, we all got busy devouring the food. Everything was delicious, and it didn't take long for everyone's spirits to rise. The two bottles of wine that Mrs. Moody opened up also helped. Conversation may not have been as animated as before, but at least we managed to keep it going.

The ice cream I'd brought along for the weekend was the perfect ending to the meal. Everyone loved the Cappuccino Crunch, but my tablemates were fiercely divided on the Honey Lavender. Interestingly, the women seemed to like it, while the men appeared to be put off by it. Maybe it was because of the actual flavor, but I supposed it also could have been because of its association with flowers. After all, machismo is still very much alive and well. The Meyer Lemon ice cream with the raspberry balsamic vinegar, a luscious combination of sweetness and tartness as far as I'm concerned, was also controversial. This one, the men seemed to favor.

As for the bananas and peanut butter flavor, absolutely everyone loved it. Apparently Elvis was still King, even in the world of ice cream.

By the time we'd polished off most of the food, the lights were still out.

"*Now* what are we going to do?" Franny asked, sounding truly distressed. "How are we going to find our way back to our rooms when all we've got to help us see is the dim light from these candles?"

Three seconds later, Mrs. Moody came back into the dining room. This time, Tarleton was trailing behind her, carrying a large cardboard box.

"There you go," Gordon said dryly. "Our buddy Tarleton is going to personally carry each one of us to our room."

"I've brought flashlights," Mrs. Moody explained, ignoring his comment. "They're so much safer than candles."

"I feel better already," Franny said once each of us was grasping a flashlight. Instinctively we all turned them on, partly to test whether they worked and partly just to reassure ourselves that we now had the means to make our way through the long, pitch-black corridors of Mohawk.

"Now that we can see again," Naveen said, "there is no reason for us all to disappear into our rooms. I suggest that we gather in one of the common areas for conversation and parlor games."

"Parlor games?" Yoko repeated. "What are those?"

"Why, they are games that people play together in an interactive way," Naveen explained patiently. "Charades, backgammon, Twenty Questions . . ."

"The kind people used to play back in the good old days before video games were invented," Gordon interjected. "They can actually be kind of a hoot."

I was surprised. Given the level of the man's people skills, I'd have thought he was much more the *Angry Birds* type than the Clue type.

Then again, Gordon struck me as someone who was probably really good at Monopoly. The board game Battleship, too.

"I noticed that there's a bunch of board games in the Lakeside Room," Jake said. "That's one of the sitting rooms near the Great Room."

"I hope they have Life," Franny said excitedly. "That's my favorite board game."

"Not Candy Land?" Gordon sneered.

His snarkiness was really starting to become annoying. And why he had it out for poor Franny was beyond me. She was obviously far away from his concept of the ideal woman, at least if his girlfriend Bethany was any indicator. But that didn't mean he had to treat her with such disdain.

"I love Candy Land!" Franny gushed. "Of course, I haven't played it since I was about ten years old."

"And we won't be playing it tonight, either," Bethany said dryly.

"I'm always up for a game of poker," Gordon said. "For money, of course."

"I suggest that we all gather in the Lakeside Room in a few minutes, the way Naveen suggested," I said. "Then we can decide what games we'll play."

After muttering agreement, our little band of seven headed out of the dining room, each one of us clutching our flashlight.

"I'm going back to my room for a few minutes," I told Jake. "I want to change out of this dress into something more comfortable."

"I'll meet you in the Lakeside Room then," Jake said agreeably, leaning over to give me a quick kiss.

My heart fluttered. Maybe I was still weighing the pros and the cons about being with Jake. But at the moment, the pros were looking pretty darned good.

I trotted down the long corridor, following the dim light from my flashlight. If Mohawk had felt a bit eerie before, in the dark it felt positively spooky. Weirdly shaped shadows kept jumping out at me, only to turn out to be from a staircase or a random chair placed in a corner. Pelting rain continued to hammer at the windows. Every once in a while, the hallway was lit up by a brilliant flash of lightning, followed by a booming clap of thunder so loud that it practically made the walls vibrate.

I made it back to my room, unlocked the door and went inside. I was there just long enough to pull off the dress and put on the comfortable stretchy outfit I'd had on before. Then I retraced my steps, hurrying back to the common area.

While I'd never been one of those people who's afraid of the dark, this was one time that I didn't like the feeling of being all alone. Not with this terrifying storm raging outside, combined with the fact that it had trapped me inside a huge, unfamiliar place with a bunch of people I didn't know. Once again I was grateful that at least Jake was here.

As I neared the lobby, I saw that a silver candelabra had been placed on the reception desk. It was outfitted with five white candles, their pale flames flickering. But that was the only light I saw. There were no beams from other guests' flashlights, which meant there was no one else in the immediate area.

I quickened my step, more anxious than ever to find the others.

Suddenly the piercing sound of a scream cut through the silent darkness.

I froze. It was definitely Franny's voice. But unlike last time, this was a scream that sounded serious.

I ran in the direction the scream seemed to have come from. I'd only gone a few feet when I realized that someone had joined me. Glancing to my left, I saw that Jake was heading toward the sound, too.

"That was definitely Franny," he said. "Maybe she just discovered that Mohawk's board game collection doesn't include Life."

"It sounds a lot worse than that," I replied.

Sure enough, as Jake and I hurried into the Maple Tree Room, we found Franny. She had dropped to the floor, the position of her body indicating that she had slumped to her knees. Even in the pale light from our flashlights, I could see that her expression was stricken, her eyes open wide and her mouth twisted into a big "O" so that she looked like the distraught man in the famous Munch painting, *The Scream*.

Next to her, lying crumpled on the carpet, was a body.

Bethany La Montaine's body.

"What happened?" I demanded. "Was there an accident? Is Bethany ill?"

It was only then that I moved the beam of my flashlight over Bethany's body. And what I saw caused me to gasp.

The front of her dress was completely bathed in blood, the fabric tainted a sickening shade of dark red.

I knelt down to get a better look, ran my flashlight along her body. She had apparently been stabbed. Multiple times. Focusing the flashlight on her face, I studied her expression. Her dull eyes stared straight ahead. When I put two fingers on her neck, right where her carotid artery was, I couldn't feel a pulse.

I was no expert, but I was pretty sure that Bethany was dead.

Even so, as I rose to my feet, I said, "We need to get her some help immediately." But no one seemed to be listening.

"I—I came in here because I thought this was the Lakeside Room," Franny wailed, struggling to stand. "I thought this was where we were all supposed to meet. But as soon as I came in and shined my flashlight around the room, looking for the board games, I found—I found—"

She dissolved into hysterical sobs punctuated with sharp intakes of breath that sounded like yelps. Jake went over to her and put his arm around her shoulders.

"Let's get you out of here," he said softly, leading her out of the room. "We need to find you a chair and a big glass of water."

"And maybe a Valium," Franny said, sniffling. "If anyone has one."

As Jake helped Franny out of the room, I moved my flashlight around the room, looking for a weapon. But I couldn't spot anything that looked as if it had been used to inflict multiple stab wounds on Bethany.

"We should notify Mrs. Moody," I told Jake as I followed them out of the room, closing the door behind me. "And we should call nine-one-one, even though I don't know how any emergency vehicle could possibly get up here. Not with the storm and that big tree lying across the only road."

Jake nodded. "What do you want me to do?"

"I'll take care of the call," I said, already heading over to the row of pay phones in the lobby. "You take care of Franny."

As I expected, my call to the police turned out to be an exercise in frustration. After the dispatcher took down the information I gave her, she informed me that the local authorities were already aware that the access road to Mohawk had become impassable. Even though she promised to get someone up to the resort as soon as possible, it was pretty clear that that wasn't likely to be particularly soon at all.

When I asked about a rescue helicopter, the dispatcher snorted. "In this weather?" she said. "Not that there's anyplace for a copter to land up there even in *good* weather."

As I hung up the phone, I thought about the implications of what she had said. Not only were we all stranded at Mohawk. We were stranded here with a murderer in our midst.

My brain felt as if the fog that hovered outside had pushed its way through my ears and into my head. I was starting to feel as if I was living out one of those goofy horror flicks that Willow and I used to watch when we were teenagers.

Only this was no movie. This was real.

* * *

"What happened?" Yoko demanded as she strode into the Lakeside Room, following the beam of her flashlight.

As if trying to answer that question herself, she began casting the dim circle of light all over the room. She stopped when she spotted Franny, who had collapsed into a dignified-looking leather chair, her face in her hands and a tall glass of water on the table beside her.

Jake and I simply hovered nearby, not knowing what we should do. One thing I did think of doing was snapping some photos of poor Bethany with my cell phone. But as far as informing Mrs. Moody, I had quickly realized that I had no way of getting in touch with her, so instead I decided to wait for her to come to us. Given her past behavior, I suspected it was only a question of time before she did exactly that.

So far, she hadn't materialized. But everyone else in our little group was in the process of gathering together.

"What is going on?" Naveen demanded as he walked into the room and surveyed the peculiar scene.

"I thought I heard someone scream," Gordon said, coming in right after him. "It sounded like Franny. What unspeakable tragedy has befallen her now?"

"It actually *was* a tragedy," I told him, struggling to keep my voice even. I thought for a couple of seconds, then said, "There's been an accident."

He smirked. "Don't tell me. Someone dropped the Monopoly game and all the pieces—"

"Stop." The sharp tone of Jake's voice got everyone's attention. "Something bad has happened to Bethany."

"Bethany?" Gordon repeated. Even in the dim light from five different flashlights, I could see that all the color had drained out of his face.

"She's been hurt," Jake told him. "Badly."

"How badly?" Gordon asked, his voice wavering. "What happened?"

"Maybe you should sit down," I interjected.

"Just tell me!" he insisted.

I glanced at Jake warily. "Gordon, from the looks of things, she's been stabbed. Several times."

"How bad is it?" he asked.

I took a deep breath. "It's bad. Really bad. As bad as it can possibly be."

"You mean she's dead?" he cried.

I nodded. "We called nine-one-one, but there's really no way anyone can get here—"

"No-o-o!" he wailed. "This can't be true!"

He turned and rushed out of the room, disappearing into the darkness.

His strange reaction left us all speechless.

"Are you sure that this is what happened?" Naveen asked. "It is possible that an accident occurred."

"This was no accident," I assured him. "Someone clearly—"

It was at that moment that Mrs. Moody appeared in the doorway. "What's all the ruckus?" she asked. "Or are you just playing some game?"

"This is no game, Mrs. Moody," I replied. "Someone has murdered Bethany La Montaine."

"I see," Mrs. Moody said, her expression unchanged. Once again, another unexpected reaction. "I assume you've notified the authorities? Or were you waiting for me to fulfill that duty?"

I blinked. "I called the police, if that's what you mean. Not surprisingly, they said there was no way they could manage to get someone over here, given the storm and the closed road."

"In that case," she said, "I'll have Tarleton deal with Bethany's body."

What surprised me most was that she didn't ask any questions. She barely reacted at all, in fact, not with shock or hor-

ror or even surprise. Instead, she was acting as if one of Mohawk's guests had just spilled a glass of red wine on the Oriental carpet.

"I believe he's still working on that generator," Mrs.
Moody continued. "I'll go find him."

"But what should we do now?" Yoko asked, her voice
shrill.

Mrs. Moody stood up a little straighter. "I know that Miss
McKay was going to treat us all to an introductory lecture
this evening, but given the circumstances, I suggest that for
now we go to our rooms and turn in for the night. We've all
had quite a shock. But first thing tomorrow, each and every
one of us needs to get up and have breakfast and then attend
the morning's ice cream workshop. It's critical that we go on
with the rest of the weekend as if this terrible thing never
happened. Since none of us can leave, what other choice do
we have?"

The five of us who remained lingered in the Lakeside
Room, cloaked in an uncomfortable silence.

"Bethany La Montaine certainly had her share of enemies," Yoko said, sinking into the upholstered love seat. She
seemed to find it uncomfortable, since she immediately
grabbed one of the throw pillows decorating it and wedged it
behind her back. "But I didn't think any of them were *here*."

Her comment startled me. She was right. I'd been too
shocked by what had just happened to think about the bigger
picture.

A chill ran through me as a horrifying realization suddenly
became clear in my mind. And that was that someone had
come to Mohawk explicitly to murder Bethany.

And it was extremely likely that that person was part of
our little group.

"I guess Mrs. Moody has a point about what we should all
do next," Jake said, taking the conversation in a different di-

rection even as I remained focused on the fact that there was probably a murderer in our midst—perhaps even in this very room. "Doing the workshops and everything else that's been planned is probably the only way for us all to get through the next couple of days or however long it takes for the guys with the chainsaws to get rid of that tree so we can all get out of here."

"It seems kind of coldhearted, don't you think?" Yoko asked. "Acting as if nothing happened, the way Mrs. Moody suggested?"

"I agree with Jake," Naveen said. "After all, what is the alternative? Locking ourselves in our rooms and staring at the clock?"

I, however, had an entirely different agenda in mind. Sure, I'd teach the workshops and eat my meals with the rest of our group and do whatever else was on the schedule. But as I did, I'd be doing something else besides.

And that was trying to find out who had killed Bethany La Montaine.

After all, I was stuck at a remote resort, with no way for anyone to get in or out. And one of the people I was stranded in this place with was a killer.

What else could I do?

Chapter 4

In 1876, a confectioner from Reading,
Pennsylvania, named William Clewell patented
the first ice cream dipper. Twenty-five years later,
there were 22 patents for ice cream scoops.

—*Ice Cream Dippers, an Illustrated History and Collectors
Guide to Early Ice Cream Dippers, by Wayne Smith*

After forcing ourselves to play a pitifully half-hearted game of Monopoly, we all retired to our rooms. I expected to have trouble falling asleep. Instead, I melted into total oblivion the minute my head hit the pillow.

That is, until early Saturday morning, when I was awakened by a loud crash of thunder.

When my eyes flew open, I found myself surrounded by a dark room, even though the barely discernible hands of the old-fashioned windup clock told me it was seven thirty. Despite having left the curtains open, there was very little light coming in. Outside, there was only doom, gloom, and plenty of gray. The fog had lifted, but the low, heavy clouds I could see hovering outside were sending down torrents of rain.

Another crack of thunder and a few flashes of lightning banished any last lingering traces of sleepiness. I dragged myself out of bed, reluctant to leave behind the comfortable mattress and the warmth of the puffy down-filled duvet I'd burrowed under all night.

I knew this was going to be a tough day. And giving two workshops on the topic of ice cream was the least of it.

I felt as gloomy as the weather as twenty minutes later I made my way along the long corridors to the dining room, once again using my flashlight to guide me. My palms were damp and my heart was beating just a little bit faster than usual.

After all, I was pretty sure I'd be sharing the breakfast table with a murderer.

As I passed through the doorway of the dining room, I was glad to see that while the skies outside were still ominously dark and a hard, steady rain was still falling, the expanse of windows let in enough light that it was actually possible to see.

And what I saw was that Jake was already there, much to my relief. This was one time when I wasn't crazy about being on my own.

He sat at the same round table we'd all been at the night before, sipping a mug of coffee. Yoko was opposite him with a cup of tea and a croissant in front of her.

I gave her a nod as I sat down next to Jake. "How are you doing?" I asked him, reaching over and squeezing his hand.

"Okay, I guess," he replied. "I didn't sleep great last night."

I didn't admit that I'd fallen into a deep sleep as soon as I'd gotten into bed. I supposed it was because I had found every aspect of the previous day utterly exhausting, from spending the afternoon preparing for the weekend to making the treacherous drive up the mountain—and of course to the unspeakable events that followed.

"But the coffee's helping," he added with a grin. "I guess they have gas stoves here and Mrs. Moody was able to light them with a match and boil water. She set up a pretty nice spread over there, too. Muffins, fresh fruit, yogurt, cereal . . .'"

I glanced over and saw that there was, indeed, an impressive breakfast buffet in the corner. It consisted entirely of foods that didn't require electric appliances like toasters or waffle makers to prepare. First, however, I needed coffee, just like Jake. I was glad he shared my appreciation for the true breakfast of champions.

I poured myself a big, steaming mug of the magic stuff, then doctored it up with enough cream and sugar that it closely resembled melted ice cream. As I sat back down next to Jake, Naveen strode into the dining room. Even though it wasn't even eight a.m. yet, he was dressed in a suit and tie. His face looked freshly shaved and his hair had been meticulously combed.

"Good morning," he said, nodding at the three of us as he pulled out a chair. "Although given the circumstances, that might not be the most appropriate thing to say."

"Clichés work just fine in situations like this," Yoko said mechanically. She had barely glanced up from her cup of tea. "Good morning to you, too."

A few seconds later, Gordon shuffled in. If Naveen was the poster boy for good grooming, Gordon looked so disheveled that it was clear that he'd had a terrible night. His hair was uncombed, his square jaw was covered in dark stubble, and he looked as if he might have slept in the white T-shirt he was wearing. As he got closer, I saw that he had it on inside out. I also saw that his eyes were red.

"Hey, everybody," he said, running his hand through his hair self-consciously as if he'd just realized that he wasn't at home, grabbing breakfast in his own kitchen.

He went right over to the coffeepot, filled a mug, and gulped half of it down. Black.

"How are you holding up?" I asked him gently as soon as he sat down.

He shrugged. "I think I'm still in shock. I haven't been able to process any of this."

I nodded. This was something I knew about since I'd suffered a few losses of my own. My parents died when I was still a child. My father, who I was very close to, passed away when I was five years old. That was when my mother, my two older sisters, and I had moved in with my grandmother. Then, five years later, I lost my mom.

"I don't think I slept more than a few minutes here and there," Gordon went on, shaking his head as if trying to shake off his dazed feeling. "I kept reaching across the bed for Bethany. But every time—"

His sentence ended in a choking sound. I did my best to comfort him by putting my hand on his back. But I knew it was unlikely that he even noticed.

It was almost a relief when the last member of our little group came bustling in. And even though the room was steeped in sadness and solemnity, the energy that Franny brought in with her managed to cut through it like a breath of fresh air.

"Good morning, everybody!" she said. "Do you believe that this crazy storm is still raging? I was fast asleep at around seven thirty, but there was this really loud crack of thunder that—"

She froze as if it was only now that she'd remembered that someone had been murdered the night before. "Oh, I'm sorry," she said, dropping into a chair. "I was so caught up in thinking about the storm that I actually forgot . . ."

She cast a sympathetic look at Gordon. But a few seconds later, the buffet table seemed to catch her eye.

"Croissants!" she cried. "Oh my gosh, I love croissants. And I hardly ever eat them because they're so fattening. Well, I guess they're okay if you only eat them occasionally, but somehow I never—and strawberries! And raspberries and blueberries . . . and is that whipped cream? Wow, this place is so amazing! It's everything I hoped it would be."

As usual, food was turning out to be an excellent distraction. Everyone helped themselves to breakfast. Franny piled so much food onto her plate that I was surprised she could lift it. Naveen, meanwhile, was simply having tea and a blueberry muffin.

We had all sat down at the table, eating and mumbling a peculiar version of small talk, when Mrs. Moody suddenly appeared. I felt her presence behind me, rather than actually hearing her come into the room. Once again, she seemed to have floated in. Or materialized out of thin air.

"I'm glad to see that you all made it to breakfast," Mrs. Moody said, addressing the whole group. "I was afraid that after the horrendous night, some of you would prefer to hide away in your rooms.

"But I'm a strong believer in staying on track," she went on. "There's no point in dwelling on things we can't change or things we can't control. So I still intend to conduct the rest of the weekend as planned." Glancing at me, she said, "Kate, I assume you'll be ready to teach the first workshop promptly at nine thirty?"

"Of course," I told her. "I'll finish setting everything up right after breakfast."

"Good," she replied with a curt nod. "If you need any help, Tarleton will be available."

"I think I'm good," I assured her quickly. As far as I was concerned, the less interaction with Tarleton, the better.

"And now I'll leave you to—"

"Why don't you join us for breakfast?" Naveen interjected. "That is, if your schedule permits."

Mrs. Moody looked surprised by his invitation. And pleased.

"I can certainly spare a few minutes," she said, actually smiling a bit. "Since you've been kind enough to invite me."

She poured herself a cup of tea, then sat down at our table.

Even though there were seven of us, however, no one seemed capable of finding a way to break the heavy silence that hung over us like one of those dark rainclouds outside.

Personally, I was finding the silence painful. If there was one thing we needed, it was conversation. And given that I was anxious to find out as much as I could about the other members of our little group, I was more than willing to be the one to get the ball rolling.

"So you work in a library," I said, turning to Franny. "I bet you're one of those people who's always loved books."

"Oh, yes!" she gushed, chattering away even though she was still chewing a mouthful of strawberries and whipped cream. "Always. Ever since I was a little girl. When I was growing up, I spent more time at the library than just about anywhere else. I loved everything about it. The smell of the books, the comfortable chairs and the big tables . . . even the fact that everyone was supposed to be quiet or else talk really softly. The library always felt like a sacred place somehow."

"I, too, am a big reader," Naveen commented. "I recently arranged for a carpenter to cover an entire wall of my study with shelving simply to accommodate my ever-growing collection."

"How about you, Franny?" Jake asked. "Do you have a big collection of books at home, too? Or do you prefer reading e-books?"

She squirmed in her seat a little. "Actually, I rarely buy books. I mostly just get them from the library where I work."

"Ah, so you are your own best customer," Naveen observed.

Franny shrugged. "I guess I never got out of the habit of getting all my books at the library. There was never much money in my family, so buying books was a luxury we simply couldn't afford. Maybe that's another reason I decided to work in a library. Not only are libraries places where I've always felt comfortable; I knew that working in one would also allow me to spend my life helping other people who love reading as much as I always have."

"So you grew up poor, huh?" Gordon commented, the bluntness of his words making me cringe. "What was *that* like?"

Somehow he managed to make not having been born with a silver spoon in one's mouth sound like some kind of interesting quirk.

Surprisingly, Franny didn't seem offended. "It wasn't that bad," she said. "At least, not when I was a little girl. I thought everybody lived the way we did, doing things like driving around the better neighborhoods in town the night before trash pickup to look through the things other people were throwing out. My folks and I would find the best stuff! I had a white dresser with flowers painted on it that we got off somebody's curb. It only had three legs, and the paint was a little chipped, but it was beautiful. I had that dresser until I went away to college. We got all kinds of amazing things. Furniture, lamps, toys . . . I even got one of the prettiest winter coats I've ever owned from someone else's trash barrel! Sometimes we even drove all the way into Minneapolis and St. Paul so we could check out the really fancy neighborhoods. That was definitely where the best stuff was!"

The expression on Gordon's face made it clear that he wished he'd never asked. Fortunately, he remained silent, burying his scornful expression in his coffee mug.

"And my mom taught me all kinds of useful tricks about doing things economically," Franny went on. "Like how to use cheaper cuts of meats to make really great meals. And how to reuse things. We were recycling long before it was in style! We would rinse off plastic wrap and plastic bags so we could use them again. And did you know that empty peanut butter jars make great drinking glasses?" Smiling broadly, she added, "Sometimes I think I should write a book about all the inventive things people can do to save money."

"You said you didn't mind not having a lot of money when you were a little kid," Yoko commented. I was surprised she'd even been listening. She had pretty much remained expressionless ever since I'd come into the room. "Does that mean your family's lifestyle started to bother you once you grew up?"

"Oh, just a little," Franny replied, waving one hand in the air. "You know, like in high school, when the other girls had things I couldn't have."

"Like a car?" Jake asked.

"Like a gym suit," she replied. "Those things are expensive, you know? And the students are required to buy them themselves, believe it or not. Fortunately, my school had a way of helping kids like me pay for extras like that."

No one seemed to know what to say.

Fortunately, Franny was chatty enough that that didn't matter. "But now that I'm grown up," she went on, "I believe that it was *good* that I grew up without much in the way of material things. It helped make me who I am."

"And who is that, exactly?" Gordon asked dryly.

"Someone who enjoys living a simple life," she replied with a shrug. "A *quiet* life. One that isn't based on acquiring things."

"In that case, I'm surprised you even came here for this weekend," Gordon commented. "Given what a *quiet* life you lead." From the way he said "quiet," it was clear that he meant "dull."

"I wasn't going to come, at least at first," Franny chirped. "When I got the flyer in the mail, I almost threw it away."

Naveen looked surprised. "You got a flyer about this weekend in the mail?"

"Well, sure." As if to prove her point, Franny reached into her big floppy purse and pulled out a somewhat wrinkled business-size envelope. From it she extracted a single page with simple computer graphics. Frankly, I thought it looked kind of amateurish. I knew that Emma, my creative niece, could have done a much better job.

"Did someone mail that to you?" Yoko asked, frowning.

"Why, yes," Franny replied. "Didn't all of you get one of these flyers in the mail?"

"Not I," Naveen said.

"I didn't, either," Yoko said. "I found out about this workshop by checking the website. I do that from time to time, just to see what kinds of programs Mohawk has planned."

"I, meanwhile, thought that spending an entire weekend thinking of nothing more taxing than ice cream sounded like a perfect respite from the demands of everyday life," Naveen said with a smile. "Especially since ice cream has always been one of my favorite foods."

"And I just came because Bethany dragged me here," Gordon added.

It was unanimous. No one besides Franny had received a special invitation in the mail.

Franny frowned. "Maybe I'm on a mailing list that none of you happen to be on," she said. Turning to Mrs. Moody, she asked, "Is that something Mohawk does? Find people that might be interested in a certain topic and reach out to them by mail?"

Mrs. Moody just offered her usual wan smile. "I'm sure I wouldn't know," she said. "That's something the marketing people would deal with, not me. I'm just concerned with the day-to-day goings-on here."

While everyone else accepted her response, moving on to talk about snail mail in general and junk mail in particular, I was confused by her answer. I assumed it was the general manager's job to know pretty much everything that was going on. Then again, I supposed it was possible that Mrs. Moody's job really did only concern keeping the hotel's guests satisfied once they had gotten here, not enticing them to come in the first place.

Even so, I made a point of getting as good a look as I could at the handwritten address on the envelope Franny had received her flyer in.

I also found myself wondering if Bethany had received a personal invitation to the weekend, just like Franny. If so, was it possible that Franny was also on the killer's list?

I was still pondering that possibility when I heard Mrs. Moody ask Gordon how he was doing. He gave her pretty much the same answer he'd given me.

But then he added, "Bethany was such an amazing woman. She was one of those rare people who was smart, beautiful, warm, generous—"

Yoko let out a snort. The sound she made was barely audible, as if it was involuntary, but we all heard it.

As if trying to explain her strange reaction, she said, "The cosmetics industry might be all about making women look pretty, but behind the scenes, it's a cutthroat business just like any other. It's a four-hundred-billion-dollar-a-year industry. And whenever there's lots of money involved, there's plenty of backstabbing. Which means someone like Bethany wouldn't have lasted more than a few years if she wasn't a tough cookie."

"You seem to know a lot about the world of cosmetics," Franny commented.

Yoko was silent for a few seconds. "I work in cosmetics," she finally said.

"Really!" Franny said brightly. "How exciting! Is that what you sell on the internet?"

Yoko nodded. "That's right. I run a website called Athena's Beauty. Athena is the goddess of wisdom, after all. Also poetry, art, and war, but it's the wisdom part I like the best. I sell the finest beauty products from all over the world. Moisturizers from France. Eye shadow and lipsticks that are used by the top makeup artists in Hollywood. Hair products that are made with the highest-quality Moroccan argan oil available, created by hand in a tiny family-run company in Marrakesh. My website is the only place where you can buy a special foundation created by one of the most in-demand dermatologists in New York. The stuff is capable of covering every blemish imaginable. Even scars and beauty marks."

"Are you the founder of the company?" Naveen asked.

"Yes, I am," Yoko said proudly. "And it's doing fabulously, if I do say so myself.

"As a matter of fact," she added, "I have a bunch of samples I could give you, if anyone is interested. They're right here in this bag I have with me . . ." She grabbed a big tote bag off the floor and plopped it into her lap.

"I'm interested!" Franny exclaimed.

I must admit, I was up for a few freebies myself. But I was glad I didn't have to be the one who gave Yoko the green light to be as generous as she wanted.

Yoko was already reaching into her bag, pulling out fistfuls of small plastic bottles in various colors and shapes. "Here we go. These are part of a new line I've been investigating. It's called Lush Luxury. There's shampoo, conditioner, hand lotion, body lotion, facial moisturizer . . ."

She handed several small bottles to Franny, then passed a few on to Mrs. Moody and me.

"Thank you!" Franny gushed. "This is so nice of you."

"It's very nice," Mrs. Moody agreed. "How thoughtful of you to include all of us in your generosity."

"I gave Tarleton a few samples before, too, since the line also includes men's products," Yoko noted. "That's something really new for me. Shaving cream, aftershave, men's cologne, moisturizer . . ." She was already distributing small rectangular bottles to each one of the men at the table. The packaging on these utilized more neutral shades, ranging from tan to brown.

"You are indeed very generous," Naveen said, as gracious as usual.

Gordon just stuck his into his pants pocket without comment.

"Did you already have a background in cosmetics when you started your own company?" Jake asked Yoko. "I'm mainly asking because I'm about to jump into a new venture of my own—kind of a boutique farm stand, if there is such a thing—and I'm curious about how other people have launched their own companies."

Once again, Yoko seemed reluctant to answer what seemed like a simple, straightforward question. "I spent a couple of years working at La Montaine."

Gordon blinked. "So you knew Bethany through work," he said, his voice flat.

This time, Yoko didn't answer at all. She simply nodded.

I, meanwhile, was fiendishly scribbling mental notes. So *that* was why Bethany and Yoko had recognized each other. They had worked together—which meant that the two women had a history.

"That's quite a coincidence," Franny said brightly. "I mean the two of you running into each other again like this, at such an unlikely place!"

Or not, I thought. But I kept my observations to myself.

"When did you work at La Montaine?" Gordon asked. "I didn't know the name of every single person Bethany ever worked with, of course, but I don't remember her mentioning you."

"It was a while ago," Yoko answered. "I left the company three years ago. That's when I started Athena's Beauty."

Gordon nodded. "I didn't even meet Bethany until two years ago. No wonder your name and face weren't familiar to me."

But they had been familiar to Bethany, I thought. And she had reacted with something along the lines of horror upon seeing Yoko Wallace again.

I was about to ask a probing question or two when the lights suddenly flashed on, seemingly from every fixture in the entire room. The huge chandeliers, the wall sconces, and even the overhead lights that were out in the hallway were ablaze with what seemed like startling brightness.

"Hey, the power is back on!" Jake cried.

"Yay!" Yoko cried. "I can get online again!"

You go, Tarleton, I thought.

Mrs. Moody stood up to leave, saying, "I hope you'll all excuse me. Now that everything is up and running once again, I have plenty of work to catch up on."

I did, too. Now that the lights were back on, there was no excuse for all of us not to do exactly what we'd decided to do: continue with the weekend as if the terrible event of the night before had never occurred.

Which for me meant teaching workshops on the light-hearted topic of ice cream. It wasn't going to be easy, but it was what I had been brought here to do.

Chapter 5

Dixie Cups, two flavors of ice cream in a
disposable paper cup, are named after the cup,
which was invented in 1907 as a hygienic way
to drink water. The Ice Cream Dixie was popular-
ized by a successful radio show, "Dixie Circus,"
that was aired on Friday nights. Dixies were
also advertised in magazines like the *Saturday
Evening Post* and *Good Housekeeping.*

—*https://sites.lafayette.edu/dixiecollection/company-history/*

As Jake and I walked out of the dining room, he rubbed
his hands together and asked, "Okay, so where do I
start?"

In response to my look of confusion, he added, "I'm here
as your assistant, right? So what can I do to assist you?"

"This morning is going to be a breeze," I told him. "There
isn't much I need to do to prepare. It's not as if I'll be doing a
demonstration or anything hands-on. Instead, I thought I'd
launch the weekend with the introductory lecture I was planning to give last night. I'll be talking about the history of ice
cream, the difference between ice cream and custard and
gelato, various ice cream desserts, and an overview of how
they're made, that kind of thing. As far as I'm concerned, you
can just relax until nine thirty, when I'll start. And then, what

I need most is for you to sit in the audience and send me vibes of moral support."

I thought he might be disappointed, but instead he lit up. "Great! In that case, I'll spend the next hour or so taking a tour of the grounds."

"You're going outside?" I cried, alarmed. "But it's still pouring out there! And it's windy and foggy and—"

"Don't worry," he insisted. "I'm not going mountain climbing. I'm just taking a little stroll."

"Please be careful," I warned. "I don't want any tree branches falling on you."

As soon as he'd hurried off to his room to grab his coat and, hopefully, an umbrella, I made a beeline for the Great Room. Given its tremendous size, I decided to follow through on my first instinct, which was establishing a class-room feeling by creating a more intimate space in one corner. And I still thought the area closest to the wall of windows in back would work best.

First I dragged a big rectangular table over to the area. That was going to serve as my lectern. Then I set up a row of chairs so they were facing it. Even though I only expected there to be five people in the audience—Jake, Franny, Yoko, Gordon, and Naveen—I set up seven chairs. For all I knew, Mrs. Moody might turn out to have a secret passion for ice cream. Tarleton, too.

Once that was done, I grabbed the boxes I'd had the fore-sight to label with a big numeral 1 to designate that they were the materials I needed for my first lecture.

I began laying out various handouts, with different subjects printed on different colored paper. The topics ranged from a time line of ice cream history to a definition of terms ranging from *affogato* to zabaglione. (Zabaglione isn't actually ice cream. It's an Italian custard, but since it can be served frozen, I considered it worth mentioning.) Thanks to my multitalented niece, Emma, who was as proficient with computers as she was with art and design, each one of the handouts looked like a work of art.

I'd just finished when I heard someone come in. Glancing up, I saw Naveen walking toward me. He was carrying a mug of coffee and yesterday's edition of the *New York Times*.

"I hope I am not intruding," he said congenially. "I must admit that spending so much time in the company of others is starting to wear me down. The thought of sitting in a room with someone who's involved in her own activities without requiring any input from me strikes me as luxuriously restful."

I laughed. "It's quite a group, isn't it?" More earnestly, I added, "And given what happened last night, well, that just complicates the dynamic even further."

"Indeed." Naveen lowered his bulky form into one of the seats that constituted the front and only row. "And please feel free to ignore me. Unless, of course, there is something I can do to help. I value my downtime, but that does not mean I do not enjoy being useful to others."

"I think I've got everything under control," I assured him. "Aside from the butterflies in my stomach, that is. To be perfectly honest, I've never done this kind of thing before."

"There is no reason to be nervous," Naveen said. "Just keep in mind that no one has any preconceived notions of how your presentation will go but you. Whatever you do, they will accept it as the norm."

"That's a good point," I said. "It sounds as if you've done some public speaking of your own."

"I have," he replied. "As a young man, when I was still living in London, I started a small company."

"Really! So you're an entrepreneur, just like me," I commented. "I don't suppose you were in the ice cream business."

He hesitated. "Actually, I was an inventor. I worked in the tech field, and I developed a new type of daisy wheel. In those days, when home computers were still a brand-new phenomenon, the printers people used at home were called daisy wheel printers. They had a small plastic disk that actually had all the letters and symbols from a typewriter on the edges. The printer worked by impressing each letter on a piece of paper, one at a time."

"I've heard of those," I said.

"Alas, I am afraid I did not have the foresight to keep up with the changing technology," Naveen continued. "Which is why my business eventually failed. However, it did give me many opportunities to speak in public, which is how I became such an expert that I feel free to advise you."

I laughed. "You certainly gave me a helpful tip."

"You also have a real advantage," he added. "I used to bore people with computer-speak. You, however, are going to treat us all to an overview of the wonderful world of ice cream this morning. Is that correct?"

"That's right," I said. "I figured that talking about ice cream, rather than serving it, was a good idea. After all, nine thirty in the morning is kind of early for people to start eating it. Personally, I'm a big fan of gulping down a hefty dose of Cappuccino Crunch for breakfast, but I understand that not everyone feels that way.

"So I prepared a lecture," I continued. "But that's exactly what it is: a lecture. I'll be making it more interesting with a few visuals, thanks to PowerPoint. I prepared a formal presentation because I assumed I'd be giving a talk to a roomful of people. But with only a few attendees, I'm going to have to make some adjustments. Try to make it more casual. And a little more interactive."

"I have no doubt that you are up to the challenge," he replied. "And I was sincere in my offer. If there is any way in which I can assist you, please do not hesitate to inform me."

"Thanks." I began rifling through the note cards I'd brought along in case it turned out that a slideshow or PowerPoint presentation seemed too businesslike for a venue like this.

"But there is one question you can answer for me," Naveen said, "something I can not help being curious about. Do you consider yourself someone who has a better sense of taste than most people? What I mean to ask is, are your taste buds more sensitive than most people's? I would think that would be something that would make you better than most people at developing new varieties of ice cream or coming up with delightful ways of combining different flavors."

I glanced up from my note cards and thought for a few seconds. "I guess I do have a pretty highly developed sense of taste," I finally said. "I do feel that I'm pretty tuned into the subtleties of different flavors. For example, I'm really good at differentiating between various types of chocolate. At this point, I can pretty much tell what percent cocoa is in a particular piece of the stuff. Everybody can probably tell the difference between milk chocolate and dark chocolate, but I bet that in a blind taste test I could tell you whether a piece of dark chocolate was made with sixty-five percent cocoa bean or seventy percent.

"I can differentiate between different qualities of chocolate, too," I went on. I had to admit that I hadn't really thought about any of this before. But now that Naveen had brought it up, I was surprised by how important these natural abilities were to me, especially given my chosen line of work. "Inexpensive chocolate just doesn't taste as good as the high quality stuff. Which means I end up using the high-priced stuff in the ice cream I make at my shop, much to my accountant's dismay."

Naveen laughed. "How about your sense of smell? Does that play an important part in your work, as well?"

"I guess it does," I said. Once again, this was something I'd never actually thought about much, but I now realized was actually pretty important when it came to developing new flavors. "If I make an unusual flavor of ice cream—like one that uses a spice with a strong presence like cardamom or basil—I'm pretty tuned in to whether or not the smell of that spice might be overwhelming to my customers. So I guess that without consciously paying attention to my sense of smell, it has become more developed along with my sense of taste."

"Fascinating," Naveen observed. "What about that chap you brought along as your assistant, the gentleman called Jake? Does he work at your shop, helping you develop new flavors, too?"

"No," I replied. "He's actually my boyfriend. Although maybe that's a bit of an exaggeration, since we just started seeing each other."

Naveen's bushy black eyebrows shot up. "Really. Given how comfortable the two of you seem together, I would have thought you had known each other for a long time."

I hesitated. "We've actually known each other since high school," I said. "It's a long story."

"I like long stories," Naveen said, smiling as he settled back in his chair.

I chuckled. "Since we only have a little time, I'll give you the short version of the long story. Jake and I were high school sweethearts. We separated at the end of our senior year and lost touch for fifteen years." With a little shrug, I added, "Now we're giving it another go."

"And is the spark still there?" Naveen asked. "Are things going well?"

"So far, they're going extremely well." While I genuinely liked this man, we barely knew each other. I didn't see any reason to tell him about the nagging doubts that continued to plague me.

"Good," he replied. "You both seem like nice people. I hope you've found yourself the right person. And that Jake has, as well."

"How about you?" I asked. "Are you married?"

"Alas, no. Divorced." With a little grimace, he added, "I am afraid I am one of those boring men who prefers reading and thinking and working to socializing or playing tennis or joining a book club. And so after twenty years, my wife decided to find a partner whose interests were more in line with hers.

"But I am finding that the solitary life suits me just fine," he added. "I enjoy being a bachelor. I can spend all the time I want reading, and most Saturday nights I am in bed by nine, watching the BBC's coverage of the week's news." Nodding toward my display of handouts, he added, "I can also indulge in such sinful pastimes as eating ice cream for dinner. I have done that more times than I care to admit."

"A man after my own heart," I said. "Do you have any children?"

His expression immediately darkened. He was silent for what seemed like a very long time.

"I have a daughter," he finally said. His voice was so somber that it was barely audible.

I remained silent, not sure what to say about his strange response. But before I had a chance to come up with anything, he started speaking again.

"She was always such a star," he said, his eyes taking on a faraway look. "From the time Sana was a little girl, she was special. Even in her kindergarten class picture, she looks like she's glowing. She radiated everything that's good about being alive. She was smart, funny, lively, compassionate . . . and so accomplished. She went to Wellesley, then did a graduate degree at Columbia."

"She sounds like an amazing person," I ventured, still not sure of how to respond.

"She seemed like someone who was destined for great things," Naveen continued, still solemn. "Above all, I saw her as someone who was capable of leading a truly happy life. At least that's what everyone who knew her expected."

Suddenly his entire demeanor suddenly changed.

"But enough about me!" he said, suddenly so jovial that I found the transition jarring. "Tell me more about this ice cream business of yours."

I was much more interested in talking about him than I was in talking about me. But once I got started, I found the story spilling out.

"I grew up here in the Hudson Valley, in a town called Wolfert's Roost," I began. "I lost both my parents while I was still very young—my father when I was five and my mother when I was ten—so my grandmother ended up playing a huge role in my life. After going to college in New Paltz, I moved to New York and ended up having a career in public relations, which I really enjoyed.

"But last March, my grandmother—I've always called her Grams—fell coming down some stairs," I went on. "It immediately became clear that continuing to live by herself wasn't the best idea. So I gave up my career and my apartment and moved back to Wolfert's Roost. Once things at home settled into a routine, I decided it was time to live out a lifelong fantasy. Last spring I rented the perfect store smack in the middle of downtown, oversaw some renovations and *voilà*! In June, just six months ago, I opened the Lickety Splits Ice Cream Shoppe." Grinning, I concluded, "And it's turning out to be the best decision I've ever made!"

". . . And ice cream has been my absolute favorite food my entire life," I suddenly heard Franny saying, her voice growing louder and louder as she got closer. "When I was a child, I used to save the pennies I found on the ground, stashing them away until I had enough to buy an ice cream cone at the local convenience store. Even now, I try to eat ice cream every single day!"

Glancing at the wooden clock on the mantel, I saw that it was almost nine thirty. And filing in right behind Franny were Yoko and Gordon, the rest of my audience.

As the other three took their seats alongside Naveen, it occurred to me that not only was I looking at the audience for my lecture on ice cream. I was also standing eye-to-eye with a lineup of suspects in Bethany La Montaine's murder.

By nine thirty, my five-member audience was seated and looking up at me expectantly. Franny sat in the very center, her legs uncrossed and her back arrow-straight. Her eyes were bright and she was clutching a pad of paper and a pen, clearly ready to take notes on whatever I said. Naveen was next to her, looking just as intent but a bit more relaxed.

Gordon, meanwhile, sat with his right leg crossed, his ankle over his left knee. He looked like he was posing for an illustration of what man-spreading is. One arm was slung across the empty seat beside him. He already looked bored, as if the only reason he was in this room was that there wasn't anything else to do. I couldn't help noticing how quickly he had seemed to recover from the events of the evening before. Or maybe he was still in shock.

As for Yoko, I was having trouble reading her. Aside from Gordon, who had simply come to Mohawk to accompany Bethany, she struck me as the most unlikely of all the attendees at this ice-cream-themed weekend. Still, she was here, and she looked as ready to hear what I had to say as anyone else.

Even though Jake sat all the way to my left, grinning at me as if this was all a great adventure, I suddenly felt very nervous.

When I'd worked in public relations, I had done plenty of public speaking. Whenever the firm I worked for put on an event, more often than not I was the person who stood up in front of the crowd once everyone was assembled. Sometimes, I didn't have to do any more than introduce someone. For example, at a dinner held by the Bermuda Tourist Bureau, designed to encourage travel writers to visit the island and write articles about the desirability of vacationing there, my role was to introduce a speaker from the organization. When a major iced tea company launched a new line of tropical flavors, ranging from yummy mango to not-so-successful pineapple, I organized a picnic and invited food writers. At that event, all I had to do was bring the firm's director of marketing onto the stage.

But other times, I was the one who conducted the entire event, complete with a PowerPoint presentation. Then there were the pitches my firm made to existing or prospective clients, sharing the ideas we'd come up with to promote whatever it was they wanted to spread the word about.

However, I'd left that job—and that life—months ago. And I hadn't had to stand up in front of a group since.

You can do this, I told myself. I took a few deep breaths, following the advice I was always getting from Willow, who in addition to being my best friend since junior high school was also our hometown's resident yoga instructor. And it actually seemed to be working, at least enough that I remembered to check the note cards I was holding in my somewhat clammy hands.

"Good morning!" I said brightly. "As you all know by now, my name is Kate McKay, and I have the pleasure of running an ice cream emporium nearby called the Lickety Splits Ice Cream Shoppe. I love ice cream and everything associated with it, so I'm pleased to have this opportunity to share some of what I've learned about my favorite topic with you.

"I'd like to start with a bit of history," I went on, already starting to relax. "When did people start enjoying ice cream— or at least an early version of it? It might surprise you to learn that the version of ice cream we know of today actually began in China. The emperors of the Tang dynasty, which lasted from about 600 to 900 AD, reportedly ate what was referred to as a 'frozen milk-like confection' made with milk from a cow, a goat, or a buffalo. It also contained flower and camphor, which came from evergreen trees. The ingredients were mixed together in metal tubs and frozen in a pool of ice . . ."

Franny was earnestly scrawling notes. Naveen was nodding, the expression on his face pensive. Even Gordon and Yoko looked interested in what I was saying.

I really *can* do this, I thought, feeling my nervousness dissolve. And from that moment on, giving my talk on ice cream was exhilaratingly enjoyable.

A half hour later, I'd pretty much covered the entire history of ice cream, complete with a few amusing anecdotes about various kings, emperors, and United States presidents who were passionate about ice cream. At least I hoped they were amusing. It was hard to tell if the chuckles that came from the audience were sincere or merely politeness.

Next on the agenda was ice cream in the world today: which countries consume the most (New Zealand is number one, per capita, with the United States in second place), the different forms like mochi in Japan and *kulfi* in India, and the different types of ice cream treats and flavors that are available nowadays. But first, I decided, my audience needed a break. Or at least I needed a break.

"Let's take a ten-minute breather," I suggested. "You can get up and stretch, if you feel the need. I know I'd like to get some water and rest my voice for a bit before I go on."

"This is so much fun!" Franny gushed. "And I'm learning so much!"

"I'm glad," I told her sincerely.

Everyone in the audience stood up, seemingly more than ready to follow my advice about doing some leg stretching. Yoko immediately buried her face in her laptop, while Jake and Naveen strolled over to the window and began talking animatedly about the storm. Gordon, meanwhile, strode out of the Great Room, back toward the lobby.

I assumed that, like me, he was in search of a restroom. Yet just in case I was wrong, I decided to follow him, remaining far enough behind that he wasn't likely to notice.

I quickly saw that my impulse had been spot-on. The men's room was not his intended destination. Instead, he ducked into one of the telephone booths off the lobby and pulled the glass-paned door closed.

Under ordinary circumstances, I would have wandered off so he could make his phone call in private. But given the fact that a murder had occurred here just hours ago—and Gordon was high on the list of suspects, simply because out of everyone at Mohawk, he was the individual who had been closest to the victim—I decided to do a little eavesdropping.

So I loitered outside the phone booth's glass-windowed door, pretending to be searching for something in my purse while, in reality, I was leaning in as far as I could without looking as if I was listening in on his conversation.

"It's me," I heard him say after a few seconds. He was keeping his voice low, which made it harder to hear than I'd hoped. "Listen," he continued. "Something has happened. Something—bad."

He was silent, no doubt because the person at the other end of the line was expressing curiosity about what this "bad" thing was.

"It's Bethany," he said, his voice still low. "She's been— last night, she was murdered." Another long pause followed before he burst out with, "Of course it wasn't me! Don't be ridiculous! Why on earth would I want anything bad to happen to the woman I love . . ." His voice suddenly grew even quieter. ". . . Not to mention the woman who was my own personal goose who laid the golden egg." Chuckling, he added, "And not just one, either. She was turning out one golden egg after another."

By this point my heart was pounding so hard that the wooden floor was practically vibrating. *So Gordon was more than simply Bethany's beau!* I thought. She was also providing him with something valuable that had nothing to do with the L-word.

And from what I knew of human nature, chances were good that that something was money.

"I know, I know," Gordon was saying. "The timing is lousy." The man he was talking to—and the sounds coming from the other end of the line were so loud that even from where I stood, I could tell they were the sounds of an angry male voice—was obviously upset.

"You're jumping to too many conclusions," Gordon finally said. "I'm just saying that things are a little sensitive at the moment. But this is temporary, I promise. Calm down. I give you my word that—"

There was another pause as the man at the other end of the conversation did some more yelling.

"Okay, so maybe my word *isn't* worth much," Gordon finally interjected. "But I can find a way around this . . . No, I don't know what that is. But all I need is a little time . . . No, I haven't forgotten . . . Listen, I *know*, but . . . I *know* . . ."

All of a sudden, I got the feeling that someone was watching me. And while I'd been at Mohawk for only a short time, I'd already learned who that someone was likely to be.

Sure enough, I turned around and found myself face-to-face with Mrs. Moody.

"Ms. McKay?" she said sharply. "Aren't you supposed to be conducting a workshop?"

"That's exactly what I'm doing, Mrs. Moody," I replied cheerfully, quickly snapping my purse shut. "But the first part of the morning was pretty intense, so I gave everyone a ten-minute break."

Just then Franny drifted by. A few sheets of toilet paper that had gotten stuck to the bottom of her shoe trailed behind her.

"Look, here's Franny, no doubt back from the restroom," I said brightly. "I suppose it's almost time to get things underway again."

I guess Gordon had heard our little interaction, or at least he'd heard people speaking nearby.

"I've got to go," I heard him say at some point during my short conversation with Mrs. Moody.

But I'd already heard enough. As I jogged after Franny so I could suggest that she rid herself of her souvenir of Mohawk's ladies' room before I dashed off there myself, I was already determined to corner Gordon the first chance I got.

The man was hiding something. And while he had already held a prominent place on my list of suspects, his name was suddenly glaring as brightly as if it had been lit up in neon.

* * *

"Nice job," Jake told me after the workshop had ended and my small but devoted audience had learned more about ice cream than they'd probably ever thought possible. "I'm not turning out to be much of an assistant, though, am I?"

I laughed. "That was the easiest workshop of the entire weekend. All I had to do was stand there and talk. This afternoon, we're doing a hands-on workshop. I'm going to be demonstrating the basics of making ice cream at home, so I'll need you to do the heavy lifting. I'll also take advantage of your scooping abilities."

"That's what I'm here for," he said. "You're not the first person who's thought of me as the strong, silent type."

"That's not *all* you're here for," I replied, dropping my voice in an attempt at sounding seductive. "You know, we have a little time before lunch. How about meeting me in the Lakeside Room in about ten minutes for a bit of that fireside cuddling that's been on my to-do list ever since we got here?"

Jake grinned. "Cuddling. Now there's something else I'm good at."

I spent a few minutes rearranging the area I'd staked out as my classroom. For this afternoon's lessons in ice cream making, I'd need a much bigger table, one that everyone could stand around. Fortunately, there was one near the fireplace that looked perfect.

As I left the Great Room and headed toward the Mountainview Room, I found myself really looking forward to having some quiet time with Jake. Being with someone who I knew so well, especially when everyone else in this place was a stranger, felt reassuring. This weekend certainly wasn't turning out the way either of us had anticipated. We'd expected interesting people, engaging ice cream workshops, a few expeditions around the grounds, and a chance to enjoy each other's company. Murder, needless to say, had never been on the schedule.

But that's exactly what we had ended up dealing with. True, we were all doing our best to get through the next couple of days, mainly by acting as if everything was normal. But the fact that there was a body on the premises, along with a cold-blooded killer, was impossible to forget.

Meanwhile, the storm that continued to rage outside was an ongoing reminder that we were all stuck here. Together.

I was trying to find a way to compartmentalize the reality of the situation so I could focus on the romantic rendezvous that was next on the agenda as I passed by the Mountainview Room. Out of the corner of my eye, I saw that there was someone inside. Automatically, I turned my head.

What I saw made me freeze.

Tarleton was sitting in a big comfortable chair, gazing out the window. Not that there was anything unusual about the man doing nothing but—well, nothing.

What surprised me was that Mrs. Moody was standing right behind him, staring out at the same view of the dreary day outside.

As she did, she was distractedly stroking his hair.

The gesture didn't only startle me because showing affection seemed so completely out of character for her. I was even more shocked because Tarleton was Mrs. Moody's employee.

At least, that was what she had claimed.

Was it possible that there was more to their relationship than stern employer and passive underling? My first thought was that there was something romantic between them. After all, that was the most obvious conclusion.

But Mrs. Moody appeared to be in her mid to late sixties. Tarleton, meanwhile, was probably in his thirties or even early forties. And while a December-May romance wasn't totally out of the question, that explanation struck me as most unlikely.

Yet whatever the circumstances were, the realization that I'd just come to was truly surprising. And that was that there was a softer side to Mrs. Moody, something I never would have expected in a million years.

Chapter 6

In the spring of 2018, a South Korean
convenience chain began selling an ice cream bar
that it claims cures hangovers. The Gyeondyo-bar
is made with a grapefruit-flavored ice cream and
contains Oriental raisin tree fruit juice, the active
ingredient. In South Korea, Oriental raisin tree
juice has been considered a cure for hangovers
for centuries.

—http://www.thisisinsider.com/cure-your-hangover-by-
eating-an-ice-cream-bar-south-korea-2018-3

I tried to put the strange little scene I'd just witnessed out of
my mind. Instead, I focused on the romantic interlude that
lay ahead of me, which was much more tantalizing.

Jake was already in the Lakeside Room, sitting on the
brown upholstered couch that faced the fireplace. No man-
spreading here. He was sitting off to one side, clearly having
made a point of leaving enough room for me, his partner in
cuddling.

A roaring fire raged in the fireplace, casting the room in a
golden glow and making those crackling noises that sound
like fall. Outside, the rain continued to come down in torrents.

If there was ever a day to curl up on a cozy couch in front

of a fireplace, this was it. I couldn't imagine anything more romantic.

I was so determined to enjoy every second of it that I wasn't even going to let the looming specter of the terrible events of the night before get in our way. I needed to focus on Jake. I reminded myself that I'd decided a few weeks earlier to give my relationship with him a chance, and I owed it to both of us not to give in to my reservations and fears and whatever else was standing in my way, and do exactly that.

Jake and I had first become a couple during our junior year of high school, when he invited me to the Halloween Dance. Actually, the way he'd done it turned out to be pretty dramatic.

I was in the midst of being taunted by our school's number-one mean girl, Ashley Winthrop. As I'd stood at my locker at the end of a school day, wrestling with a couple of heavy textbooks, she lingered nearby with two of her gal pals, bragging loudly about having not one, not two, but three invitations to the dance and pretending to feel sorry for the "unpopular girls," as she put it, who hadn't had any invitations at all. She had just finished asking me if I was going, her smirk making it clear that she thought she already had her answer, when Jake Pratt walked over to me and asked me to the dance right in front of her.

And Jake wasn't just anyone. He was our high school's star baseball player. And thanks to his talent in sports—not to mention his lean, muscular build, his amazingly blue eyes, and his easygoing personality—he was one of the most sought-after boys at Modderplaatz High. He was also daringly independent, choosing not to be lured into any particular clique. And that included the one Ashley presided over, the group that had somehow managed to convince everyone else that they were the cool, popular, all-powerful kids.

As Ashley had witnessed Jake asking uncool me to the Halloween Dance, she had looked like a balloon that had suddenly sprung a leak. But I had known even then that it wasn't Ashley's reaction that made this an important moment. This was about Jake and me.

The night of the Halloween Dance was magical. *We* were magical, something that he and I both understood immediately. The inevitability of the two of us being together was sealed that very night with our first kiss, which in my mind remains one of the most memorable events of my life.

And for the next year and a half, we weren't just any couple. We were one of those totally inseparable, soul-mates-joined-at-the-hip couples that everyone accepts as a has-to-be pairing like salt and pepper, peanut butter and jelly, and hot fudge sundaes and a cherry on top.

That is, until prom night.

There was no question about Jake and me going to the prom together. And preparing for that special night had made me feel like a real grown-up for the first time ever. Finding the perfect blue dress, luxuriating in a long, hot bubble bath, getting my hair styled professionally, carefully applying more makeup than I had ever worn before . . .

But Jake never showed.

I waited, all dressed up and ready to go. Grams and I sat together, watching the clock, making small talk, and most of all making excuses for Jake's uncharacteristic lateness. Finally, it had gotten late enough that I gave up, tearing off the blue dress and dissolving into inconsolable tears.

I didn't see Jake for another fifteen years. I didn't get a phone call, a text, an email, a letter, or even a post on my Facebook page.

Then, a few months after I'd come back home to Wolfert's Roost, I'd stumbled upon him once again. I unexpectedly found him standing behind the counter of the organic dairy he now ran. It was only shortly afterward that I finally learned what had happened that devastating night. Jake's father, a longtime alcoholic, had been in a terrible car accident, one that had left three people injured, including a little girl. Jake had spent the evening with his dad at the police station, still wearing his tux. And he'd been so ashamed about his family's problem ruining what was supposed to be one of the most special nights in our young lives that he'd been afraid to face me.

I'd found it really hard to get over the pain of that night. The years that followed, too. While missing prom night had been traumatic enough for a high school girl like me, I'd found Jake's silence during all those years afterward even more hurtful. My anger was aggravated further by recently learning that he had been living in New York City some of the time that I was living there, too. He had been working as a criminal defense lawyer in a high-powered Manhattan law firm during several of the years that I'd been residing in a shoebox-sized apartment on the Upper East Side, working at a public relations firm.

But after witnessing how steadfast Jake Pratt had been over the past few months, standing by me in a number of trying moments, I'd come to appreciate him all over again. To see him as the warm, caring, funny, supportive and, yes, attractive, man he was.

Which was why I'd told myself that it was time to forgive him.

Yet even though your brain may tell you to do one thing, that doesn't necessarily mean that your heart will follow. And my heart was still sitting on the fence about Jake, at least a little.

In my mind, this weekend was part of exploring whether or not I could make a real commitment to him—or at least to sincerely giving our relationship a try. This would be the most time he and I had spent together since high school. So far, all we'd done together was go out on old-fashioned-style dates. We'd gone to a couple of movies, we'd tried Peruvian and Cuban and Basque restaurants in various towns all over the Hudson Valley, and we'd poked around farmers markets and craft fairs.

We'd also taken lots of long walks along the Hudson River. On those, we usually brought along a chaperone: Digger, my household's resident canine charmer, a terrier mix who gave new meaning to the term "high-energy." In addition, we'd spent plenty of evenings hanging out at either his house or mine, watching TV and eating ice cream and just enjoying each other's company and getting to know each other all over again.

But this was the first time Jake and I had actually gone away together. Which meant it was also the first time we would be spending more than a few hours in each other's company. In a way, this weekend at Mohawk was sort of a test.

"So how was your walk?" I asked as I plopped down beside him, kicked off my shoes, and curled up against the soft couch and his not-so-soft shoulder.

He grimaced. "It wasn't much of a walk. It was more like a reconnaissance mission, dodging the rain by dashing from one overhang to another while I tried to see as much of the grounds as possible. I'm afraid I didn't get very far.

"But what I did manage to see looked really cool," he went on. "The lake is fantastic. We should come back here sometime when the weather is better so we can enjoy it. We could go canoeing or kayaking or paddleboarding. And there are plenty of great hiking trails, too. I bet it's great here in the spring."

I nodded. But my stomach tightened over the enthusiasm with which Jake was making long-term plans for the two of us. Like five or six months away, which suddenly seemed like a very long time.

Relax! I told myself. *The man is just making conversation.*

"One of the coolest things I found," he continued, "is a maze."

"Are you talking about a maze for kids?" I asked, not sure what he meant.

"Better," he replied. "It's a maze for everybody. It's huge, made out of tall hedges. Like something out of a movie, you know?"

I did know. I had seen that kind of thing in lots of movies. English movies, mostly, from what I recalled. I thought of hedge mazes as being popular at English castles and manor houses, the kind of thing Jane Austen's characters might encounter.

"It'd be fun to get lost in one of those," I commented.

"It'd be fun to get lost in one with *you*," Jake said, leaning over and kissing me. This wasn't one of those chaste kisses that was suitable for prying eyes like Mrs. Moody's. This was a seriously mushy kiss. I immediately felt guilty, as if I was carrying on inappropriately.

For a minute or two, we sat together in silence, simply enjoying being together as we watched the fire as intently as if it was the hottest new release from Netflix.

"There's something I've been meaning to ask you," Jake finally said, "but it seems like kind of a dumb question."

"Ask me anything," I said. But that knot that had formed earlier was back. And this time, it was the size of a scoop of Rocky Road. A really generous scoop.

"I guess I should have asked you sooner," Jake said, suddenly as bashful as my favorite of the Seven Dwarfs, "but somehow the time never seemed right."

I was starting to get *really* nervous.

But then he took a deep breath and asked, "What exactly does a person who works for a public relations firm *do?*"

I burst out laughing. "That question is a lot easier to answer than some of the things I was thinking you were going to ask me!" I told him, a wave of relief washing over me. "The whole point of public relations is getting the clients' names in front of people. Not by paying for coverage, like with advertisements, but by having people who work in media write things about them. Or talk about them, in the case of television.

"Let's say a client who's an actor has a new film out," I went on. "Or that the client is a company that just came out with a new product. An advertising agency would buy ads in magazines or on websites or on TV to spread the word. But the job of the public relations firm I worked for was to contact people—writers, editors, bloggers, producers, people who cover whatever is going on in the world—and pitch stories. Like, 'Harold Hunk, who just starred in such-and-such movie, grew up in your town. Wouldn't you like to do a feature on the local news about how a local boy made good?' Or for a new electronics product, we might get in touch with someone who writes for a tech website and say, 'I know you handle the column on Ten New Great Things to Look Out For This Month. Can I send you some information about my client's exciting new gizmo that makes it possible to read people's minds while you're talking to them on the phone?'"

"Interesting," Jake commented. "I never thought about how things like that work, but now I get it."

"We also put together events, which was one of my favorite parts of the job," I added. "Like we'd hold a launch party for a new product and invite journalists who write about that industry. I especially enjoyed launching new restaurants, since we'd basically throw a big party that showed the place off and invite everyone who wrote about food or things to do in New York."

"But it sounds like public relations is basically all about keeping people's names and faces out there," Jake said. "In a positive way."

"Exactly," I agreed.

"That sounds sort of cool," he commented. Grinning, he added, "But I think spending your days making and selling ice cream is a much better use of your time. Not to mention your creativity."

I laughed. "I'm with you on that."

Suddenly the mood changed. "I've got some other ideas on good uses of your time, too," he said, snuggling a little closer.

"Oh, really?" I said. "I'd be interested in hearing about those."

He leaned forward and was about to plant another one of those romantic kisses when I suddenly got the creepy feeling that someone was watching us.

A half a second later, I heard someone cough.

I whirled around, coming this close to knocking my shoulder into Jake's jaw. Sure enough, we weren't alone. Mrs. Moody was standing right behind us.

"Goodness! You two are in here!" she said. "I'm sorry. I had no idea the room was occupied. I was just coming in to check the fire."

"We're doing great with the fire," Jake assured her. "I'll keep an eye on it. I promise."

She smiled at him. "I'm sure you will. You're obviously an able-bodied young man."

My eyebrows shot up, but I remained silent.

"Since everything appears to be in order, I'll leave you two to enjoy Mohawk," Mrs. Moody said. "Don't forget that lunch is at noon, and the next workshop begins promptly at one thirty."

"Boy, she's good at sneaking around," Jake commented after glancing over his shoulder to make sure she was gone. "I'm starting to wonder if that woman is a vampire."

"That thought has already crossed my mind once or twice," I added. "Tarleton, too."

"Maybe the job requirements for working at Mohawk are being able to work through the night—and not eating any of the food," Jake joked. "At least, the normal food."

"I did notice that she checked my pulse before showing me to my room," I added.

"Somewhere on the premises, probably in a room down in the basement, there's a coffin with her name on it," he said. "And probably one right next to it for her pal Tarleton."

I was already getting tired of talking about Mrs. Moody. Especially since the time I knew I'd have to spend alone with Jake was turning out to be a lot scarcer than I'd expected. And I was finding it a lot less threatening and a lot more enjoyable than I'd expected.

"So here I am," I said, pretending to be thinking out loud, "lying in front of a roaring fire with an attractive man . . ."

"An *able-bodied* man," Jake interjected, grinning.

I cast him a look of disdain. "Well, at least a *young* man. Mrs. Moody got that part right."

"Hey, I'm extremely able-bodied," he insisted. "Not that I know what that means, exactly. I mean, I can lug around a ten-gallon drum of organic milk. I can lug around a calf, for goodness' sake. Does that make me able-bodied?"

"Somehow, I don't think Mrs. Moody was referring to your ability to haul heavy cans," I replied. "Or livestock."

"Which brings us right back to where we were before we were so rudely interrupted," Jake said.

Once again, he leaned forward and was about to kiss me when I heard another cough.

"I was afraid you two might be getting bored," I heard Mrs. Moody say.

I jerked my head around and found her standing behind us again. Only this time, she was carrying a tray with two mugs and a pitcher.

"I've brought you some hot chocolate," she announced. "I thought it was just the thing for a dark, rainy Saturday."

"If you're eight years old," Jake muttered softly.

In a louder voice, he said, "That's so thoughtful, Mrs. Moody. Thank you."

I was impressed by his ability to be polite even in a situation like this one. But I nearly jumped through the ceiling when he added, "Would you care to join us?"

I wondered if Mrs. Moody could see the daggers that were shooting out of my eyeballs as I cast what was supposed to be a meaningful look at him. He didn't seem to notice.

"Why, thank you, Jake," she replied as she set down the tray on the table in front of us. She sounded almost flirty. "But I have so many tasks to attend to that I simply don't have the time for any lollygagging."

The moment she left us alone again, I turned to Jake and teasingly told him, "I'm beginning to think that Mrs. Moody has a crush on you."

"She's going to have to update her vocabulary if she expects to get anywhere with me," Jake said. "I mean, lollygagging? Have we gone back in time? Are we in the nineteenth century, a time when people had more time to lollygag?"

"They didn't actually do much lollygagging back in those days," I said. "They were too busy rolling hoops and churning butter and holding greased pig races."

"Ah," Jake said with a sigh. "Good times."

We each picked up a mug and took a sip of hot chocolate. My eyes immediately grew big and round.

"This is awful!" I sputtered, forcing myself to swallow it even though I was much more inclined to spit it out.

"There's no sugar in it, for one thing," Jake said.

"And it's much too strong," I added. "And believe me, when it comes to chocolate, I rarely feel that way!"

Jake and I exchanged looks of horror, then burst out laughing.

"Good old Mrs. Moody!" I cried.

"That woman is the devil!" Jake exclaimed. "Either that or this is just another example of how she failed to inherit the nurturing gene."

"My theory is that she's trying to sabotage us," I said. "Do you think she's jealous?"

Jake smiled. "I definitely think she is. I'm convinced that the moment she laid eyes on me, she decided I was her idea of the perfect man. And she figured she wasn't going to let some . . . some ice cream empress stand in the way of her finding the romance she's always longed for . . ."

"Oh, so you think you're that irresistible?" I asked, my voice dripping with sarcasm.

"I don't actually know if I'm irresistible," he replied thoughtfully. He put his mug back on the tray, wriggled closer to me, and wrapped his arms around me. "But I sure intend to find out."

Even though my Saturday morning workshop had provided a temporary break from the group's somber mood, as soon as I sat down with the rest of the group at the lunch table I noticed that the same bleak feeling had returned.

Every member of our group had retreated into silence. Yoko stared longingly at her phone, as if she was desperately trying to will it back to life. Naveen appeared to be lost in thought, while Gordon's sullen expression reflected his usual disdain for the rest of us. Even Jake, my last hope, seemed to be at a loss for words as our little group of six sat at the big round table in the middle of the cavernous dining room. Everyone picked half-heartedly at the plates they'd filled from the tremendous platters set out, buffet style, on a large table.

I took my time choosing from the display of food, not in a hurry to rejoin the group. Finally, I had no choice but to sit down and eat. As soon as I did, I happened to glance over at Franny. I was greatly relieved to see that she looked as if she was about to burst.

"Is everything all right, Franny?" I asked, hoping to start up something resembling a conversation.

"Everything is more than all right," she replied. Two dots of bright pink dotted her cheeks. "I've been thinking about whether or not I should share something important in my life with all of you. And I finally decided that I'm so excited about it that there's no way I can keep from doing exactly that!"

"I'm so glad," Gordon mumbled sarcastically.

As usual, Franny was a master at simply ignoring him. Her eyes were shining brightly as she announced, "I've developed what I call my secret plan."

"A secret plan?" Gordon repeated, his tone mocking. "That sounds so mysterious. Like something a ten-year-old would write about in her diary."

"Personally, I'm always developing secret plans," I commented cheerfully, rushing to Franny's defense. "Of course, most of those plans are related to ice cream. But I'm always obsessing about something or other, like trying to put together the details of an innovative new product for my shop or a good way of helping out my grandmother or my niece . . . "

"My secret plan is much bigger than that," Franny insisted. She seemed oblivious to the scornful look on Gordon's face. "I've decided to give my entire life a major overhaul."

"Switching to a different brand of laundry soap, are you?" Gordon said with a sneer.

"I've told my landlord I won't be renewing the lease on my apartment," Franny told us all triumphantly. "And I've quit my job at the library. I've decided to force myself to create a whole new life for myself. A new location, a new career . . . a whole new me."

Even though I barely knew the woman, the dramatic changes she had decided to make all at once caused me to shudder. Her rash actions struck me as something even a stronger, more self-confident, more capable person would be foolhardy to take.

Everyone else in the room appeared to feel the same way. A heavy silence had fallen over us, as if we were all speechless.

"But you must have some idea of where you'd like to live and what you'd like to do," Jake said gently. "Everyone has fantasies about the paths they feel they would have followed if only they knew then what they knew now."

Out of the corner of my eye, I could see that he was casting me a meaningful look. I had a feeling I knew exactly what he was referring to, which is why I made a point of not meeting his eyes.

"I'd live in Hawaii, if I had it to do all over again," Yoko said. "I should have moved there right after I'd finished school. Instead of going into the cosmetics field, I should have started a career in the hospitality industry. Managing a trendy restaurant in Honolulu or running a cool boutique hotel somewhere on the Big Island . . ."

In other words, you would have followed in Mrs. Moody's footsteps, I was tempted to comment. But I kept my mouth shut.

"I sometimes think I should have remained in London," Naveen said thoughtfully, holding his fork poised in midair. "I have never felt completely at home here in America. Maybe my fantasy isn't as romantic as living on a tropical island, but I agree with Jake that it is inevitable that as we grow older we question the decisions we made earlier on in our lives."

"Not me," Gordon boasted. "I'm one hundred percent satisfied with my life."

"Except for the fact that you have just lost the woman you love," Naveen noted. His voice was mild but his underlying message was unmistakable.

"Oh, right," Gordon said, clearly deflated. "There's that, of course."

This time, when Jake managed to catch my eye, he and I exchanged a look of total disbelief.

"But aside from that," Gordon went on, waving his hand in the air as if Naveen had just brought up some minor, barely incidental detail, "I love my career, my apartment in Manhattan, the success I've enjoyed . . . I can't think of a better life. At least, in terms of what I want to get out of it."

Jake turned to Franny. "If you're moving out of your apartment in Minnesota," he said, "where will you go when this weekend is over?"

Gordon snorted. "Assuming we ever get out of this place," he said. "I find myself wondering if we all died and ended up in hell. Confined in this creepy building, stuck inside with just a handful of people, most of them . . ." He stopped himself mid-insult. "Most of them total strangers," he finished weakly. "Then, of course, there's what happened to Bethany. Which I'm sure I'll never get over."

He didn't sound very convincing. I wondered if anyone else noticed. Aside from Jake, that is, who cast me another horrified look.

Franny was nodding enthusiastically. "It's just like *No Exit*," she said earnestly. "Do you know it? The play by the French writer Jean-Paul Sartre? It's about three people who died and are spending eternity in a tiny room, driving each other crazy by not getting what they want out of each other . . . in the end, one of the characters concludes, 'Hell is other people.'"

"The difference is that, unlike us, those three people were all put in that room together intentionally to make each other miserable," Gordon interjected. "We're just here randomly."

I had to admit that I was surprised that he was familiar with Sartre's work. Then again, he'd probably gone to an excellent prep school. Even though my impression of him was that he had always been a party boy, I supposed there was a chance there had been some fallout from a solid education.

"Besides," Gordon went on, "in the play the characters are all people who are lying to each other about the kind of people they really are and what terrible things they've done in their lives. We, meanwhile, are just—"

Suddenly he stopped. A distinct flush had come to his cheeks, making me wonder if he was speaking about more than just Jean-Paul Sartre's play.

Fortunately for him, Jake seemed to be finding all these tangents frustrating. "So where do you plan to go, Franny?" he asked once again.

I expected her to give a vague answer, listing a bunch of possibilities. Instead, her face lit up as she said, "New York City."

It took us all a second or two to digest her answer.

"Really!" Gordon said, sounding skeptical. "There's no place in the world like the Big Apple, but it's a tough place to live."

Yoko nodded. "That old saying about 'if you can make it there, you can make it anywhere' often seems painfully true."

Naveen chimed in with, "I love New York, too. But it is a very competitive, fast-paced city. Extremely expensive, too."

But Franny's expression was still one of excitement. "I've always dreamed of living in New York," she said. "Ever since I was a little girl. I see every single movie that comes out that's been filmed there, I love reading books that are set there . . . I even have a guidebook that I've practically memorized. Did you know that both the Metropolitan Museum of Art and the Museum of Modern Art, two of the most magnificent museums in the world, are open seven days a week? That means that art lovers are never stopped from seeing some of the most magnificent artwork in the world!"

"Still, that's not exactly a reason to move there," Jake commented. "Especially if you're someone who doesn't know anyone there or have a place to live. Not to mention if you're someone who doesn't have a job."

"But that's the most exciting part of my secret plan," Franny said, the two pink dots reappearing on her cheeks. "Unfortunately, it's the one part I can't tell anyone about." She glanced around the room, no doubt noting the less-than-enthusiastic looks on our faces. Yoko looked horrified, Jake and Naveen looked worried, and Gordon looked as if he was about to burst out laughing.

"I think it's a great idea," I suddenly said. "Franny, if it's something you've always wanted to do, I say go for it. I have a feeling that you're a very levelheaded person, and I suspect that the really secret part of that plan of yours includes all the details of where to live and how to get a job and everything else you'll need to make your dream come true."

She smiled at me, clearly grateful for my support.

"I lived in New York myself for a few years," I went on.

"In fact, I just moved away from there, up to the Hudson Valley, less than a year ago. I loved living there. It was one of the happiest periods of my life. There's nothing like the excitement of the city. Of course there are challenges, especially the expense of living there. But plenty of people do it. Every day aspiring actors and dancers and writers move there. So do people who are looking to make a career in finance or marketing or media.

"And of course there are plenty of regular people with regular jobs who live there, too," I noted. "Schoolteachers and accountants and librarians. They all find a way to do it, and there's absolutely no reason why you shouldn't be able to do exactly the same thing."

Franny just smiled at me again. But this time, she said nothing.

The soft thud of footsteps against the wooden floor caused me to turn around. I saw that Mrs. Moody had just walked in and was heading in our direction.

"I thought I'd check and see how everyone is doing," she said as she neared our table. She pulled her thin lips into a straight line that I thought was supposed to be a smile. It seemed to require great effort on her part.

"We are doing well," Naveen said heartily. "We are all enjoying a wonderful meal that was prepared by your first-rate chef."

"I'm so glad," Mrs. Moody said, so wooden that her reply almost sounded like sarcasm.

"We were also being treated to the fascinating tale of Franny's upcoming life change," Gordon added with a smirk. "She's about to embark on an exciting new chapter."

"That's right," Franny said. "I'm moving to New York."

"Goodness," Mrs. Moody commented. "That really is a major change. Moving to the largest city in the country from the fourth largest city in Minnesota—"

Gordon jerked his head back in that annoying gesture that means *wha-a-a-?* "How do you know that obscure little factoid?" he asked. "Is memorizing little-known information about Minnesota your hobby or something?"

"I was just wondering that myself," Jake interjected. "Where is it that you live now, Franny?"

"Duluth," she replied. "And it really is Minnesota's fourth largest city." She looked as surprised as the rest of us.

All six of us were staring at Mrs. Moody, surprised by her impressive expertise in the area of Minnesota trivia.

At the moment, the woman's face showed more expression than I'd ever seen on it before. She reminded me of the proverbial deer in the headlights. In other words, she looked as if she'd been caught.

"I spent some time living in the Midwest," she finally replied. It was as if she was spilling some deep, dark secret that she'd had no choice but to reveal.

"In Minnesota, I assume," Naveen commented.

Mrs. Moody hesitated. "Yes. But it was a long, long time ago."

"Now isn't that a coincidence," Gordon said. "Two Minnesotans! Hey, do they have a whimsical nickname for people who live there? Like Hoosiers in Indiana or Buckeyes in Ohio?"

"Not that I'm aware of," Mrs. Moody replied sullenly.

"I've always wondered who comes up with those names," Gordon went on. "I mean, is there some guy whose job it is to think up words like that? And how about names for cars? Now that would be a plum job! Can you imagine working for Toyota or BMW and sitting around all day, thinking up names for cars? Like the word 'Prius.' What the heck does *that* mean? Or 'Jetta,' as in the Volkswagen Jetta . . . ?"

I was irritated that Gordon had managed to turn the conversation around so that it was focused on him. I was much more interested in the strange coincidence that I'd just learned about, that both Mrs. Moody and Franny had roots in the same part of the country.

Was *it a coincidence?* I wondered. I only hoped I'd be able to figure that out.

That, plus a whole lot of other things.

Chapter 7

In 1929, Greek immigrant Tom Carvelas was
selling frozen custard out of a homemade trailer
near Hartsdale, New York, on Memorial Day.
When he got a flat tire, he started selling his
melting ice cream. Surprisingly, sales rocketed.
Soon afterward, he built his first ice cream store
at that same location. He later invented the
"Custard King" ice cream freezer for dispensing
his soft-serve desserts.

—*http://www.retroland.com/carvel/*

It was time to get serious.

The more time I spent at Mohawk, the clearer it became
that I was wandering around in a maze of intrigue. The more
I walked through that maze, the more twists and turns I encountered. Not only had it become increasingly fascinating;
it involved me because I was stuck in that maze along with all
the suspects.

I was already having trouble keeping track of all that I'd
learned so far. In an effort to sort it all out, I sought out the
softest upholstered chair in the Mountainside Room, which
fortunately happened to be placed directly in front of the
fireplace. I plopped my computer onto my lap as if it were a
purring pussycat, opened a brand-new page in Word, and
started typing.

Gordon Bradley, I wrote first. **Boyfriend. Doesn't seem particularly upset. Mysterious telephone call.**

Then I added, **In trouble? What was he getting from Bethany besides a relationship?**

Next, I typed Yoko's name, followed by, **Unlikely workshop attendee. Worked in cosmetics business, currently runs online cosmetics company.** I thought for another few seconds, then added, **Coincidence that she works in same industry?**

Naveen was next. I actually felt a sense of dread as I typed the letters of his name. I liked him. We were becoming friends. Out of all the people here, he was the one I least wanted to have been involved in Bethany's murder.

Still, I had to include him. So I wrote down, **What happened to his daughter?** I didn't see how that tied into Bethany, but it was the only thing I had to go on at this point. I made a mental note to try to find out more about the distressing turn that Sana Sharma's life had taken.

Next I wrote down Franny's name. She, too, seemed to have little or nothing to do with Bethany La Montaine or her glamorous world. And her enthusiasm for ice cream certainly seemed sincere. But once again, she was someone I had to consider a suspect simply because she was here.

Besides, she was the person who had discovered Bethany's body. That automatically put her on the list of suspects, even though it looked as if she had merely been the victim of being in the wrong place at the wrong time.

Then there was Mrs. Moody. I didn't really have much on her aside from her general creepiness. The same went for Tarleton. Still, I added both their names to my list.

I read through what I'd just written, hoping for some insights. Instead, all I saw in front of me was a lot of fits and starts. There was nothing there that came even close to being conclusive. Or even particularly helpful.

It was obvious that I was just getting started with peeling back the layers of this onion that was the truth behind Bethany La Montaine's death. Therefore, I was ready to move on to the next obvious step in any quest for knowledge.

It was time to google.

Fortunately, here in the lobby I was able to connect to Mohawk's WiFi with ease. The Google home page had just appeared on my screen and I was about to type in the words "Merle Moody" when I suddenly got that creepy-crawly feeling on the back of my neck, even though I hadn't seen or heard anything in particular.

It was that impossible-to-ignore feeling that I was being watched.

I whirled around. Sure enough, Mrs. Moody was standing right behind me, her eyes fixed on my computer screen.

She was spying on me.

"Hello, Mrs. Moody," I said cheerfully as I slammed my laptop shut. Doing my best to keep the irritation out of my voice, I added, "I didn't hear you come in."

"The carpets are so thick here at Mohawk," she replied, her voice low and even. "That's one of the many things I love about this place."

I'm sure it is, I thought wryly. *It makes it so much easier to sneak up on people.*

"I always find it interesting to see the way people use the internet," Mrs. Moody commented. Glancing up, I saw that she was wearing a funny half-smile. "I'm always surprised by the kinds of things they spend their time looking into."

"It's certainly an efficient way to get information," I said. Not to mention a great way of allowing certain people to spy on other people by secretly peering over their shoulders to see what they were using it for. "But it sounds as if you're not exactly a big fan."

Mrs. Moody sniffed. "If you ask me, people mainly use it to waste time," she replied crisply. "And I'm certainly not a 'big fan,' as you put it, of wasting time."

"You're right," I said, rising to my feet. "I should be doing something other than staring at a computer screen. I should be taking advantage of my lovely surroundings."

It was only then that I noticed that she was carrying a book. "Or maybe I should curl up with a good book instead of my laptop. It looks as if that's what you've got planned."

A stricken look crossed her face. I got the feeling she was horrified by having had something personal revealed. She glanced down at the book in her hand, acting as guilty as if she'd been carrying around a loaded gun. "This? This is for later. I still have work to do. I never read while I'm on the job."

Even though she was holding the thick volume close to her thigh with the cover facing inward, the words that were printed on the back of the thick paperback clued me in to what the book was.

The fact that sour Mrs. Moody was reading *Gone with the Wind* was a shock. Almost as jolting as seeing her ruffle Tarleton's hair.

Maybe I hadn't had a chance to learn much by googling. But I had learned something important about Mrs. Moody: Despite her icy demeanor, the woman had a romantic side. Or at least a side that wasn't entirely consistent with the image she presented to the rest of the world.

There was something else I'd learned, as well. And that was that when it came to looking into the backgrounds of the people on my list of suspects, I was going to have to get a little more creative.

In the meantime, duty called. Duty in the form of my position as instructor, lecturer, and workshop leader at the We All Scream for Ice Cream weekend.

Which meant that I really needed to get busy setting things up for my one thirty workshop on How to Make Ice Cream at Home.

Unlike the morning's lecture, this one was going to take a

lot more planning. Instead of passively listening, the way the workshop participants had during the morning session, in the afternoon session they were actually going to be making ice cream.

Fortunately, I'd brought along everything I would need to make that happen. That, in fact, was the main reason I'd had to load up my truck with all the boxes and bags that Jake and I had ended up dragging into the hotel all by ourselves.

I'd brought along three different ice cream makers. One was a top-of-the-line electric Cuisinart, a magnificent machine that made making ice cream at home a snap. The second was a Donvier ice cream maker, a manual device that was not as high-tech but was equally effective. The third was an old-fashioned ice cream maker that looked liked a wooden barrel. It could have passed as a decoration in Adventureland at one of the Disney theme parks. However, it was outfitted with an electric motor that did most of the work, just like the higher-priced Cuisinart model.

I'd also brought enough ice cream–making ingredients for a group that was much larger than the one that had materialized. Not only cream and milk and sugar, either. I'd also packed up a big box of powdered cocoa, nuts, and a variety of other flavorings and add-ins.

There were other necessary items I'd lugged here, as well, an assortment of necessities ranging from plastic bags to ice cream scoops to measuring cups. I was pretty sure I'd thought of everything. Unfortunately, I wouldn't know for sure until we were all up to our elbows in partially made ice cream. Still, I figured that if I'd forgotten something crucial, I could find it in Mohawk's kitchen.

I was less nervous about keeping the group engaged during this workshop. It was partly because that morning's lecture had already gone off without a hitch. It was a good reminder that playing the role of teacher, at least in my chosen field of ice cream, was something I could easily handle. But even more important was the fact that in this afternoon's workshop, I'd be keeping everyone busy. Instead of the eyes of the audience being fixed on me the entire time, the participants would quickly become engaged in making ice cream. And if that wasn't enough to make a group of people happy, I didn't know what was.

"This workshop should be really terrific," Jake commented as he picked up the packing boxes and stacked them neatly in a corner of the Great Room.

"I hope so," I replied.

Placing my hands on my hips, I surveyed all the items I'd arranged on the big table that everyone would be standing around for most of the afternoon. The ice cream makers were in the center, the ingredients were off to one side, and the other miscellaneous things we would need were scattered here and there to make them accessible to whoever needed them.

Grimacing, I explained, "One thing that I'm a little worried about is that this will be the first time everyone will have to interact together so intensely, at least aside from meals."

"And our meals together have been—shall we say, interesting," Jake said, grinning. "Let's be sure to keep Gordon as far away from Franny as possible."

I lowered my voice as I added, "And let's try to keep Mrs. Moody and Tarleton as far away from everyone as possible."

Jake laughed. "It's likely that they'll be too busy to come to this afternoon's workshop. Fixing generators, doing paperwork, haunting the hallways . . ."

"I hope you're right," I replied. "Still, once there's ice cream around, people have a way of turning up. Especially when it's homemade."

Not only would the workshop participants have a chance to try their hand at making ice cream. If all went according to plan, they were also going to have the chance to devour what they'd created. It didn't take long to magically turn milk and cream and sugar into ice cream. The plan was to make it, freeze it, and then serve it at four o'clock teatime, along with the traditional tea, cookies, and sherry. I had a feeling that the ice cream was going to outshine the other snacks.

Jake and I had just finished setting up as people began straggling in. It was interesting to see that they were all becoming much more comfortable with each other, even though it was hard to imagine a more varied group of individuals. Age, interest, background, temperament . . . the members of this crew had little in common.

Yet Yoko and Franny strolled in together, animatedly talking about whether Mohawk's resistance to making technology more accessible to its guests was a plus or a minus. Gordon and Naveen wandered in next, earnestly discussing some topic I couldn't overhear well enough to discern. Whatever it was, they were both clearly finding their conversation absorbing.

Not surprisingly, all the workshop attendees sat down in the exact same seats they had sat in that morning. People tended to do that. I supposed it had something to do with our animal instincts about staking out our own territory.

I jumped right in as soon as everyone was settled.

"Welcome back, everyone," I began. "This afternoon's workshop will focus on how to make ice cream. And that's exactly what you'll be doing, so I hope you're all ready to do a little work. But I promise that this is really enjoyable work. And the best part will come later on, at afternoon tea, when you all get to eat what you've made."

The looks on their faces ranged from surprisingly interested—that was Gordon—to bursting with eagerness, as was the case with Franny. From the vibe in the room, I could already tell that this workshop was going to be a huge success.

"I'll start by telling you about what supplies you need in order to make ice cream at home," I went on, stepping over to the display of three ice cream makers. "I've printed a list of tools and ingredients that I'll hand out later, but let's begin with these machines.

"Each one of these can do the job just fine, and you'll have a chance to try them all in a little while." I waved my hand over them, Vanna White–style. "Whether you're using a fancy electric ice cream maker like the Cuisinart or something lower-tech like this manual Danvier, which requires cranking the ice cream mixture by hand, what you're mainly doing is adding air.

"And the key to success is keeping everything as cold as possible," I continued. "The containers should be left in the freezer at least overnight. Personally, for home-use models I prefer chilling them for at least twenty-four hours to make sure they're really, really cold before you use them. Ice cream has a bit of an attitude, and it doesn't believe in cutting corners."

I paused, hoping to get a laugh. Naveen and Franny both came through. From Jake, I got an appreciative smile.

"The ingredients should be kept cold, too," I continued. "It's a good idea to keep everything in the refrigerator for at least a couple of hours before getting started—not only the milk and cream, of course, but also anything else you plan to add. Even better, put all the ingredients into the freezer for a half hour or so before you begin. Just make sure nothing actually freezes."

I talked a bit more about the ins and outs of using an ice cream maker. Franny was taking notes, while Yoko, Naveen, and Jake were simply listening intently. Gordon, meanwhile, appeared to be daydreaming. I had a feeling that making ice cream at home wasn't something he was about to add to his repertoire.

"But there are other ways to make ice cream at home that don't require any special equipment at all," I added once I'd covered all the details of operating the various machines. I felt like Johnny Appleseed, gleefully spreading around something wonderful. But in my case, it wasn't fruit. It was knowledge—the knowledge that anyone could create magnificent ice cream just by using the things most people already have in their kitchen.

"Two of the most popular ways are the freeze-and-stir method and the plastic bag method," I went on. "Their names pretty much tell you everything you need to know. With freeze and stir, you basically mix the ingredients together in a stainless steel bowl and then stick them in the freezer for about forty-five minutes. By that point, you should notice that the mixture is starting to freeze around the edges. That's your cue to take it out and stir it really hard with a spatula. Put it back in the freezer, and keep taking it out and stirring it again every half hour. In two to three hours, you'll end up with what's commonly known as ice cream."

I was rewarded with another chuckle from Franny and Naveen, although this time it was a considerably more modest one.

"The plastic bag method is similar, in that once again it's all about keeping the ingredients you've mixed together cold and in motion," I announced, holding up a plastic bag in case anyone was unsure about the latest in Ziploc technology. "There is a downside, however. It's not unheard of for the bag to either split open or leak at the top. That can result in a very messy kitchen.

"But as long as you're aware of the risks," I went on, "all you have to do is put the mixture into a quart-size Ziploc-type bag. Make sure you squeeze out as much air as you can, and please make sure you seal it tightly! Put this bag inside a second quart bag, also taking care to get out as much of the air as possible and then closing it up. Put the double-bagged mixture into a big gallon-size bag and fill it with at least four cups of crushed ice. Then throw in about four tablespoons of coarse salt, which lowers the freezing point of the ice and makes everything extra cold."

At that point, I held my hands out and shrugged. "And that's pretty much it! That's how simple it is to make ice cream. You mix together a few ingredients—a few *cold* ingredients—you add air while keeping everything as cold as possible, and *voilà*, you've got ice cream!

"Now who's up for trying the plastic bag method?" I asked heartily. "Hopefully someone who isn't wearing their best clothes . . ."

Given the frolicsome time the group appeared to be having from that point on, you'd have thought I'd just introduced a group of kindergarteners to the concept of finger painting. Everyone from Naveen to Gordon got into making their own ice cream, chattering away about possible ingredients and offering advice on how each person could make their concoction even better.

Franny had planned to opt for simple chocolate, but the group encouraged her to be more adventurous. She finally relented, adding chocolate chips, marshmallow fluff, and crumbled graham crackers to create the ice cream version of s'mores. Meanwhile, Naveen went for mocha, adding cocoa powder, which I encouraged him to sift first, along with instant espresso powder. When he shyly asked if it would be appropriate to add a few nuts, the other members of the group went wild over the idea.

Yoko also started with chocolate, adding plenty of Nutella to give it a lovely hazelnut flavor. Gordon went for mint chip, made by adding peppermint extract and a whole lot of chocolate chips. Jake enthusiastically blended in strawberries, raspberries, and blueberries for what he named Berry, Berry Good ice cream.

Once everyone had had a chance to create their own ice cream flavor, we took the mixtures to the next level. Two of the concoctions, Naveen's and Yoko's, were taken to the freezer by Jake so that in a half hour everyone would have a chance to try both the freeze-and-stir method and the slightly terrifying plastic bag method. The other three mixtures went into the Cuisinart, the Donvier, and the old-fashioned-looking machine.

Once we were completely done and Jake had brought the finished products back to the kitchen for storage in the freezer, the expressions on everyone's faces made me feel positively triumphant. This hands-on workshop had clearly been a success. Franny looked exhilarated, Gordon appeared more relaxed than I'd seen him since he'd arrived, and Naveen seemed completely contented. Even Yoko had loosened up from the experience.

"So as you can see," I said, once again standing in front of them in teacher mode, "there's no reason not to make ice cream at home anytime you feel like it. Now that you've done it, you know how easy it is.

"Of course, that doesn't mean you should stop going to ice cream shops like mine," I added. "That's the last thing you should do!"

When I glanced at my watch and saw that it was almost four o'clock, I was astonished. The hours had raced by and it was already time for afternoon tea. In fact, Tarleton was hovering outside, ready to wheel in carts with tea service, trays of cookies, and sherry. I was pleased to see that the cart also had elegant glass ice cream dishes stacked on it. I was looking forward to sampling everyone's concoctions as much as the rest of the group undoubtedly was.

"I can't wait to wolf down my Berry, Berry Good ice

cream," Jake commented as we packed away the last of the supplies. "By the way, I had no idea that making ice cream was almost as much fun as eating it."

"I'm glad you enjoyed it," I said. "I'm always looking for assistants in the shop, so let me know when you're ready to turn pro."

He laughed. "Let's see how well it turned out before you put me on the payroll," he said. "And it looks like that moment is almost upon us. Are you ready to gorge?"

"I am," I replied. "But first there's something I have to do. Why don't I meet you back in the Great Room in a few minutes?"

"Sure," he agreed. "I'm going to find a computer and check a few football scores."

I headed for one of the pay phones. Now that my official responsibilities for the afternoon were done, I was back to thinking about investigating Bethany La Montaine's murder.

It was time to call in the experts.

So I went into the tiny phone booth, closed the door firmly, and dialed my niece's cell phone number.

Emma had shown up unexpectedly six months earlier, soon after Lickety Splits had first opened. A dispute with her parents, who included my oldest sister, Julie, had prompted her to run away from home right after high school graduation, seeking refuge with Grams and me. It seemed her parents were determined that she begin college in the fall, while Emma wanted to take some time off to get a better idea of where she wanted her life to go. She had a passion for both art and computers and wasn't sure which direction made more sense for her—or whether some other field interested her even more.

Not only had she instantly become a welcome addition to our small household; she had also turned into my best, most reliable, and pretty much only employee. I realized in retrospect that running my own ice cream shop would have been a lot more challenging without her at my side.

But thanks to her skill with computers, Emma was also a crackerjack researcher. That young woman would be capable of tracking down pretty much any piece of information I asked her for. And I suddenly found myself with a very long list.

But it wasn't until I got her on the phone that I realized how concerned she and my grandmother had been about me.

"Kate!" she practically shrieked into the phone. "Why haven't we heard from you? Grams and I have been worried sick! This storm has wreaked havoc with the entire Hudson Valley! The whole New York metropolitan area, in fact! Trees are down, power is out all over the place, there's flooding and—and . . . are you okay?"

"I'm fine," I assured her.

I could picture her in my mind: her forehead wrinkled with concern as she clutched her cell phone to her ear, nestling it in her halo of wonderfully explosive dark curls streaked with blue.

"I'm sorry I haven't gotten in touch," I told her. "But cell phone service here is pretty much nonexistent, since we're way up in the mountains. And we lost electricity last night, probably because some wires were downed . . ."

"It sounds awful!" Emma wailed. "Why don't you just come home?"

I hesitated. "It's not that simple," I told her, doing my best to keep my voice even. "You see, a big tree fell across the road that connects Mohawk with the rest of the world. Until a crew with the right equipment can make it over to clear it away, I'm afraid we're all stuck up here."

"Is Jake there?" Emma demanded. "Do you have enough food?" And then, after another second, "Is it boring?"

Apparently, word of Bethany La Montaine's demise had

not yet reached the rest of the world. I wasn't surprised. In addition, I was greatly relieved, since I didn't want Emma and Grams worrying about me any more than they already were.

"No, Emma, it's not the least bit boring," I replied. "There are fewer guests here than there were supposed to be, but even so I've been able to run the ice cream workshops I'd planned. I've already taught two. One was a general lecture on ice cream—the history, different types, that kind of thing—and the other was a hands-on session in which people actually made their own ice cream. That one was a huge success.

"And Jake is indeed here," I went on. "We're finding some time to be together, just enjoying the place. As for your other question, so far we have plenty of food, including lots of ice cream. So all in all it's not exactly terrible being stranded up here. Mohawk is a lovely place, with fireplaces in practically every room and beautiful views of the lake—when it's not too foggy to see beyond a couple of feet, of course—and a charming old-fashioned ambiance . . ."

"I'm just glad you're safe," Emma said. "And I'm thrilled that Jake is there with you. It's always good to have backup."

She had a point. And I had to admit that I'd been greatly appreciative that Jake had been there the entire weekend. And it wasn't only because he was backup.

"But there's a reason why I called," I continued. "Other than to let you know that I'm okay, I mean. Since you're such a computer whiz, I wondered if you could help me out by doing a little research."

"There's nothing I'd like more," Emma replied enthusiastically. "With this terrible weather, I made an executive decision not to open Lickety Splits today. I didn't think there would be many ice cream eaters out braving the wind and rain." I could already hear her clicking away on the keys of her laptop. "Let me just open a new page so I can write down whatever you . . . okay, ready!"

I took a deep breath and checked the notes I'd scribbled on a piece of paper from the Mohawk Mountain Resort pad I'd found on my night table. "I'm interested in finding out more about some of the people who are here at Mohawk with me," I said, trying to sound casual. "One of them is the general manager, Merle Moody. I'd like you to look into her past. I'm particularly interested in what she was doing while she lived in Minnesota. That would have been back in the 1980s."

"The 1980s!" Emma repeated. "That's ancient history!"

"I know," I said, even though that wasn't exactly how I would have classified that particular decade. "But I'm hoping you can find out why she was there."

"I'll do my best," Emma said, sounding uncertain. "What else would you like me to research?"

"I'd like you to find out whatever you can about a gentleman named Naveen Sharma. And his daughter. Her name is Sana."

"Got it," Emma replied. "I'm writing all these names down."

"Great," I said. "I have three more: Yoko Wallace, Gordon Bradley, and Franny Schneffer. Let me spell them for you, just to make sure . . ."

I was curious about Tarleton, too, but I didn't know his whole name. Just for the heck of it, after I'd spelled out all the other names, I added, "Here's one more, but you might not find anything at all. See if you can find out anything about Tarleton Moody."

"Okay, so that's six names," Emma said. She paused for a moment, then added, "Maybe it's just a crazy coincidence, but this list reminds me of the kind you've put together in the past. And those lists have always been lists of suspects. I don't suppose—"

"Of course not!" I cried. "I'm just trying to find out more about the backgrounds of the people who are here at Mohawk. All this is nothing more than my general nosiness."

I felt bad lying to my niece. But I reminded myself that I was only doing so in order to protect her. It was simply a way of keeping her from worrying about me any more than she already was.

Besides, I thought, *it's only a little lie. A lie that hardly counts at all.*

And the benefits of putting my ace researcher on the case, I knew, greatly outweighed any guilt I may have felt about not being completely honest about what was really going on here at Mohawk.

Chapter 8

America's Ice Cream & Dairy Farm Museum at
Elm Farm in Medina, Ohio, featured a 1900s
soda fountain, early ice cream freezers, milk and
ice cream delivery trucks, and other ice cream
paraphernalia. The museum closed in 2012.

*—Everybody Loves Ice Cream: the Whole Scoop on
America's Favorite Treat by Shannon Jackson Arnold*

Not surprisingly, the afternoon's ice cream tasting was a
huge success.

By four o'clock, we had all reconvened in the Great Room.
The already grand space looked as if it had been converted
into a set for *Downton Abbey*. Two large tables had been set
up across from each other, each covered with a cream-
colored lace tablecloth. Lined up on one were canisters containing the various flavors of ice cream the workshop participants had just created. Alongside them were large glass
bowls of toppings: hot fudge and caramel syrup, smaller
bowls of nuts, M&M's, and sprinkles. The ornate ice cream
dishes I'd spotted earlier were lined up beside a row of shining silver spoons.

Laid out on the other table was everything needed for tea:
a tall, elegant silver urn, delicate white cups and saucers decorated with pink roses, a tray displaying at least eight differ-

ent varieties of tea bags, and a second tray piled high with cookies. A glass carafe at the other end held a translucent liquid I assumed was sherry. Small stemmed cordial glasses stood in a circle around it. The comfiest chairs in the room had been moved closer to the huge fireplace, as if saluting the roaring fire that was doing a valiant job of chasing away the gloominess of the gray, rainy afternoon.

The entire group immediately descended upon the ice cream table. We all eagerly scooped out a sampling of each flavor, then grabbed spoons and dug in. Even Gordon looked as if he'd turned into a little kid on Christmas morning. Ice cream has a way of doing that to people.

Still, Gordon couldn't help being Gordon.

"Mine is definitely the best," he announced, holding up a spoonful of his overly green mint chip to demonstrate. "But the others are all pretty good, too. Especially the berry thing that Jake made. I really like the big chunks of fruit. And the Nutella ice cream that Yoko came up with is kind of amazing." Begrudgingly, he added, "Franny's s'mores flavor concoction isn't bad, either."

"I love Nutella's combination of chocolate and hazelnut flavors," Yoko chimed in. "But that's mainly because hazelnut is my absolute favorite, especially when it's paired with chocolate. But I also love Naveen's. The mocha has just the right balance of chocolate and coffee. And his idea about adding nuts was a real brainstorm."

"I love them all pretty much equally," Franny said generously. "Of course I'm partial to my own, since I used my favorite things to make it. But they're all so darned tasty. Good job, everybody!"

Mrs. Moody didn't actually partake of any of the ice cream. Instead, she stood in a distant corner, watching us as she sipped the cup of tea she had poured herself. No sugar.

Not even any milk. But she did shoot me a look of approval, along with a nod. I was strangely pleased.

Once everyone had had a chance to gorge on ice cream, they moved on to the other offerings. Naveen, Yoko, and Franny chatted together congenially as they helped themselves to tea. I noticed that Yoko opted for a glass of sherry, as well. Gordon, meanwhile, grumbled about the lack of coffee. He did help himself to a handful of the butter cookies, however. They looked homemade. And if the expression on his face after he took his first bite was any indication, they must have been pretty good.

"I love the way ice cream brings everybody together," I commented to Franny, who came over to me after pouring herself a cup of tea and grabbing a few cookies. I was still hovering near the ice cream table, wondering if going back for more would make me look appreciative of my students' efforts or simply gluttonous.

"It really does help people bond," Franny agreed, taking a big bite of one of the cookies. "You're so lucky to have built an entire career around ice cream!"

"Believe me, I feel that way every day," I told her. "I've always loved it, ever since I was a child. Of course, aside from its wonderful texture and terrific flavor and perfect amount of sweetness and creaminess, it also has emotional meaning. My dad and I shared a passion for ice cream. We both ate it every chance we got. One of my fondest memories is the wonderfully lopsided ice cream cake he made me for my fourth birthday." Sighing, I added, "I still remember that cake like it was yesterday."

Franny smiled. "Do you and your father still eat ice cream together?"

I shook my head. "He passed away when I was five years old." Even now, after all these years, talking about him made me tear up.

"I'm so sorry!" Franny cried. "That must have been terrible for you."

"It was," I said. "I lost my mother at a young age, too. That was when I was ten." By this point, I was mumbling into my ice cream. I hadn't expected to share my life story with anyone this weekend.

"But what about you?" I asked abruptly, speaking with a cheerfulness that sounded forced even to me. "Are you close to your parents? Do they live near you?"

"We're pretty close," she replied after what struck me as a surprisingly long hesitation. She paused again, then added, "Of course, we're fairly different types of people. That's not surprising, I suppose, since I was adopted."

Even though she had undoubtedly made that simple statement hundreds or even thousands of times before, the words she spoke were so filled with emotion that just saying them caused her entire demeanor to change. Yet it was impossible for me to read what was behind her strong reaction—gratitude, anger, resentment, or something else entirely.

"But my adoptive parents are great," she added quickly. "The Schneffers aren't rich or anything, as I mentioned at breakfast. But they've always been totally supportive of everything I did. It's just that they were so . . . so . . ."

I remained silent, waiting for her to finish her sentence. But instead, she smiled sadly and said, "I don't know about other people who've been adopted, but I've never stopped feeling . . . I guess the word is *disjointed*. What I mean is, I've always felt as if the fact that I wasn't raised by my biological parents made everything about my life feel a little off. It's as if I'm living the wrong life or something. Or maybe that . . . I don't know, it's hard to explain."

I remained silent. While I'd had my share of upheavals in my own life, I knew that everyone's experience was different.

I couldn't compare my own feelings of loss—and at times that same disjointedness that Franny had mentioned—to what she or anyone else might have gone through.

Yet she and I definitely had something in common. I had been raised by my mother and grandmother from age five on, and then solely by my grandmother from age ten. Which meant that I, too, had missed out on the traditional mother-and-father experience for most of my childhood.

Even so, our experiences had been different enough that I didn't feel right commenting on hers. So instead, I simply said, "I guess we all have plenty of baggage from our childhood that we can't help but carry around with us for the rest of our lives."

I was actually glad that Mrs. Moody chose that moment to head over in our direction, walking with such determination that I instinctively felt guilty.

"There's some ice cream left over," she announced haughtily. "Shall I have Tarleton dispose of it? Or is it worth saving?"

"Don't throw it out!" Franny cried before I had a chance to answer. "We all put so much effort into making it—and we're all positively thrilled about the way it turned out! Let's serve it again at dinner, for dessert. I'm sure everyone would love that. I know I would!"

I felt like hugging her. Given the strong positive reaction from one of the paying customers, Mrs. Moody couldn't help but comply. And Franny's enthusiastic endorsement of my efforts spoke more loudly than anything I could have said.

"Very well," Mrs. Moody said, forcing her mouth into what almost looked like a real smile. "Then that's what we'll do."

I smiled back. But my smile was sincere.

* * *

I continued standing off to the side, watching the group that had gathered for afternoon tea with ice cream—a definite improvement over the classic afternoon tea, as far as I was concerned. Before long, the participants began to wander off, no doubt exhausted from the demands of the day. Not to mention full of ice cream.

Once everyone had drifted away, I lingered in the Great Room by myself for a few minutes, enjoying the silence and the remains of my tea. Then I decided to continue this much-needed bit of solitude in one of the smaller sitting rooms.

As I wandered into the Fireside Room, I assumed that I was still alone. So I was surprised when I noticed what looked like an elbow sticking out of the side of a chair that was facing away from me. I was pretty sure that elbow belonged to Yoko.

"I'm sorry," I said automatically. "I didn't realize anyone else was in here."

A sleek black head of perfectly straight hair bobbed up from behind the back of the chair. Sure enough, Yoko craned her neck around. Once she saw that it was me who had come in, she smiled.

"Hey, Kate," she said. "It's just me. You're welcome to come in."

"Thanks. I think I will."

As I dropped into the big comfy upholstered chair next to hers, I saw that a bottle of sherry sat on the low table between us. It was nearly empty. I noticed then that Yoko was cradling a round-bottomed brandy snifter in one hand, a glass that was capable of holding a lot more liquid than the tiny cordial glasses I'd seen at afternoon tea. Those details, along with the somewhat foggy look in her eyes, led me to conclude that she'd been hitting the sherry a little too hard.

"There's such a thing as too much togetherness," she said, her words a bit slurred.

As I started to apologize for my presence, she added, "Not you. You're not the one I was talking about. It's that awful Mrs. Moody. The only person here who's worse than that horrible woman is Franny. Although, come to think of it, Gordon is no prize either."

She frowned, then paused to sip more sherry. "Which brings us to Bethany La Montaine."

"I was surprised to find out that you already knew Bethany," I said, trying to sound casual. "What a coincidence that you both ended up coming here this weekend. I mean, what are the chances of two old friends running into each other at something like this?"

Yoko's eyes blazed. "Friend?" she repeated, spitting out the word. "*Friend?* Bethany and I were anything but *friends.*"

I had already figured that out. The lack of warmth between them had been clear from Bethany's shocked reaction when she'd first spotted Yoko at dinner Friday night, as well as in Yoko's iciness while she was in Bethany's presence.

But I pretended to be oblivious, saying, "I suppose working with someone day in and day out can sometimes reveal their worst qualities, as well as their best . . ."

Yoko snorted. "You have no idea," she said bitterly. "Bethany was a monster."

I blinked, startled by the severity of her words.

But I didn't even have to ask her to explain. "Everybody at the firm knew what Bethany La Montaine was like," she said, her voice still fueled by fury. "The woman gave new meaning to the word 'back-stabber.' I saw her steal people's ideas and present them as her own without even glancing at the person who'd actually come up with it. I saw her berate employees in a conference room full of people, practically reducing grown men to tears."

She shuddered, as if the mere memory of her days at La Montaine Cosmetics was still traumatizing. "Anyone who worked at La Montaine learned pretty early on that the safest thing to do was to stay on Bethany's good side," she said. "Or better yet, to steer clear of her altogether.

"But Bethany really had it out for me," Yoko went on, her voice growing even angrier. "From the very start, I was high on her list of people she considered enemies. Although I suspect the correct word is rivals."

"I'm surprised that the two of you were, uh, rivals," I commented. "For one thing, she's so much older than you. I would just assume she had a much higher position in the company than you did. After all, you're only in your twenties while she'd been working at La Montaine Cosmetics for nearly two decades."

Not sure if I was treading into a place I shouldn't, I added, "Besides, she was the boss's daughter."

"That was exactly the problem," Yoko replied. Proudly, she added, "Bethany's mother, Gloria, saw me as a rising star. After I'd been there for only a few weeks, I started coming up with one fabulous idea after another. For example, Bethany was hell-bent on keeping the Fleurs de France line in department stores. But that concept is totally old-school. Nobody my age buys cosmetics in stores! We all shop online. So I proposed making a major shift, selling Fleurs de France exclusively through La Montaine's website. True, that was a few years ago, before it was as obvious as it is now that online shopping was destined to dominate the market in most industries. But even though I knew exactly what was happening in terms of the way people shop, Bethany couldn't see the writing on the wall.

"So she and I went head-to-head on that issue," Yoko continued. "Gloria sided with me. And in the end Fleurs de France did develop its own website. And it did really well."

"But I take it Bethany wasn't as pleased with your foresight as her mother was," I said, hoping to drag more out of her. Although the way things were going, "drag" wasn't exactly the right word. Not when Yoko seemed more than happy to have someone listen to her complain about her former "rival," as she put it.

"Not only wasn't she pleased, she finally managed to get me banished from her mother's company altogether," she said icily.

I gasped. "How did she do that?"

Yoko took a deep breath. "Gloria La Montaine is really into *things*, if you know what I mean. I swear, if she had to choose between her own mother and her Birkin bag, I'm convinced that she'd have to think long and hard."

I knew all about Birkin bags. They were leather tote bags made by the ultra-luxury designer Hermès and named after a singer and actress named Jane Birkin. The story behind their creation was that back in the 1980s, Birkin was seated next to one of the company's top executives while flying from Paris to London. During the flight, she complained about what a hard time she'd had trying to find the right leather weekend bag. The result was a black leather tote that was named after her. But the leather bag had quickly become a serious status symbol. That was mainly because the price started around twelve hundred dollars and went up into the hundreds of thousands, depending on how rare a particular model was.

"But the thing that Gloria treasured above all else," Yoko went on, "was this collection of little boxes she kept in her office. She brought in a special antique table just for displaying those stupid boxes. I don't even think they were that valuable. At least, not all of them. But apparently she'd started collecting them when she was a little girl, so they really meant a lot to her. She had tiny Limoges boxes and Wedgwood boxes and other upscale brands. But she also had hand-carved wooden boxes that weren't expensive but that she'd picked up on trips to India and Mexico and other places she'd visited."

I nodded to show I knew what she meant. And I did. My grandmother had also traveled all over the world, and she'd accumulated a collection of souvenirs that she displayed in three curio cabinets in the living room. Inexpensive trinkets, mostly, like ceramic pitchers from Greece and colorful wooden animals from Mexico. But while they may not have been worth much in dollars, I knew they were priceless to her in terms of the wonderful memories she associated with them.

"Anyway, one day Gloria started ranting and raving about how someone had stolen a few of her boxes," Yoko continued. "Of course, no one had any idea what she was talking about. The last thing any of her employees would have ever done was steal any of her stupid boxes. Even if they had been worth something, which they weren't, we all knew how much they meant to her."

I had a feeling I knew where this story was going. But I kept listening.

"So a day or two after we all first heard about the missing boxes, Bethany and I were sitting in a meeting with Gloria and a bunch of other executives," Yoko continued. "I was there to pitch another one of my brilliant ideas: packaging La Montaine's products in boxes and jars that weren't only made from recycled materials, but were made to be used for some other purpose after they'd been emptied. Recycling-

Plus, I called it. Like selling moisturizer in such a pretty glass jar that it could be used as a vase—or even to keep jewelry. Or putting astringent in a ceramic jar with a handle that could be used as a coffee mug after the product inside was all used up."

Her expression became faraway, as if she could actually see the scene she was describing right in front of her. "So there we all were, sitting in the conference room around this big table, and it was my turn to tell everyone about my idea. I put my briefcase on top, opened it up to take out my notes—and out spilled five or six of Gloria's beloved boxes."

Her face crumpled at the memory. "You can imagine what happened next," she went on. "All hell broke loose. Gloria started screaming at me, calling me a thief and an ingrate and a betrayer and a bunch of other names I can't bring myself to repeat. She ordered me to leave the room immediately, saying that I was fired and that she'd make sure I was blacklisted and that I'd never work in the cosmetics industry again."

"Oh my," I said breathlessly. "It sounds as if she never even gave you a chance to explain."

"She never would have believed me, even if I'd tried," Yoko said, tearing up. "For one thing, she never would have believed that her horrid daughter was behind it.

"But there was never a doubt in my mind that Bethany had planned all this," she added. "I can still picture her sitting at that conference table, wearing this disgusting smirk as she watched the whole scene. I can just imagine what she told her mother afterward: that she'd known all along that I was trouble, that the company was better off without me, that Gloria was right to make sure I'd never work in the beauty business again."

"And Bethany was back to being the golden girl again," I commented.

"Exactly."

"But you certainly showed them," I noted. "It sounds as if your company, Athena's Beauty, is a huge success."

Yoko opened her mouth to speak, then immediately snapped it shut. "That's right," she said. "It is."

But her words sounded hollow. Something about the way she'd first reacted, before she'd had the presence of mind to stop herself, even in her inebriated state, made me wonder if Athena's Beauty really was doing as well as she claimed.

Picking up the bottle of sherry, Yoko said, "I suggest that we toast my company and my success and the fact that, in the end, *I'm* the one who became the success story, not Bethany."

As she poured me some sherry, I commented, "By the way, it was really sweet of you to hand out those samples at breakfast this morning. Everyone was tickled."

She laughed. "That stuff is junk."

Startled, I asked, "What do you mean?"

"I mean exactly that: It's junk," she repeated. "Those were samples from a new manufacturer I was considering working with. But they're awful. I guess you haven't opened any of the bottles yet, but if you do you'll see immediately that they smell terrible. In fact, the reason I had them with me was that this weekend one of the things on my to-do list was writing the company a nasty email. I was going to name each product, one by one, and tell them why I couldn't possibly consider selling any of them on my website."

So much for generosity, I thought as Yoko handed me a glass of sherry.

"So let's toast my success!" she bubbled. "To me—and a long, lucrative future for Athena's Beauty!"

I lightly clinked my glass against hers. "To you," I said, trying not to sound too sarcastic.

But as I went through the motions of celebrating her good

fortune, I couldn't help mulling over what I'd just learned: that Yoko had hated Bethany. Even though she'd gone on to start her own cosmetics company, the terrible thing that had happened to her at La Montaine Cosmetics still hurt.

The question was, was Yoko's animosity toward Bethany strong enough to motivate her to kill her?

Chapter 9

Kulfi, a frozen dairy dessert from the Indian
subcontinent, is popular all over India, Sri Lanka,
Pakistan, Bangladesh, Nepal, Myanmar, and the
Middle East. While it is similar to ice cream, it is
creamier and more dense. The most traditional
flavors are cream, rose, mango, cardamom,
saffron, and pistachio.

—*https://en.wikipedia.org/wiki/Kulfi*

I decided that like everyone else I would head back to my
room for some serious alone time. I left Yoko sprawled out
in her chair to drown her bitter memories in what remained
of the sherry.

But as soon as I walked out of the Fireside Room, I spotted
Gordon Bradley heading toward one of the other lounge
areas.

Which offered me the perfect opportunity to cozy up to
him to see what I could find out about him, Bethany, and
their relationship. So much for my chance for some alone
time.

"Gordon!" I called after him. "I'm so glad I ran into you.
We haven't really had a chance to chat."

He turned, looking surprised. And not exactly pleased. I
guess he'd been hoping for some alone time, too.

"It looks like you're about to relax in the Mountainside Room," I said as I caught up with him. "Mind if I join you? I'm up for a little break myself."

"Uh, sure," he said. After all, he didn't have much choice.

"Great." I flashed him my biggest smile.

He and I settled into side-by-side chairs in front of the Mountainside Room's fireplace. We exchanged some polite small talk about how beautiful Mohawk was, how inviting the fireplace was, and how comfortable the chairs were. A long silence followed.

It was Gordon who finally broke it. "I just made one of the most difficult phone calls of my life," he said. "I finally got up the courage to call Gloria La Montaine and tell her what happened to her daughter."

Of course. Someone had to break the news to her family. And it made sense that it had been Gordon, the only person who was here at Mohawk who had had a personal relationship with Bethany.

"That must have been awful," I said sympathetically. "I don't even have to ask you how she took the news."

"No," he agreed. "I'm sure you can imagine how our conversation went." He grimaced, then added, "Not surprisingly, it wasn't a very long conversation. Gloria fell apart and needed to get off the phone right away."

"Gordon, you're doing an absolutely valiant job of getting through this weekend," I told him. "You must be devastated, and yet you're managing to go through the motions as if nothing had happened."

He cast me an odd glance. I wondered if he was picking up on my thinly veiled criticism or if this was just his usual way of dealing with conversations that centered around feelings.

"I don't have much choice, do I?" he replied. "If I hid away in my room, counting the minutes until I could get out of this place, it would be worse. At least having things to do and other people around is a distraction." He thought for a few seconds, then added, "That ice cream we made today was pretty good, too."

I laughed. "It looks as if I may have succeeded in creating one more ice cream aficionado. Hopefully I've turned you into someone who's going to start spending every spare moment in the kitchen whipping up batches of homemade ice cream."

"I doubt that," he said, grimacing.

"What *do* you do with your spare time?" I asked chattily.

"Spare time?" he repeated with a wry smile. "What's that?"

"Ah," I said. "So you're one of those workaholic types."

"I suppose I am." Gazing into the fire, he added, "I guess that's something Bethany and I had in common."

"She did seem passionate about her career," I commented, nodding. "And I understand completely. I'm the same way about my career."

When he didn't respond, I threw out a line that I hoped would get him talking. "You two appeared to be very much in love."

A shocked look crossed his face. "Really? We did?"

I shot him a shocked look of my own. "You sound surprised."

I noticed that his cheeks turned just a tiny bit pink. "It's just that neither one of us was particularly demonstrative," he said. "In fact, sometimes when we'd go out to dinner or a party, people around us would assume we were business partners, rather than, you know, a couple."

"But you two were crazy about each other, right?" I prompted.

Once again, he looked uncomfortable. "Bethany and I were very . . . compatible." Quickly, he added, "What I mean is, we were two people who saw the world in the same way.

We loved our work and that was what came first. The challenge of being successful, of coming out on top, those were the things that got us both leaping out of bed before the alarm rang every morning."

Personally, I preferred coffee. Then again, I was clearly on a very different wavelength than people like Gordon and Bethany.

"Was your relationship serious?" I asked. "I mean, did the two of you ever talk about getting married?"

"She brought it up once or twice," he said. Squirming in his chair, he added, "And it was definitely something to consider. I loved Bethany. I really did. Sure, she had her bad points. But everybody does."

"And what exactly were her bad points?" I asked gently.

It didn't take him long to answer. "I guess the main one was that she was pretty much wrapped up in herself," he said. "But I never thought it was her fault. After all, she'd been spoiled rotten from the day she was born." He sighed. "Still, it was only going to get worse from here on in."

"Why is that?" I asked.

"Her mother, Gloria La Montaine, was getting ready to retire," Gordon replied. "And her plan was to make Bethany her replacement."

My eyebrows immediately shot upward. But I managed to sound calm as I mumbled, "Really?"

"That's right," he said. "Gloria was gearing up to hand over the title of President and CEO of La Montaine Cosmetics to her daughter. And while Bethany had always had whatever she wanted in terms of material things, she was about to become an incredibly powerful business magnate with all the respect and wealth and everything else that go along with it."

He was silent for a few seconds, just thinking. "When it came to our relationship," he finally said, "I guess I was starting to worry about how it would all play out. I was mainly concerned about Bethany's ambition spiraling out of control. You know, like whoever played the role of her husband was invariably going to become less important to her than running a cosmetics empire."

My mind was racing. And it wasn't Gordon and Bethany's possible future as husband and wife that I was most concerned with. "Who else knew that Bethany was about to take over at La Montaine?"

"Anybody who has access to a computer and enough time and interest to read Bethany's blog," Gordon replied with a contemptuous snort. "That woman had no sense of limits, and she wrote about every single aspect of her life for anyone in the world to see. That translated to things like her plans to come here to Mohawk for the weekend, of course. But it also included the fact that her mother was getting ready to make her the new head of La Montaine Cosmetics."

I blinked. "I don't know much about how big corporations work, but isn't a decision like that up to more than one person? Like other employees—or stockholders?"

Gordon shook his head. "There are no stockholders. La Montaine Cosmetics never went public. As big as it is, it's still a privately owned company." He laughed coldly. "Gloria had no intention of ever sharing any of the power. She ran the whole place herself. So naming her replacement was her decision and hers alone. And no one else besides her daughter was even in the running to take over the company."

I was silent for a while, mulling over what I'd just learned. I couldn't help but wonder if Bethany's career being on the verge of skyrocketing had played a role in her murder.

Yet the timing of her demise would have made much more sense if there had been other people who were competing for the job as Gloria's replacement. People who might have been jealous of Bethany's familial ties to the previous boss. People like other high-level employees at the firm, or maybe an executive at another company who was hoping to snag that plum position, or perhaps someone else who was closely involved in La Montaine's business dealings . . .

Gordon, for example.

But I believed what he had said about Gloria not even considering handing over the cosmetics empire she had built to anyone but Bethany. Besides, none of the people who made up the pool of suspects struck me as likely contenders for a high-level position like that.

Even Yoko, the only person here who worked in the field of cosmetics, had left La Montaine long before now. And given what had happened there, thanks to Bethany's deviousness, it wouldn't exactly have put her on the short list even if she still worked there. Then there was the simple fact that Yoko was still in her twenties. No matter how sharp she was, with only a few years of experience she would hardly have been in a position to run an enterprise of that size.

Which all led me to conclude that Bethany's murder probably hadn't been related to her impending rise in the business world after all.

As Gordon and I lapsed into silence, both of us staring at the crackling fire, I found myself feeling deflated. I had just learned something about Bethany La Montaine that seemed significant, yet there was no way I could fit it into the terrible tragedy that she had met up with. So I decided that I would just tuck this piece of information away at the back of mind, considering it one more piece of a frustratingly difficult puzzle that I was beginning to feel I would never succeed in piecing together.

I rushed into dinner at ten minutes after seven, flustered over being late. Once I'd gone back to my room, I'd lain down on the bed, wanting to focus on the conversations I'd just had with Yoko and Gordon in an attempt at seeing some angle, some clue, that I'd missed up until that point. Instead, I fell asleep as soon as my head hit the pillow.

It wasn't until 6:55 that I emerged from a wonderfully deep and rejuvenating nap. I was instantly thrown into panic mode, hurrying to zip myself into my pastel flowered dress, brush my hair, and sprint through the long hallways toward the dining room.

When I arrived, as breathless as if I'd just run a marathon, I saw that everyone else in our group had already sat down together at the big round table. And while Jake was smiling and chatting away amiably, I picked up on a heaviness that hung over the other guests. All of us being trapped together, with the murder of a member of our group hovering in the background no less, wasn't exactly making it easy to act as if nothing out of the ordinary was going on.

"Sorry I'm late," I declared as I pulled out the one remaining empty chair and sat down. "I fell asleep."

"Who could blame you?" Franny chirped, as usual doing her best to put a positive spin on things. "You've been working nonstop since the moment you got here."

"And doing a very fine job," Naveen added.

Yoko just stared at me, her eyes bleary. I got the feeling that she hadn't been able to fit in a nap between sherry hour and dinner, since sherry hour had lasted so much longer than it was supposed to.

Still, the arrival of a new person—that would be me— seemed to liven things up a bit. The conversation immediately turned to speculation about what the dinner offerings might be tonight. Some people claimed that they were too full of ice cream to eat more than a few bites. Others insisted that they didn't expect to have the slightest problem digging into whatever was put in front of them.

And then, just as the mood was shifting to something

along the lines of animated, a dark cloud suddenly descended. In other words, Mrs. Moody appeared in the doorway.

"I forgot to mention that I invited Mrs. Moody to join us for dinner tonight," Franny said, glancing over at the new arrival. By way of explanation, she added, "Our little group has spent so much time in each other's company that I thought it would be refreshing to have someone else join us."

Jake shot me an amused look that told me he was thinking the same thing I was thinking: that the word "refreshing" should never be used in reference to Mrs. Moody.

"An excellent idea, Franny," Naveen said. "I am sorry I did not think of it myself."

Gordon just grunted. Yoko, meanwhile, was too busy downing a big glass of water to speak. I would have bet a three-gallon tub of chocolate marshmallow fudge ice cream that she wished she had some ibuprofen to go with it.

As Mrs. Moody headed toward our table, I saw that once again she was carrying a book with her. And that it was the same one I'd seen her holding before: *Gone with the Wind.*

Franny noticed, too. As soon as Mrs. Moody sat down, she commented, "I see you're reading *Gone with the Wind.* That's one of my favorite books of all time."

"It's one of my favorites, too," Mrs. Moody said. She actually smiled. And it was a *dreamy* smile, something I never would have suspected the woman was capable of. "I must have read it twenty times. And I've seen the movie at least thirty times."

I was a big fan of the book, too, having first read it when I was twelve. Just like everyone else in the universe, I'd been totally charmed by Scarlett O'Hara's spunkiness and her transition from self-centered Southern belle to survivor. Rhett Butler wasn't bad, either.

"I happen to know all kinds of interesting trivia about the movie version of *Gone with the Wind,*" Franny told us, her eyes shining. "For example, did you know that a chapter of a group called the United Daughters of the Confederacy that was based in Ocala, Florida, staged a protest over a British actress playing Scarlett O'Hara? But when they were told that Katherine Hepburn was next on the list, they thought it would be even worse if a Yankee played the role!"

"Fascinating," Gordon said dryly.

"Here's another fun fact," Franny went on, either not noticing or not caring that no one else seemed particularly interested in what she was saying. Aside from me, of course, and, presumably, Mrs. Moody. "Leslie Howard hated playing Ashley Wilkes! He felt he was too old and that he wasn't handsome enough. He'd also had his fill of playing weak men. But David O. Selznick, the movie's producer, offered him a credit as a producer in another film he was going to make, so he went along with it." She paused to take a breath. "Leslie Howard actually hated the entire project. He said it was 'nonsense'!"

"That *is* interesting," I commented. And I meant it.

"Here's one more bit of trivia," Franny continued. "See if you can guess the answer. In the movie, which character has the opening line?" She paused, clearly expecting all of us to call out our answers. When no one did, she added, "I'll give you a clue. At the start of the film, Scarlett O'Hara is sitting on the porch, and two of her suitors are talking to her about the impending war."

"Ashley Wilkes?" I guessed, feeling bad that no one else seemed interested enough to answer. Not even Mrs. Moody was venturing any guesses, and she was clearly into the book much more than anyone else in the room.

"Nope," Franny said gaily. "Guess again."

"Rhett Butler," Yoko ventured, proving that she was absolutely clueless when it came to the classic film. Everyone who's ever seen the movie knows about the first time Clark

Gable appears on screen as the rakish and irresistible Rhett Butler. Our hearts inevitably beat a little faster as we picture him standing at the bottom of that grand staircase, gazing up at Scarlett as she drifts down.

"Nope," Franny replied. "Any more guesses?"

Silence.

"It was Brent Tarleton," she announced victoriously, "who was played by an actor named Fred Crane. Brent Tarleton was one of the Tarleton twins, just two of Scarlett O'Hara's many suitors. His brother was named Stuart . . ."

Of course! I thought, nearly blinded by the light bulb going on in my head. The Tarleton twins! *That* was why the unusual name of Mohawk's bellman had sounded so familiar!

But then another thought occurred to me. Tarleton had the same name as a character in Mrs. Moody's favorite book!

I had a sneaking suspicion that that was more than a coincidence.

I glanced over at Mrs. Moody, curious about how she was reacting to this revelation about her favorite novel and film. But she was stone-faced, sitting stiffly with her eyes fixed on the salt shaker.

I thought back to the way she'd looked as she had ruffled his hair, looking at him in what increasingly seemed to me like a loving way. Here I'd been thinking that she was merely fond of him, perhaps because they'd worked together for a long time. But now I was starting to realize that it was very likely that there was more to it.

I did a quick mental calculation. Mrs. Moody looked as if she was in her late sixties, while Tarleton appeared to be in his early forties . . .

He was the right age to be her son.

I struggled to remember if anyone had ever mentioned Tarleton's last name. Not that it mattered. After all, even if he was her son, Mrs. Moody could have remarried after Tarleton had been born, taking a new last name for herself even though he still used his biological father's last name.

But what interested me even more was the fact that Mrs. Moody hadn't introduced him as her son. Or treated him like a son, aside from that private moment I had accidentally witnessed.

And why would that be? I wondered. Was it possible that she was ashamed of him? Or maybe her secrecy had something to do with company policy. I supposed it was possible that for some reason Mohawk didn't want anyone to know that a mother and son were both working there.

But I had a hard time buying into that theory. Why would anyone care? The guests certainly wouldn't. And the other employees at Mohawk would most likely have figured out at some point that the two were related. After all, I'd come up with that conclusion after being here for only a few hours. The rest of the staff, meanwhile, worked with both of them day in and day out.

The true relationship between Mrs. Moody and Tarleton was turning out to be just one more mystery that I hoped I'd be able to solve.

When it came to mysteries, I realized, it was turning out that Mohawk was chockful of them.

"How about spending a little time together?" Jake suggested, taking my hand in his as we walked out of dinner. We were both feeling pretty mellow, thanks to a lovely meal, an excellent merlot, and as the perfect ending, a luscious dessert course that consisted of more of the group's homemade ice cream from that afternoon.

"That sounds like a great idea," I replied, giving his hand a squeeze. "What have you got in mind? More cuddling in front of a roaring fire?"

"Actually, I had something a bit more strenuous in mind," he said. "I did some more exploring. And I discovered something really exciting: There's a foosball table in the basement."

While I happen to be the opposite of athletic, foosball is a game that even I'm capable of playing. It's basically a table-top version of football or soccer, played by turning knobs that move lines of plastic players back and forth so they can "kick" the ball. It's a game I happened to be pretty good at, due largely to a near obsession with the game during my college years. Even Jake's background as our high school's star baseball player wasn't going to be all that helpful when it came to pitting my skill at wrist-flicking against his.

"You're on!" I cried.

For the next hour, Jake and I stood opposite each other at the foosball table, yelling and laughing and having a great time as we batted a plastic ball back and forth. Focusing on something so mindless and so—let's face it—unimportant was a great release. In fact, I couldn't remember the last time my ribs actually hurt from laughing so hard.

I also managed to win more games than he did. Whether that was because of my exceptional hand-eye coordination or because he was refraining from calling upon all of his, I couldn't say.

This is fun, I thought. Then immediately noticed that I'd had that thought.

Maybe the positives about being in a relationship make it worth all the negatives: the ambivalence, the anxiety, the compromises, even the occasional argument. I reminded myself to try to keep that in mind the next time I was wrestling with that wicked ambivalence.

"Enough!" I finally cried, noticing that my wrists were getting tired. And I had serious wrist power, given all the time I'd put in with an ice cream scoop. "I'm clearly the superior player, and there's no need for me to continue to humiliate you with my impressive foosball-playing skills."

Jake grinned. "Next time, we'll play a different game. How about arm wrestling? Or touch football? Or chess?"

"No, no, and yes," I replied. "But for now, I'm completely exhausted and in desperate need of some sleep."

"In that case, I'll shuffle off to my room in the hinterlands," Jake said. "Good night, Kate." He took my face gently in his hands, then leaned forward and planted the sweetest, softest kiss imaginable on my lips.

I could feel myself melting like a soft-serve cone on a hot August day.

"Good night, Jake," I said, my voice a hoarse whisper.

I still felt as if I were floating, or at least walking a few inches off the ground, as I made my way back to my room. Reaching it required passing through the lobby. As I walked past the doors that opened onto the Great Room, still feeling a bit dazed, I happened to glance inside.

I expected it to be covered in dark shadows with no one inside. Instead, I noticed the glow of a laptop computer screen in one corner, the only light in the entire room. Even though I was tired and still feeling a little dazed from Jake's amazing kiss, I couldn't resist the urge to duck inside and see who was there.

As my eyes adjusted to the dim light, I saw that Yoko was sitting at a wonderfully old-fashioned wooden table with ornately carved legs. The fact that someone was staring at a computer screen at that table, rather than writing poetry with a quill or reading a leather-bound first edition of some classic novel, just seemed wrong.

She was hunched over the screen of her laptop, so involved in whatever she was looking at that she didn't appear to have noticed that someone else had come into the room.

I jumped when I suddenly heard her cry, "No! Not again!"

Tentatively I walked over to her. "Is everything all right?" I asked in a gentle voice.

She glanced up at me for all of two seconds, then went back to looking at her screen. "No, everything is *not* all right," she replied bitterly. "Someone is trying to ruin me!"

Chapter 10

The Eskimo Pie, which Christian Nelson invented
in Iowa in 1920, was originally called "I-Scream
Bars." The name changed when he partnered with
confectioner Russell Stover.

*—Everybody Loves Ice Cream: The Whole Scoop
on America's Favorite Treat, by Shannon Jackson Arnold*

I ventured closer and peered at the computer, curious to see
what Yoko was looking at. And even more importantly, to
find out what had led her to draw such an extreme conclusion.

So I was surprised by the image that filled the screen. It
was a line of lipsticks in different shades of pink, starting
with the palest pastel and ending with a color so startling
that it reminded me of neon. As for the slim tubes that contained them, they were shiny white enamel with irregular
black polka dots that gave them a clean, slightly edgy look.

"What are those?" I asked, even though I was pretty sure I
already knew.

"Lipsticks," Yoko replied sharply. But in a softer voice she
added, "Or to be more specific, they're my newest line. I call
them Lingering Lipsticks, which is meant to communicate
that they stay on all day. I worked hard to come up with a
name that implied that they, you know, make other people
want to kiss you a lot."

"They look very . . . nice," I said, not sure exactly how to compliment what to me looked like nothing more than an ordinary bunch of lipsticks.

"They're more than nice," Yoko insisted. "They're revolutionary. They're made with this new ingredient that's totally organic and totally pure and totally a secret. They really do stay on all day. You can eat a three-course meal in my Lingering Lipsticks and by dessert they'll look just as good as when you ordered!"

"So what's the problem?" I asked.

"The problem is the negative reviews!" she shrieked. "Just look at them! People have posted one bad comment after another. Look at this one from three days ago by somebody called LadyM. It says, 'This lipstick had worn off almost before I'd left the bathroom. What a waste of money.' And this one from yesterday morning says, 'The colors look nothing like they're supposed to. I just bought In The Pink and when I put it on my lips looked BLUE!' "

By this point, I was totally confused. "But if your new lipsticks are so terrific, why are people having such bad experiences?"

"They're all phony!" Yoko exclaimed. "Like I said, someone is trying to ruin me! They're going out of their way to make my fabulous products sound terrible, even though they're wonderful."

"That's awful," I said. "But who would do such a thing?"

Yoko suddenly froze. "I have no idea," she said crisply.

With that, she slammed her laptop shut. She grabbed it, then hurried out of the room, mumbling, "I have to go make a call."

But I was bursting with curiosity. Who would go out of their way to ruin Yoko's online cosmetics company?

The gnawing feeling in the pit of my stomach gave me a clue.

I took out my phone and, with a little help from Google,

found the website for Athena's Beauty. I clicked on the link for Lingering Lipsticks and a few seconds later was staring at the same page I'd seen on Yoko's laptop.

I started reading the customer reviews. Many of them were raves. I suspected that those were the legitimate ones. However, I was much more interested in the negative reviews. I readily found the two that she had read aloud.

But I let out a gasp when I read one posting that was a bit further down on the web page.

This lipstick is junk, LipStickLady had written. **If you want a really good one, you should buy La Montaine's LipLuxurious lipsticks. Now there's a product that really performs!**

I checked the date and time of the post. It was from the morning before, about ten minutes after the previous post had been written.

It wasn't much of a leap to make the assumption that Bethany La Montaine had written this review. And it wasn't much more of a leap to assume that Yoko knew that the person who was trying to sabotage her company was none other than her former coworker.

From the looks of things, Bethany had been determined to ruin Yoko. Not only had she managed to make Yoko lose her job at La Montaine; she had also been doing her darnedest to unravel Yoko's success in reinventing herself as an entrepreneur.

Which meant that Yoko had a pretty strong motive to want Bethany *gone*.

By the time I headed back to my room, I was pretty wiped out. It had been an extraordinarily long day. And it wasn't only because of the ice cream workshops I'd conducted. Even more, it was because of my struggle to figure out what was behind Bethany La Montaine's murder.

I'd learned so much since breakfast that I was finding it impossible to sift through all the new information that was vying for space in my brain. So I was looking forward to lying in bed and trying to sort it all out. I always found that complete silence and total darkness were ideal for seeing things much more clearly than I ever could during the day, when a zillion different sights and sounds competed to distract me. And I expected that the hypnotic sound of the rain against the window would make it even easier than usual for me to focus.

As I passed through one of the long, eerily silent corridors en route to my room, I suddenly caught my breath. Someone was lurking in the shadows. At least, that was my first thought. After only a second or two, I realized that the man standing in front of the big window at the end of the corridor was Naveen.

He appeared to be gazing outside, perhaps watching the branches that were whipping around in the wind or the silvery pattern the pellets of rain were making on the glass. I was a little surprised, since I was pretty sure it was impossible to see anything more scenic, like the moon or the stars, much less anything as far away as the lake. Still, he seemed transfixed by whatever he was staring at.

"Hello, Naveen," I said, causing him to jump about six inches into the air. I realized that he hadn't been looking out the window after all. He had been lost in thought.

"Ah," he said, immediately composing himself. "If it isn't the queen of ice cream herself."

I smiled. "The queen is taking the rest of the night off," I told him. "Even I need a break from ice cream every once in a while."

"A well-deserved break, too," he said. "It is clear that you have been a most dedicated professional since you arrived, giving all of us your undivided attention."

When I wasn't busy conducting a murder investigation on the side, I thought wryly. But I just smiled.

"What about you?" I asked. "I would have thought that

after the long day we all put in, you would have gone to your room long before now."

"I was just on my way there," he replied. "But sometimes, I find that being alone can be difficult. Tonight is one of those nights."

"I know exactly what you mean," I said.

He cast me a strange look. "I hope not," he said. "What I mean is, I hope that during your lifetime you have been spared the kind of sadness that I have unfortunately experienced. The type that brings on fits of melancholia whenever you are left alone with your own thoughts for too long a time."

I had a feeling I already knew what he was referring to. And I discovered that I was right when he added, "Something about this place, maybe the solitude or the beauty or something much less tangible, is bringing up so many thoughts of my daughter."

"What happened to her?" I asked gently. Even though I'd known this man for only a bit longer than twenty-four hours, I felt as if we had made enough of an emotional connection that I could ask him that question without offending him.

He lowered himself onto the wooden window seat that jutted out from below the window, softened with a thick cushion covered in flower fabric. He gestured for me to sit down beside him.

"The graduate degree that Sana earned from Columbia University was in business," he said slowly. "An MBA. She was so intelligent and such a hard worker that she could have done anything, and I had hoped she would pursue something more challenging for her life's work. Something more creative. And something more humanitarian. But she decided it was the right path for her. She insisted that business was a field that would enable her to take advantage of both her practical side and her creative abilities.

"Of course she did wonderfully in the program," he went on. "She was a star student, just as she had always been. And when she was about to graduate, she was interviewed by half a dozen big companies in New York. And every single one of them offered her a high-level job."

"That sounds terrific," I commented.

"And not the least bit surprising," he said, his chest puffing up with pride. But his posture quickly changed. "Alas, she soon found that the business world could be a terribly cutthroat place. She merely wanted to get the tasks that were put before her done in the best way possible, but she quickly learned that too many of the people around her often had agendas of their own. In the end, it was simply too much for her."

Lowering his eyes and staring at his hands, he said, "Sana suffered a sort of breakdown."

"I'm so sorry," I said softly.

"It was heartbreaking," Naveen said. "Here was this lively, intelligent woman who suddenly could not bring herself to get out of bed. She quit her job, moved back in with her mother, and rarely left the house. Her mother and I worked together to get her into therapy, to find the best psychiatrist in the city to prescribe medication, to try to get her interested in something, anything . . ."

"Did any of it help?" I asked.

Naveen smiled sadly. "She did finally find an interest," he replied. "Unfortunately, it was something none of us could have foreseen. Something none of us who loved her would ever have wanted for her."

Before I had a chance to ask what it was, he told me, "Sana became part of a cult."

I gasped. "A cult!"

I didn't know much about cults. I thought of them as something that had been common during the 1960s and

1970s when people were experimenting with all kinds of different lifestyles. Heaven's Gate, with dozens of followers committing mass suicide because they believed it would get them to an extraterrestrial spacecraft. Jonestown, where nearly a thousand people killed themselves by voluntarily drinking Kool-Aid that was laced with cyanide. David Koresh's Branch Davidian sect in Waco, Texas, which became the scene of a deadly battle involving the Bureau of Alcohol, Tobacco, Firearms and Explosives—more commonly known as the ATF—and the Texas Army National Guard. Charles Manson, whose name has become a synonym for evil, and his murderous followers.

But then I remembered that cults were not just a thing of the past. The Nxivm sex cult, for example, which had gotten media attention fairly recently when a well-known actress was arrested for her alleged involvement with recruiting women to become sex slaves.

In a much calmer voice, I asked, "What kind of cult?"

Another sad smile. "There is only one kind of cult," Naveen said. "And that is the kind that brainwashes its members and turns them against their families and the people who love them in order to gain total control over them."

"I'm surprised that someone as intelligent and as grounded as your daughter fell for something like that," I commented.

"Ah, but that is the thing," Naveen said. "Someone like Sana does not realize what she's getting into. It starts out as something that seems innocent, like a prayer group or even a bunch of activists—for example, people who share an interest in animal rights, which was the group that attracted Sana. Not only does the person herself not have any idea of the realities of the organization; the entire situation seems so innocuous that even her friends and family do not realize what is really going on.

"And people who are already vulnerable because of their

mental state, as Sana was, make the easiest targets," he continued. "She was depressed, feeling lost and disillusioned, and pretty much isolated. But I must add that plenty of people who become involved in cults are on perfectly solid ground psychologically. They have simply come to believe that the organization offers them something they value.

"Cults are always built around one particular individual," Naveen continued. "A person, usually a man, who plays the role of authority figure. Of course, his interest in it is access to money and power and, sadly, women. There are currently over three thousand such cults in the United States. And the way they differ from legitimate groups is that rather than attempting to work toward a valid goal or to improve the lives of the members, they were created to serve the purposes of the cult's leader."

"But I still can't help wondering how a levelheaded young woman like your daughter managed to get brainwashed," I said. "Once she was involved with the group, why didn't she figure out that it wasn't what she'd first thought it was?"

"There are special techniques that are used to what is basically gaining control of other people's minds," Naveen told me. "One of the most basic ones is to deprive the person of protein. Without protein, the brain cannot function normally. That prevents the subject from exercising logical thought. The same goes for sleep deprivation. And sometimes the subject is drugged without knowing it.

"Another technique is keeping the subject from ever being alone," he continued. "Instead, a new recruit is constantly in the presence of other members of the cult. Then there is no way to make a reality check or to analyze any of the things that are going on around her. Instead, the mumbo-jumbo of the cult's philosophy is all she is exposed to. And of course the subjects are kept away from their friends, their family, anyone from their other life.

"And as is usually the case, their techniques worked," Naveen said with a slight shrug. "We lost our daughter to this misguided group that basically took over her mind."

"You must have done everything you could to get her away from them," I commented.

"Of course," Naveen replied. "Sana's mother and I even hired a professional deprogrammer to try to get her to leave the cult and return to us. His plan was to lock her into a hotel room until he used his special techniques to get her to come to her senses. To finally understand what was going on. But she managed to get away from him."

I blinked. "How did she do that?"

"With the help of other cult members," he replied. "It is amazing how far they can reach. And the lengths to which they will go to hold on to their members."

"Where is she living now?" I asked.

Naveen sighed deeply. "We are not sure. The cult she is in moves around, renting or buying farms or ranches in isolated spots. For a while, we thought she was in Arizona. But we have heard she's now in Indiana, thanks to the grapevine. And believe me, there is a grapevine. There are plenty of families that are completely distraught over losing a loved one to a cult."

"Naveen, I feel terrible," I told him sincerely. "I can't even imagine what you've been going through."

He forced a weak smile. "Thank you," he replied. "I try to find enjoyable ways to pass the time. To distract myself. Coming to Mohawk for this lovely ice cream weekend, for example."

I could sense that his mood was shifting. "Speaking of which, you have worked very hard today and I should allow you to get on with your evening. It is very late, and I am sure that you are tired. You have inspired us throughout the day, and I am completely sincere when I say that I have developed a new appreciation for ice cream." Smiling, he added, "I promise you that I will never feel the same way about it again."

I laughed. And it felt good to see him smile. I was glad that he had managed to put his sadness aside, at least for a few moments. I could see that the man's heart had been broken. And it didn't look as if it would be easily healed.

As I stood outside the door of my room, turning the key in the lock, I realized that the feeling of sadness that had fallen over me as I'd listened to Naveen's story about his daughter had returned.

Poor Naveen, I thought. *He's such a sweet man, and he obviously cares about his daughter more than anything else in the world. What a tragedy that—*

As soon as I'd gotten inside and locked the door behind me, I remembered that I had no choice but to consider him a suspect in Bethany La Montaine's murder. With or without the tragedy of what had happened to Sana.

Or maybe *because* of the tragedy.

It was only then that it struck me that I'd missed out on an important opportunity: asking Naveen exactly where his daughter had worked. Learning the name of the company at which she had had such a terrible experience that she had actually had a nervous breakdown would have been an important piece of the puzzle. Yet I'd been so absorbed in the story he'd told me, so distraught over his report on the terrible fate that had befallen his daughter, that it hadn't occurred to me to ask.

The sick feeling in the pit of my stomach told me there was a very good chance that that company had been La Montaine Cosmetics. Which would mean that Naveen deserved to be high up on my list of suspects.

Not Naveen, I thought mournfully, sinking onto the bed.

Please don't let him be the person who murdered Bethany. I hope the terrible sadness in his life didn't drive him to do something so unspeakable . . .

I was still agonizing over that thought when I heard a knock at the door. I immediately jumped up, startled by the idea of someone coming to my room so late at night.

It must be Jake, I told myself. But when I cautiously opened the door, just an inch or two, I found myself face-to-face with Tarleton.

"Tarleton!" I cried, already heading toward panic mode. "What are you doing here?"

"You have a telephone call," he replied woodenly. "In the lobby. On one of the pay phones. You're lucky that I heard it ring as I was walking by. So I answered it."

"Who is it?" I was already thinking the worst. Had something happened to Grams? Or even to Emma? My heart was already pounding with alarming speed, instantly banishing the fatigue that had been dragging me down before.

"I don't know," he replied, still not showing even the slightest sign of emotion. "It sounded like a girl."

So it *was* Emma. My heart was pounding even more furiously as I dashed past him, racing through the halls as I made a beeline for the lobby. The obvious reason my niece was calling was because of my request that she find out whatever she could about the workshop participants' backgrounds. But part of me couldn't let go of the possibility that she was calling for another reason entirely. While the distance between my room and the center of the resort always seemed long, tonight the trip seemed interminable.

As soon as I reached the lobby, I spotted the receiver of the pay phone dangling from its cord. I headed into the booth, snapped it up and barked, "Emma? Is everything all right? Is Grams okay? Are *you* okay?"

"Grams is fine," Emma replied. "So am I. In fact, everything is fine." The calm tone of her voice immediately put me at ease.

But then she added, "At least, everything is fine in *our* lives."

I immediately grasped the meaning of her intriguing statement. "You've found out something interesting, haven't you?" I demanded.

"Something *very* interesting," she replied. She hesitated for a moment before adding, "Although I'm not sure what it means. But I'm hoping that what I found out will be helpful to you . . ."

"What did you find out?" I asked, already aware that no matter what it was, she had found it important enough to warrant a phone call late on a Saturday night.

A long silence followed. And then, still speaking in a matter-of-fact tone, Emma said, "It seems this Merle Moody of yours is a kidnapper."

Chapter 11

From 1993 until 2003, Ben & Jerry's produced an ice cream called Wavy Gravy that was named after an entertainer who founded a circus and performing arts camp in Northern California called Camp Winnarainbow. The ice cream consisted of a base of caramel, cashew nut, and Brazil nut ice cream with a chocolate hazelnut fudge swirl. Sales helped fund scholarships for underprivileged children at the camp.

—*https://en.wikipedia.org/wiki/Wavy_Gravy*

A strange feeling had come over me, as if I'd somehow been transported into another state of being. Emma's announcement was *that* strange.

"I'm listening," I told her.

At the other end of the line, I heard her take a deep breath. "Forty years ago," she said, "the story about Merle Moody and her kidnapping of a baby boy was headline news. But maybe I'd better go back to the beginning."

Frankly, I was so anxious to hear about Mrs. Moody's history as a kidnapper that I would have preferred to start with what had happened at the end. But I realized that having some context, a way of fully understanding whatever information Emma had uncovered, made much more sense.

"I started out my research by trying to find a connection between Merle Moody and the state of Minnesota, just like you asked me to," Emma told me. As usual, she was taking a logical approach. "It seems she lived there in the late seventies and the early eighties, back when she was in her twenties. She was a social worker. At least, that was her official title. But what I discovered is that after working for the city of Minneapolis for a couple of years, she went to work for a lawyer who handled private adoptions."

"I don't know much about how adoption works," I commented, thinking aloud. "So I'm afraid I don't know the difference between private adoptions and any other kind of adoption."

"I do," she said. "At least, I do now. Thank you, Google."

Once again, my niece was turning out to be a true gem in the realm of research.

"It seems that most people who decide to adopt a child go through a state-run adoption agency," Emma explained. "But a second option is adopting through an attorney. Adoption can also be done privately when, for example, a woman who's pregnant wants a certain kind of family to adopt her baby—like maybe she feels strongly about the child being raised in a particular religion or even in a specific part of the country.

"There are other advantages, as well," my niece went on. "For one thing, the process of adopting privately, through a lawyer, goes much faster than using a state agency. But what's even more important is that with an independent adoption—that's another term for using a lawyer rather than an agency—fewer constraints are put on the person who wants to adopt."

"I would expect that government agencies look into the prospective families' backgrounds pretty carefully," I mused.

"Things like their income and employment history, but also everything else they've ever done."

"Exactly," Emma agreed. "And state adoption agencies have their own criteria when it comes to people who want to adopt, like their marital status or their age or their sexual orientation. I'm sure they even consider whether the person who wants to adopt has a criminal record. But with an independent adoption, none of that stuff matters."

"Go on," I prompted.

"So the lawyer Merle Moody went to work for, the one who handled private adoptions, was a man named Terrance Shelton," Emma continued. "But the reason I even found her name online is that while she was working for him, a lawsuit was filed against both Shelton and Merle Moody." She hesitated before adding, "And then, about a year after the lawsuit was filed, Merle Moody was charged with kidnapping."

I grabbed a pen and the pad of paper. I was still trying to digest what I was hearing as I commented, "It sounds like there are still a lot of blanks for you to fill in."

"I can send you links to some of the websites I found," Emma offered.

"It's better if you just tell me what you found out," I told her. I was on the verge of admitting to her that I was being watched—by none other than the woman she had been researching. But I stopped myself. After all, there was no reason to make her worry. At least, not any more than she already undoubtedly was.

Once again, Emma took a deep breath. "The mother of the baby boy who had been put up for adoption sued Merle Moody and the lawyer she worked for because she claimed that the baby hadn't actually been placed with the couple she'd agreed to allow to adopt her son. And for a long time, no one knew *who* he was living with. But a few months later, the mother claimed that Merle Moody hadn't placed him at all. She pressed kidnapping charges, saying that Merle had kept him for herself and that Terrance Shelton had been complicit."

I gasped. "So she actually kidnapped him? As in grabbing him and running and hiding him away . . . ?"

"Not technically," Emma said. "According to the lawsuit, the mother claimed that the lawyer, this Terrance Shelton, had fudged the paperwork after the birth mother had signed it. She sued because she claimed that he had changed the names in the contract from the couple she'd wanted to adopt her son to Merle Moody." She paused. "And once she'd figured out what had happened to her missing baby, the police arrested Merle Moody for kidnapping. Shelton was also arrested on a lesser charge. Something about abusing his role as an attorney."

I was scribbling away as quickly as I could. "How did the mother figure out what had happened to her baby?"

"She hired a private detective," Emma replied. "Somehow, she'd had a hunch about Merle Moody. I guess she'd acted strange during their meetings. But the mother had her followed and—well, she eventually figured out that Merle was hiding the baby in her tiny apartment, taking care of him herself."

I was speechless. Was it really possible that Mrs. Moody had kidnapped Tarleton? It was difficult to believe that anyone was guilty of such a horrendous act.

Yet it made perfect sense, based on what I'd observed for myself. When Mrs. Moody thought no one was looking, she treated Tarleton like a son. As for the timing of the newspaper articles Emma had found, he was certainly the right age.

"Did the mother win the lawsuit?" I asked.

"I wasn't able to find anything about that," Emma replied. "I'm pretty sure that that's because the case was settled out of court. But if the mother was paid a settlement, and I suspect that that was how it would have been resolved, I wasn't able to find any information about the details."

"What about the kidnapping charge?" I asked. "Did Mrs. Moody stand trial? Did she serve time?"

"Yes, there was a trial," Emma said. "But no, she didn't serve time."

I found that as surprising as everything else I was hearing. "Why not? It sounds as if what she had done was illegal."

"Technically, it was," Emma replied. "But this was such an unusual case that the judge concluded that he couldn't treat it like an ordinary kidnapping. Instead, his findings were that since Merle Moody had already acted as the boy's mother for over a year, it wouldn't make sense to take him away from her and place him with another family. But he did insist upon psychological counseling and—let me see, I think there was some pretty serious oversight, as well. You know, home visits, evaluations of the boy's progress, that kind of thing. But it seems that overall, the court determined that she had been doing a perfectly fine job of raising him so far and that in this instance she should be allowed to continue as the boy's adoptive mother."

My brain was spinning. And one of the main reasons was that I felt I had completely misjudged Mrs. Moody. Here I'd thought she was as hard as nails. Creepy, even. Yet she had wanted a baby so badly that she had actually taken a little boy, risking arrest and even risking eventually losing him.

"There was something else that the judge said that I found interesting," Emma commented. "It seems that Merle Moody was given a chance to testify on her own behalf during the trial. And what she said really touched him."

"What was that?" I asked.

"She told the court that it was pretty clear from the start that that baby had some fairly serious learning disabilities," Emma said. "Merle Moody said that while she sometimes thought about giving the baby back to the couple who had originally wanted to adopt him, she was afraid that they would find him 'imperfect' and reject him. She told the judge that no matter what, she was prepared to dedicate herself totally to raising the boy, making sure he got all the love and care in the entire universe if that was what he needed. The judge said in his findings that the phrase she'd used, 'all the love and care in the entire universe,' had particularly touched him. To him, that meant she had been a good mother to him and that she would continue to be totally devoted to him. That was one of the main reasons he felt it was in the child's best interest for him to remain with her."

Emma was silent for a few seconds before asking, "Is that helpful, Kate?"

"*Very* helpful, Emma," I assured her. "You are truly amazing when it comes to finding your way around the internet. I don't know what I'd do without you."

"Thanks!" she cried. I could tell from the pride in her voice how pleased she was that she'd been so helpful.

"There's one more thing," I added. "Could you do me a favor and track down contact information for the lawyer who was involved in all this? I believe you said his name was Terrance Shelton?"

"Since my skill set happens to include reading minds," Emma quipped, "I already did that. I had a feeling that you might want to follow up on this. So I tracked down the only Terrance Shelton who was ever an attorney in Minnesota. In fact, it looks like he still lives there." She rattled off an email address and a telephone number. I jotted down both.

"I'll keep doing more research," she continued. "I know there are other people you said you were interested in finding out more about . . ."

But I was only half listening, since I was deep in thought.

And not only about what I'd just learned from Emma's crackerjack research.

I realized that while what I'd learned answered some of the questions I'd had about Mrs. Moody and Tarleton, there was one question that it didn't come close to answering. And that was whether it was possible that the surprising act that Merle Moody had committed almost forty years earlier was somehow connected to Bethany La Montaine's murder.

As soon as I got into bed, I fell into a deep sleep. But it wasn't as restful as I had hoped. Instead, I was tormented by bad dreams. And the workshop participants all played starring roles.

In the dream that was the most realistic—that is, the one that caused me to wake up in a panic, gasping for breath and horrified to find that my heart was beating at a sickening rate—was a nightmare in which I was stranded at Mohawk, just as I was in reality. But in the dream, Gordon and Yoko and Naveen and Franny had all turned into zombies. Mrs. Moody and Tarleton, too. And they were all coming after me, shuffling in my direction as I dashed around the sprawling building, desperately trying to find a place to hide.

Even when I caught my breath and managed to calm my pounding heart, I still didn't feel comforted. After all, aside from the zombie part, my horrible dream wasn't that far from the truth.

So it was a great relief to glance outside the window and discover that the rain had finally stopped. The sky was still gray and a thick fog made it impossible to see most of the lake, but at least there seemed to be a lull in the storm.

Maybe I'll actually get out of here at some point, I thought grimly as I brushed my teeth, the tile floor ice-cold beneath my bare feet.

But part of me hoped that wouldn't happen until I'd somehow managed to figure out who had killed Bethany. While I'd been holed up at Mohawk for only a little more than thirty-six hours, I'd gotten to know all the workshop participants better than I'd expected. True, it was largely because someone had been murdered—and each and every one of them was a suspect. Yet I'd already invested so much in trying to learn everything I could about their relationship with the victim, meanwhile finding out so much about them, that I was achingly curious to know who had really been behind the deadly deed.

Even though reading about it in the newspaper in a few days would have satisfied my curiosity, I was so enmeshed in this place and the people who were all stuck in it together that I wanted to answer the question myself.

Sunday morning brunch was generally a high point of vacationers' stay at Mohawk. This little factoid was one I had learned on the resort's website.

According to the chatty write-up on the Dining page, the highly acclaimed brunch consisted of a mind-boggling buffet that started with fresh fruit, some of the pieces cut into the shapes of flowers and leaves, and ended with no fewer than six varieties of coffee cake.

But the true highlight, it seemed, was an omelet station. The man who presided over it had apparently played the same role for more than two decades, coming in only on this one day of the week. He would don a white apron and a chef's cap, then whip up unimaginably fluffy concoctions that featured any and every possible combination of more than twenty-seven different add-ins.

Today, the man who was reportedly a veritable egg genius was nowhere to be found. Thanks to the downed tree that still lay across the resort's only access road, it seemed that we were going to have to settle for a considerably simpler meal.

In fact, it was the exact same breakfast buffet as the day before.

Yet as soon as I sat down at the table, it became clear to me that the disappointing brunch menu could not be blamed for the heavy mood that still hung over the room.

"Good morning," I said cheerfully as I lay my napkin in my lap. But while my greeting was meant for everyone, I was looking at Jake. And directing my big smile at him.

"Right back at ya," he replied, grinning back. "I hope you slept well."

I decided not to share the details of my nightmare. Instead, I just nodded. "How is everyone else this morning?" I asked, glancing around the table.

"Just dandy!" Franny exclaimed.

"Very well, thank you," Naveen added.

Yoko, meanwhile, mumbled something that sounded a lot like, "Fine."

Gordon snorted. "I feel like I'm in a Hitchcock movie," he grumbled, keeping his eyes fixed on his plate. The two fried eggs sitting in the middle of it appeared to be staring right back at him like a pair of unblinking yellow eyes. "It's not bad enough that Bethany was murdered. Now the rest of us are still stuck here under the same roof as her killer. This nightmare just won't end."

"It is truly an excruciating situation," Naveen agreed. He, too, struck me as uncharacteristically sullen. I wondered if telling me the painful story of what had happened to his daughter was responsible for his bad mood. Or maybe it was something else. Something like the fact that he was the person responsible for Bethany's death.

I decided to make a priority of asking him the important question I'd neglected to ask him the night before. That was the one about where Sana had been working when she had

had the breakdown that had ultimately resulted in her becoming involved with a cult.

"It's hard for all of us," Franny chirped. "But I think we
all have no choice but to just continue with what we've been
doing all weekend: making the best of things."

She looked over at me, beaming. "Kate, are you going to
lead another one of your fun and fabulous workshops this
morning?"

"That's the plan," I replied, slathering a plump sesame
bagel with cream cheese. "Although I can't promise that it'll
be either fun or fabulous."

"I'm sure it will be both," she insisted.

She reached into her purse and pulled out an envelope that
I immediately recognized. It was the one with the Mohawk
brochure about this ice cream weekend that someone had
mysteriously sent her.

"Let's see," she said. "What's the topic this morning? Oh,
here it is. 'Secret Tricks of the Ice Cream Trade.'"

"That's what I'm prepared to talk about," I said. But I was
eyeing the envelope. More specifically, the handwriting on it.
It had occurred to me that if I could match that writing to
someone else's, I would know who had gone out of his or her
way to make sure that Franny was going to be here this
weekend.

As for the reason why someone had been so determined to
make sure she was in attendance, that was another matter
entirely. But I couldn't help suspecting that somehow it had
something to do with Bethany La Montaine.

"Can I see that for a second?" I asked, trying to sound casual. "I want to make sure I cover everything that's listed in
the brochure."

"It's actually pretty general," she said. "It just says that
you're giving an inside look at the magical world of making
ice cream, and that we'll learn a bunch of tricks we can use at

home." But she dutifully handed me the brochure, along with the envelope.

"Thanks." I placed both the brochure and the envelope in my lap, then pretended that I was focused on slathering my bagel with more cream cheese. "I read something interesting recently," I said, hoping to distract Franny and everyone else. "In the 1880s, the most famous restaurant in New York City was a place called Delmonico's. It was considered pretty cutting-edge back in the day. And they used to serve asparagus ice cream. They also served a flavor called pumpernickel rye."

"Ewww," Yoko cried, glancing up from the big cup of coffee she'd been absorbed in up until that point. I got the feeling the caffeine had finally kicked in. That was certainly something I could relate to.

"My thoughts exactly," I said. "I try to keep an open mind about possible new flavors, but I don't see either of those two making it onto Lickety Splits's menu anytime soon."

Just as I'd hoped, the conversation immediately turned to other unlikely flavors for ice cream. At least Franny and Yoko seemed interested in speculating about possibilities. Gordon still seemed cranky, while Naveen was as subdued as he'd been since I'd sat down. Fortunately, Jake jumped in with a few ideas of his own, helping to move the conversation along.

"How about herbal flavors?" Jake suggested. "Kate makes a mean Honey Lavender. And she adds basil to peach sorbet.

"Then there's this other flavor she came up with," he went on excitedly. "She named it Berry Blizzard. It's mainly a delicious strawberry ice cream made with fresh strawberries, but it also has raspberries and blueberries in it. But the best part, the secret ingredient, is a tiny touch of spice. Cardamom and cinnamon, right, Kate?"

"You really are giving away all my secrets," I said, laughing.

"But there must be tons of other possibilities, too," Jake said.

"I saw sage gelato at an artisanal shop in Brooklyn once," Yoko volunteered.

Franny's eyes grew round. "Did you try it?"

Yoko shook her head. "But now I wish I had. It was probably terrific."

"I'm not so sure," Franny countered. "It sounds kind of . . . weird, don't you think?"

"So you are not in favor of combining exotic spices with ice cream?" Gordon asked wryly. "Too dangerous?"

"Well, cinnamon would be okay," Franny replied. "Using it with berries in that thing Jake described sounds kind of interesting . . ."

I decided to take advantage of the animated conversation going on around me to consult with Naveen.

"I wanted to thank you for being so honest with me about your daughter last night," I said to him, keeping my voice low enough that the others couldn't hear me. "It must have been very difficult to talk about."

He offered me a sad smile. "It is, but you strike me as a sympathetic listener," he said. "I had a sense that you would understand."

"There is something I thought of asking you after I got to my room," I said. "If you don't mind, that is."

"Not at all," he assured me.

"Who was Sana working for when she had the terrible experience you told me about?" I was doing my best to sound casual. But my heart was pounding with such force I was sure I was having a 'Tell-Tale Heart' moment and that everyone at the table could hear it pounding. I only hoped that Naveen would answer me truthfully.

"This is quite a coincidence," he replied. "She worked for Bethany La Montaine."

It was exactly the response I had been expecting.

I just nodded. But my thoughts were in turmoil. On the one hand, I was relieved that Naveen had been honest. The fact that he hadn't even tried to hide the truth told me that he was as honorable a person as I thought.

Yet at the same time, his admission that his daughter had been working at La Montaine Cosmetics when she experienced her breakdown tied him to the murder victim in a most incriminating way. He had just given me a strong motive for killing Bethany.

Revenge. One of the most common motivations for murder.

My thoughts were interrupted by Franny focusing in on me and asking, "Could I have my brochure back? I like to keep referring to it, just so I know what there is to look forward to."

"Of course," I said. I reached into my lap, picked it up, and handed it to her.

But I made a point of leaving the envelope in my lap.

"Thanks," she said, apparently not noticing. She was already standing up, gathering up her sweater and her purse as she got ready to leave. "I drank so much coffee this morning that I'm going to have to stop off at the ladies' before I come to the workshop," she said, cheerfully sharing what's commonly known as too much information. "I'll see all of you there!"

I gave her a little wave as she turned to leave. But with the other hand I covered up the envelope. After all, I was hoping it would turn out to be a clue in this convoluted puzzle I was trying to solve. But first, I had to do a little sneaking around.

Instead of seeing the Sunday morning workshop as a welcome distraction, I was so caught up in my quest to figure out who had killed Bethany that I just wanted to get it over with.

I wasn't the only one who seemed to be a little tired of ice cream. As I faced my audience, sitting in their usual places in the Great Room, I noticed that Gordon looked as if he was half asleep. He was slumped over in his chair, listing slightly to one side and barely keeping his eyes open. I didn't know if he was bored or had simply had a poor night's sleep. Yoko also looked kind of dazed, although I found her so hard to read in general that the blank expression on her face could have meant anything.

Naveen was his usual well-behaved self, sitting up straight in his chair and holding a pad of paper in his lap so he could take notes on the gems of wisdom he was expecting me to dispense. But somehow his eyes had lost their shine. Even Jake was looking a bit ragged around the edges. I had a feeling that if he hadn't been so determined to be 100 percent supportive, he would have found something else to do.

The only person who actually looked happy to be there was Franny. In fact, I got the impression that the woman couldn't learn enough about ice cream. Even now, after all the time this eclectic little group had spent in each other's company—under what could only be considered the worst possible set of circumstances—she alone appeared to be as enthusiastic about the We All Scream for Ice Cream weekend as she had been when she'd first arrived.

Despite the air of lethargy that permeated the room, I was amused to note that the members of the group had clearly all tried out the scented products that Yoko had handed out to them. I also realized that she hadn't been exaggerating when she'd complained that they were too awful to even consider selling on her website. As I walked around distributing a handout I'd printed in advance, I discovered that Franny gave off the odor of a bouquet of lavender that was about ready for the compost heap. Naveen brought to mind a spice shop with a broken ventilation system. Gordon, meanwhile, smelled like a woodland creature in heat. Then again, maybe he always smelled that way.

Fortunately, once I was standing in front of my creatively scented audience, I started to get into my role of teacher—and the joy of spreading the word about the wonders of ice cream. For this workshop, I had promised to share what I'd enticingly referred to as secrets. In reality, it was more like I was going to demonstrate some unusual yet easy-to-make ice cream concoctions.

I started out with a demonstration that I knew would be a real crowd-pleaser. And sure enough, it was. I showed the group how easy it is to make that wonderful thin chocolate shell that's part of classic ice cream creations like the Brown Bonnet that Carvel has been serving up for decades and the luscious coating that Good Humor and other manufacturers put on their ice cream bars on a stick. It also comes in a fancier, and considerably more expensive, form: individual single-serving cups that a hostess who's channeling Martha Stewart can fill with ice cream so she can impress the heck out of her guests.

The chocolate shell is surprisingly simple to make. All that's required is mixing together two ingredients, chocolate chips and coconut oil, and heating them. Then, it's a lot of fun to drizzle the hot mixture over ice cream and watch it harden into a shiny shell.

Pouring it over chilled ceramic or glass cups results in the elegant chocolate dishes, something that can be used as a receptacle as well as something to eat. Another variation is dipping an ice-cold spoon into the hot mixture, instantly coating it with chocolate. It's an amazing accompaniment to anything ice cream related, turning even an ordinary dish of chocolate, vanilla, or strawberry straight out of the local supermarket's freezer into something special.

Just as I had expected, the group was beyond enthusiastic

about this marvelous technique. From the way they'd carried on, you'd have thought I'd just turned straw into gold. All the signs of lethargy that had caused my audience to droop only minutes before vanished. And their excitement was contagious, making me a more animated and more engaged speaker.

Next, I demonstrated some lesser-known desserts that incorporated ice cream. I started with *affogato*, a simple Italian dessert that is basically ice cream smothered in espresso. But there's plenty of room for creativity—for example, adding a favorite liqueur such as Kahlúa or Baileys Irish Cream or topping the whole thing off with crushed almonds or chocolate chips. For my demonstration, I used Cappuccino Crunch ice cream. Since it's already coffee flavored, it's the ideal match for the actual espresso that it's combined with.

All in all, the workshop ended up going surprisingly well. Not only was I relieved; I was also a little surprised. It was amazing that all the participants managed to put aside the strangeness of our situation. Then again, ice cream is pretty powerful stuff. It's hard for anyone to be in a bad mood while they're eating it—or even thinking about it, learning about it, or watching someone else do creative things with it.

Throwing myself into the anxiety-free world of ice cream relaxed me, too. In fact, I was so involved in what I was doing that for a while, at least, I actually managed to forget about the envelope in my pocket.

It wasn't until the workshop was winding down that I thought about it again. I also remembered that there was something important I had to get done before the group dispersed.

Fortunately, I'd come up with what I thought was a true brainstorm.

"The ice cream flavors everyone came up with yesterday were so creative," I said to my tiny audience, doing my best to sound matter-of-fact. "Would you mind jotting them down on this sheet of paper I'm about to pass around? And please write your name next to your flavor. If I ever decide to 'borrow' one of them to make at Lickety Splits, I'll be sure to give you credit."

That line got a laugh. But I still felt sneaky about what I was *really* doing. As I passed a clipboard with a blank sheet of paper to Naveen, I could barely manage to look him in the eye.

By that point, I could hardly wait for the workshop to be over so I could check the handwriting of each of the participants. As soon as they had all scattered and only Jake stayed behind, I pulled out the envelope.

"What are you up to?" he asked, coming over to where I was standing. On the table in front of me were the envelope and the handwritten list of flavors.

"A little sleuthing," I told him. "I'm trying to figure out who sent that brochure to Franny. Someone was trying to lure her here and I'm dying to know why."

Jake joined me at peering at both pieces of paper, leaning over them the same way I was. Methodically I looked at one after the other. But even before I'd had a chance to actually study them, simply scanning the five different handwritings had pretty much told me that this wasn't going to be as easy as I'd hoped. Naveen's writing was too neat and methodical, Gordon's was a scribble, Yoko's was curly letters with way too many flourishes, and Franny, who wasn't actually in the running, wrote on a slant.

"None of these match," I told him. "Which can only mean one thing."

"Which is . . . ?" Jake prompted.

"It has to have been Mrs. Moody who sent the phony brochure to Franny," I said. "She must be the person who wanted to make sure that she showed up here this weekend."

Thoughtfully, I added, "I've been wondering if Bethany got one of these brochures, too. Which would have meant that the person who sent them wanted to try to make sure they were both here this weekend."

I closed my eyes and let out a deep sigh. "My head is spinning," I said. "I need to step back and sort everything out. Let's go somewhere quiet, where we can be alone."

Jake's expression immediately brightened. "I like that idea!" he exclaimed.

I punched him in the arm playfully. "It's not what you think," I told him. "I want to try to process all the information I've been gathering on all the suspects in Bethany La Montaine's murder. And I'm hoping you'll be an objective listener. Maybe you'll spot something I missed. Or figure out some connection . . ."

"Not my first choice of how to spend a few stolen moments alone," he replied with a grin. "But I'll take what I can get."

Chapter 12

In 1997, Ben & Jerry's introduced Phish Food,
named for the Vermont-based rock group named
Phish. It consists of chocolate ice cream with
marshmallow swirls, caramel swirls, and fudge
fish. A portion of the flavor's sales goes toward
environmental efforts in Vermont's Lake
Champlain Watershed.

—*https://www.benjerry.com/about-us#3timeline*

Jake and I ended up in a tiny sitting room that was halfway
down the hallway that ran between the lobby and the dining room. The less-than-congenial space, not much more
than twelve feet by twelve feet, was dark and gloomy, mainly
because it had only one small window. And it didn't contain
any of the cozy amenities like a fireplace or a comfortable
couch that were so prevalent throughout the rest of the resort.

The one thing it did have was a television. No big screen,
high definition, state-of-the-art machine for Mohawk. Instead, this particular model looked as if it been manufactured
back in the days that *The Jeffersons* and *Laverne & Shirley*
graced the screen. The message was clear: *Mohawk is not
TV-friendly. We're doing our best to discourage you from
parking yourself in front of a television. Instead, we're striv-*

*ing to make you experience life instead of merely watching
other people pretend to experience it on an electronic device.
If you really must watch it, we're going to make doing so as
unappealing as possible.*

It was the perfect spot for Jake and me to have some privacy.

We settled into the two chairs that were placed side by
side, all the way across the room from the television. They
turned out to be as uncomfortable as I'd expected.

"Do you think that thing is black and white?" Jake asked,
grinning. "Hey, maybe we can catch *The Flintstones*. A TV
that's this old probably still broadcasts shows that were
made half a century ago!"

"I wonder if it even works," I added. Then I turned my attention to the reason I'd dragged Jake here in the first place.

"I can't stop thinking about Bethany La Montaine's murder," I told him. "And trying to figure out who killed her. I
feel as if I have lots of little pieces of information floating
around, but they don't fit into any anything conclusive." I let
out a long, deep sigh. "I keep coming up with the image of a
bunch of random puzzle pieces that have fallen onto the
floor. They don't form any definitive pattern that even begins
to look like an actual picture. They're just scattered all over
the place."

Thoughtfully, I added, "And one puzzle piece that's missing completely is the one with a picture of the murder
weapon."

"A knife, no doubt," Jake said, sounding equally pensive.
"I'm betting on a kitchen knife that came straight out of Mohawk's kitchen."

"Or maybe a knife that the killer brought here expressly
for the purpose of killing Bethany," I mused. "But what's
even more important than the actual murder weapon is the
relationship that each one of the guests here had with Beth-

any. Even though I still need to do some more poking around, I'm pretty sure that each and every member of our little group had a motive to kill her."

"Wow," Jake said breathlessly. He took a few moments to digest what I'd just told him, then grumbled, "If you ask me, Gordon is your man. I sure don't like that guy."

"I don't either," I said. "But that doesn't mean he's guilty."

"He's the boyfriend," Jake pointed out. "Isn't that who the cops usually consider the most likely suspect?"

"The boyfriend certainly ranks high on the list of suspects in cases like this," I replied. "And it's true that Gordon doesn't seem to have been particularly fond of Bethany, even though the two of them were supposed to be a couple."

"I got that vibe, too," Jake said.

"In fact," I went on, "I overheard him on the phone yesterday. And he referred to Bethany as 'the goose that laid the golden egg.'"

"So our hunch is correct," Jake said, frowning. "He really is—*was*—after Bethany for her money." He thought for a few seconds, then added, "I wonder if he's going to profit from Bethany's death. *Really* profit, I mean, as in inheriting a huge amount of money or getting a better job . . ."

"I found out something really interesting about Gordon," I said, shifting uncomfortably in my seat. And strangely enough, it had nothing to do with the fact that the upholstery stuffing probably hadn't been replaced since—well, since *Laverne & Shirley* went off the air. "I happened to overhear a phone conversation he was having. It was completely by chance, since I was sitting directly on the other side of the wall of the phone booth he was in. And from what I could tell, it sounds like he's in trouble."

"What kind of trouble?" Jake asked.

"I'm not sure," I said. "But during that phone call, which happened to be the same one in which his true feelings about

Bethany became clear, it sounded as if the person he was talking to was giving him a really hard time about something. From the way he talked about Bethany being a source of money, I suspect that that's also what his problem is all about."

"So good old Gordon deserves a high spot on the list of suspects for even more than simply being the victim's boyfriend," Jake commented. "What about Yoko? After all, that website she runs sells cosmetics. Did she have a bad experience with Bethany?"

"Yup," I replied. "She worked at La Montaine Cosmetics once upon a time. At least until Bethany got jealous of her becoming a rising star at the company. A star that her mother seemed to have found particularly bright."

"Uh-oh," Jake muttered. "In that case, I have a feeling that Yoko's stint with the company ended badly."

"It certainly did," I said. "While she was working there and apparently making a name for herself in the company, Bethany got jealous. So she took a few of her mother's favorite collectibles, some small boxes that meant a lot to her, out of her office. She planted them in Yoko's briefcase, where it was inevitable that they were going to be found. And they were—right in the middle of a big meeting in a conference room. Gloria was livid. She fired Yoko on the spot." I thought for a few seconds. "At least, that's how Yoko tells the story."

"I see," Jake said thoughtfully. "So Yoko has a history with Bethany, too."

"Yup." I let out a long, loud sigh. "Then there's Naveen."

A look of surprise crossed Jake's face. "Naveen?" he repeated. "He strikes me as the kindest, gentlest, most considerate person here."

"I feel the same way," I replied. "But he has a pretty good reason to have hated Bethany."

"I can't imagine him hating anyone," Jake commented. "But you clearly know something I don't know."

I nodded. "Naveen's daughter, Sana, worked at La Montaine Cosmetics after getting her business degree at Columbia. Not surprisingly, she didn't exactly have a positive experience there. In fact, Bethany apparently made Sana's life so miserable that she had a kind of breakdown."

"That's terrible!" Jake cried.

"It gets worse," I said. "After a long period of being pretty nonfunctional, Sana joined a cult. Naveen and his ex-wife, Sana's mother, have pretty much lost her. And he's as distraught as you'd expect."

"Wow," Jake muttered. "So he has as strong a motive as everyone else you've named."

"Exactly." I let out another deep sigh. "I really don't want it to be Naveen. But I can't let my feelings get in my way."

"It is important to be impartial," Jake agreed, thoughtfully. "What about Mrs. Moody? I don't think I've ever met anyone as inherently creepy in my life. Just being in the same room with her makes my skin crawl. Just being in the same *building*!"

"I know," I said, laughing. "That woman just gives off an aura of negativity, doesn't she? But there's more to it than that. I've witnessed her acting kind of strange in a few different instances. Nothing that's out-and-out incriminating, but still . . ."

"Like what?" Jake asked. "Aside from sneaking up on us with hot chocolate. Really *bad* hot chocolate."

I glanced around nervously, wanting to be sure that the ever-sneaky Mrs. Moody hadn't managed to sneak into the TV room without us noticing. I wouldn't have been surprised to find her hiding behind the television set.

"First of all, I'm pretty sure that Tarleton is her son," I said, my voice a near whisper.

"Get outta town!" Jake cried. "You mean that vampire woman actually gave birth to another human being?"

"Not exactly," I replied. "She adopted him." I paused, wondering if I should tell him the whole story. "That is, after she kidnapped him."

Jake nearly fell out of his chair. "Okay, let's go back to the beginning," he said once he'd gotten over the initial shock of the little tidbit I'd just dropped on him. "Spill it."

I told him everything. I started with how I'd observed Mrs. Moody ruffling Tarleton's hair in what I later realized was a very motherly manner. Then I told him about her passion for *Gone with the Wind*, which features a set of twins with the same unusual name as Mohawk's own reluctant bellhop.

But I saved the real whopper for last. And that was the information that Emma had uncovered online. Jake was spellbound as I told him all about Mrs. Moody taking a child away from the couple who was supposed to adopt him and raising him as her own son.

"So Mrs. Moody is even stranger than we thought," Jake said once I'd finished. "Both better and worse. She's a loving mother, but she also got that role in a way that was—well, let's just say somewhat unusual."

I nodded. "There's something else that troubles me about Mrs. Moody," I told him. "I still have to verify this, but I believe that she's the one who sent that brochure to Franny to make sure she came this weekend. I don't know why, at least not yet, but you have to admit that that's kind of odd."

"Speaking of odd," Jake said, "is Tarleton on your list of suspects?"

"He is," I replied. "Given the situation, I can't help but consider him a possibility."

"Because he's always creeping around the halls and . . . well, and not doing much else?" Jake asked, only half kidding.

"That's part of it," I said. "But also because he's part of our group, just like all the others I named. He was here at Mohawk Friday night, at the time of the murder, with the same access to the lobby area as everyone else. I don't know of any particular reason why he might have wanted to kill Bethany, but just because I haven't figured that out yet doesn't mean it's not possible."

"Which brings us to Franny," Jake observed. "Miss Cheerful herself. Who also happens to be the only person you haven't yet mentioned. And of course she's on the list of people who made it up here on this particular weekend, the weekend that Bethany was going to be here."

"Yes," I agreed. "But I haven't actually uncovered any way that she was connected to Bethany. Yet there's still something about her . . ."

Jake was thoughtful for a few minutes. "It's hard to believe that she's really all sunshine and flowers, the way she pretends to be."

"True," I agreed. "But what bothers me even more is that brochure."

"I wonder if it's a fake," Jake mused.

"It *is* a fake," I replied. "The fact that no one else got one, and that there doesn't even appear to be another copy floating around, points to that. I'm convinced that it was custom-made." I hesitated. "I've been thinking that maybe Franny made it herself, taking information about the ice cream weekend that was already posted on Mohawk's website. She could have even disguised the handwriting on the envelope or had someone else address it for her . . ."

Jake looked startled. "Why on earth would she have done that? Why would Franny have gone to all that trouble to make it look as if she was lured here by a brochure?"

"That, my friend, is what they call a mystery," I replied. "Which is why I need to find a sample of Mrs. Moody's handwriting. That's how I'll be able to figure out if she's the one who sent it. She's the only person on my list of suspects whose handwriting I haven't yet seen. I have to find out if she addressed the envelope."

"And I bet you've already come up with a way to do just that," Jake commented, smiling.

I just smiled mysteriously and held one finger up to my lips. When it came to secrets, ice cream wasn't the only area in which I had some expertise.

My plan was simple: I was going to sneak into Mrs. Moody's office and find something handwritten so I could compare that sample with the writing on the envelope. I was hoping that accomplishing my mission wouldn't take more than a minute or two.

The trick, of course, was to keep from being spotted. *Especially* by Mrs. Moody.

I casually strolled through the lobby, then ducked down the hallway that bore a sign that read, EMPLOYEES ONLY. As soon as I did, my heartbeat sped up as fast as my level of anxiety. But I kept on walking, trying to act as if I wasn't doing anything the least bit out of the ordinary.

Pretend you're Nancy Drew, I told myself.

Trying to channel a fictional character was a pretty pathetic way of trying to calm myself down. But at the moment I didn't have any other ideas.

Fortunately, I was turning out to be as lucky as Nancy so often was. There didn't appear to be a single soul around.

I just hoped my luck would hold out.

Once I was inside Mrs. Moody's office, I immediately began looking around for something handwritten. I barely glanced at my surroundings, although I couldn't help noticing that there was nothing the least bit personal in her work area. No framed photographs, no posters featuring photographs of sunsets with affirmations written on them, not even a vase of flowers or a knickknack from a vacation.

Not surprisingly, it was also annoyingly neat and organized. There wasn't a single sheet of paper on the desk, on the shelves behind it, or anywhere else I could see. Which meant I had to start opening drawers, taking my snooping to another level entirely.

Fortunately, that old Nancy Drew luck came through for me once again. The first drawer I opened contained one file after another. Of course, it helped that I chose a drawer that was the right size and shape for storing files. I did learn something from reading all those mysteries when I was growing up.

I began pulling out one file folder after another, quickly opening them and glancing inside. Not surprisingly, practically every sheet of paper I came across had been printed.

Thank you, digital age, I thought morosely, closing the file drawer. *Doesn't anyone write down anything with a pen anymore?*

I was about to try opening a different drawer, more out of desperation than as part of any grand plan, when something caught my eye. It was a small piece of lined paper with a ragged edge, stuck underneath a plain white coffee mug. It wasn't one of the usual eight-and-a-half-by-eleven white sheets that printers routinely spit out, but a scrap pulled out of a spiral pad. The kind of pad that women frequently carried around in their purses.

As soon as I grabbed it and glanced at it, I knew exactly what it was.

A grocery list. *Bananas, Brown Sugar, Flour, Tomatoes, Eggs, Butter . . .*

I held my breath as I held it side by side with the envelope. The handwriting looked the same. And if there was any doubt at all, the capital F in Franny and the one in Flour were identical.

So it *had* been Mrs. Moody who had gone out of her way to make sure Franny would be here this weekend. Franny, and no one else.

But *why*? I had yet to come up with a theory.

I was still thinking about what Mrs. Moody's ties to Franny could be, and whether or not any of this was even remotely connected to Bethany La Montaine's murder, as I put the grocery list back precisely where I'd found it and turned around to leave.

My heart sank as I realized I was suddenly standing face-to-face with a huge obstacle.

An obstacle in the form of Tarleton.

He was looming in the doorway, watching me intently.

"Hi, Tarleton!" I said brightly. Plan A was to act as if there was nothing out of the ordinary about him stumbling upon me snooping around Mrs. Moody's office. Unfortunately, plan A didn't work.

"What are you doing in here?" he asked, his voice flat. "You're not supposed to be in this office. It's private."

Given the way my mind was racing, coming up with a reasonable answer was turning out to be a tremendous challenge. "I know it's private," I replied. "But I, uh, was looking for something."

"What were you looking for?" he asked.

I glanced around the office wildly, hoping the answer to his question would magically materialize. "I was looking for, uh, a piece of paper." It wasn't the most original answer. But there were plenty of pieces of paper all around me, so it was the first thing I thought of.

"What kind of piece of paper?" he asked. "What's written on it?"

"Addresses!" I cried, fixing on the first thing that came into my head. "I was, uh, looking for a list with the home addresses of the workshop participants. I'm, uh, putting together a, uh, cookbook of ice cream recipes. And I want to be sure to send each one of them a copy."

Tarleton's confused expression softened. "That's nice of you," he said. "Could I get a copy, too? I really like ice cream."

"Of course you can!" I said, relief pouring out of me almost as freely as perspiration. "I'd be happy to send you a copy. I'll just use Mohawk as the mailing address."

He nodded. "That's a good idea." And then he frowned. "Did you find it?"

I blinked. "Did I find what?"

"The list," he replied. "The addresses of the people who are here this weekend."

"Uh, no," I told him. "But maybe I'll just ask Mrs. Moody. Yes, that's probably the best idea. I should have thought of that sooner."

He nodded. "She knows everything. I'm sure she can help you."

"You're so right," I said. "She *does* know everything. But now, I'd better go back to my room. I have to . . ."

My voice trailed off. I was sure there was a reasonable way to finish that sentence but at the moment I simply couldn't figure out what that might be.

"I spend a lot of time here at Mohawk," he said suddenly, completely out of nowhere. He sounded proud.

"I know you do," I replied. "And it's a wonderful place."

"I know everything there is to know about it, too!" he added.

"I bet you do."

"I'd be happy to show you around, if you'd like," he offered. "We could go anywhere you'd like. Not only inside, either. I also know my way around outside."

"Thank you, Tarleton. That's a really kind offer."

"I could even show you around right now," he said. "We could go outside. There's all kinds of fun stuff outside!"

"Thanks, but I don't think this is the best weather for an outdoor tour," I told him.

He shrugged. "Okay," he said cheerfully. "But let me know if you change your mind. You can even leave me a note, right here on this desk. I come in here all the time." He waved at me stiffly. "I'll see you later!"

I waved back, although the gesture I made was really more like a half-hearted hand flop.

As I sneaked out of the office, still glancing around to make sure no one else was about to pop out and surprise me, I felt a slight sense of relief. I'd done what I'd intended to do.

I only hoped that Tarleton didn't think my little escapade was worth mentioning.

Rather than holing up in my room, I decided to use the little bit of downtime I had to check my email. Having access to WiFi meant opening my laptop in the lobby, which is precisely what I did.

I didn't expect there to be much communication from the big world out there. That is, aside from the one person I was desperate to hear from: my niece.

So I was thrilled that as I was looking through emails offering me great deals on travel packages and the usual daily update on my credit card balance, a new email suddenly popped up.

It was from Emma. And the subject line read, **CALL ME NOW!**

I clicked on it, my fingers moving clumsily as I hurried to

open it. The email consisted of only four words: **It's about Naveen Sharma.**

Adrenaline was already rushing through every vein in my body. But I did my best to act as if nothing was out of the ordinary. I leaned back in my chair, stretched my arms up in the air, and dragged myself to my feet. Then I sauntered over to one of the telephone booths and dialed Emma's cell phone number.

As soon as Emma answered with, "Kate! I'm glad you called!" I could hear that her voice sounded strange. Something was wrong. *Very* wrong.

"I saw your email about Naveen Sharma," I said, keeping my voice low. "Did you find out anything about him?"

There was silence at the other end of the line. "Well, sort of. I mean, I think I did, but I'm not sure . . ."

I was immediately on alert. It wasn't like Emma to be so vague. Not my very own personal computer queen. Something was definitely up.

"What did you find, Emma?" I asked.

"I put in all the information you gave me about him," she explained, still speaking slowly. "All that stuff about him inventing the new kind of daisy wheel. And someone with that background definitely comes up." I heard her clicking keys in the background.

"In the late 1970s," she continued, "there was an Indian entrepreneur in London who started a company called Daisy Chain, Ltd. The firm manufactured a daisy wheel that was made out of some weird kind of plastic that had never been used before. It supposedly printed each letter more clearly and was far superior to anything else in the marketplace. But the company was only in business for a few years. According to what I read, other developments in the world of daisy wheel printers squeezed it out, and then other technologies pretty much made that kind of printer a thing of the past."

"That definitely sounds like Naveen's company," I said excitedly. "I hope you were able to find out some other things about him."

Emma paused to take a deep breath. "That's where it gets complicated."

"Complicated—how?" I asked.

"The daisy wheel entrepreneur with the Indian name who fits what you told me?" she said. "That person had an entirely different name."

"What name?" I prompted, not sure what all this meant.

"This guy's name was Deepak Varma," Emma said. "I found some photos of him, pictures from articles about him in tech magazines. I can mail you a photo of him if you'd like."

"Yes," I said. "Please do."

"Okay. Just give me one second . . ."

My heart was already racing. Was it possible there was a terrible mystery behind Naveen Sharma, a man I'd come to like as a friend, after all? Could it be that he, too, was hiding something?

I jumped when I heard a ping. Eagerly I stared at the image on my laptop, blinking once, then again, then once again.

The man staring back at me was Naveen Sharma, all right. Only the man I was looking at was apparently not *really* named Naveen Sharma. He was named Deepak Varma . . .

"That's him," I told Emma. "But I can't imagine why he changed his name."

Emma was silent again. "There's more," she said. "Something really . . . important."

If I'd thought my heart had been pounding hard before, that was nothing compared to the jackhammer it had just turned into.

"It seems that this man, Naveen or Deepak or whatever his real name is, was implicated in a crime a few years ago."

I was already going through a list of possible infractions. Embezzling corporate funds, harassing employees, misrepresenting his product . . .

But the sinking feeling in my stomach was a warning that I was aiming too low.

"What was the crime, Emma?" I finally got up the nerve to ask.

Emma's voice was strained as she said, "It seems he was arrested for murder."

Chapter 13

In 1866, after the Civil War, William A. Breyer
began selling hand-cranked ice cream out of his
kitchen. He soon bought a horse and wagon so he
could sell ice cream outside of his neighborhood,
outfitting the wagon with a big dinner bell to
announce his arrival. By 1918, the Breyers Ice
Cream Company was producing over one million
gallons of ice cream a year. Since 1993, Breyers
has been owned by Unilever.

—http://mentalfloss.com/article/82735/10-
frozen-facts-about-breyers-ice-cream and
www.breyers.com

My head was reeling.

Naveen Sharma—involved in another murder!

Here I'd been thinking that the revelation about Mrs.
Moody having been accused of kidnapping had cast the spot-
light of guilt directly on her. But the crime she had committed
some forty years earlier paled considerably beside what
Emma had uncovered about Naveen.

And the fact that I'd started thinking of the man as a
friend tightened the knot that had already formed in my
stomach even further.

"I should tell you up front that he was acquitted," Emma

added. "But from what I read online, it sounds like that was largely due to the prosecution messing up."

"Who was the victim?" I asked. I was having trouble speaking, largely because my mouth had become so dry.

"His business partner," Emma replied. "Apparently Naveen was the person who invented the new daisy wheel, but his partner was the one who had the business smarts. His name was—wait, let me find this—here it is, Prem Patel. The two of them knew each other from their college days. They both went to University College London, which I understand is a pretty good school."

"I'm not surprised," I commented. "Naveen seems really smart."

"The company they built, Daisy Chain, was really successful," Emma went on. "But over time, as the business started to fail because of the ways technology was changing, they began running into financial difficulties."

"Money," I said breathlessly. Another one of the top reasons for foul play.

"Naveen ended up suing Prem for mismanagement," Emma explained. "Or to be more precise, accusing him of what sounded like embezzlement."

"I take it that Naveen didn't win the lawsuit," I said.

"No, he didn't," Emma replied. "And Daisy Chain went bankrupt. It was right after that that Prem was found murdered in his own home."

"How was he killed?" I asked.

I held my breath as I waited for her to answer.

"Prem Patel was stabbed to death," Emma said, choking on her words.

The breath I'd been holding came out in a loud swoosh. The man that Naveen Sharma had been accused of murdering had been killed the exact same way as Bethany La Montaine.

"But you said that Naveen was acquitted," I said, still desperately wanting to believe that this was all just a horrible coincidence.

"Yes, he was," Emma said. "There was quite a bit of evidence that pointed to Naveen. His fingerprints were found all over the house, especially in the room in which the murder had occurred. Strands of his hair, too, along with fibers that matched clothing he owned. But the two men had been friends and business partners for years, so it made perfect sense that he had been a frequent visitor to Prem's house. And that's exactly the point that Naveen's lawyer argued.

"In the end," Emma concluded, "the main problem was that one of the police officers who showed up at the scene early on, before the homicide experts had arrived, picked up the murder weapon. He claimed he didn't understand that it was what had been used to kill Prem. But when he touched the knife, he smeared the fingerprints, which in the end made it impossible to determine whether or not Naveen was the killer. So Naveen was never actually found guilty."

"I see," I said. But that horrible sick feeling remained in the pit of my stomach.

Another thought occurred to me. "Do you know what kind of knife it was?"

"A kitchen knife," Emma replied. "Apparently the killer got it out of Prem Patel's own kitchen."

In other words, a knife that just happened to be on the premises. Just as Jake had speculated.

There were just too many parallels between the murder of Naveen's business partner and the murder of Bethany La Montaine to ignore. The fact that the man had had a good reason to be so close to the scene of the crime in both instances was alarming enough in itself. But the fact that similar weapons had been used in both murders went one major step further in eliminating the possibility of mere coincidence.

Which all added up to one simple fact: While I'd been thinking of Naveen as a friend, it was time for me to start thinking of him as a cold-blooded killer.

As soon as I ended the call with Emma, I forced myself to focus. And to remind myself that even though I had no choice but to put Naveen high on my list of suspects, the fact was that he had been acquitted of that other crime. Since he hadn't actually been found guilty, I owed him the benefit of the doubt.

In other words, I had to avoid the temptation to jump to conclusions.

Besides, there were still five other people on my list of suspects. And there was still a chance that each and every one of them could still rise to the top of that list. Which meant I couldn't let up on my investigation. Not yet.

Mrs. Moody, for example, still loomed large as a likely candidate. After all, she, too, had a past that made her seem suspicious. And thanks to Emma, I had a clear way to find out more about that past.

I stepped out of the phone booth, once again pretending to stretch my arms but actually checking around to make sure that no one was lurking in the shadows of the lobby— especially Mohawk's most skillful lurker, Mrs. Moody herself. Then I ducked back into the same booth. My hands were trembling as I punched in the telephone number that Emma had supplied me with.

"Hello," a man answered after four rings. His voice was gruff. In fact, he sounded downright irritated that someone was calling.

It wasn't the best way to start off our conversation. Even so, I took a deep breath and jumped right in.

"I'm trying to reach Terrance Shelton, the attorney," I said, sounding as matter-of-fact and businesslike as I could.

"That's me," he replied. "Although I'm not practicing anymore. No, I decided a few years ago that it was time to retire.

"I knew it was a tremendous loss to the legal field," he went on, volunteering a lot more information than I'd asked for. "But my grandchildren are so crazy about me that I finally reached a point where I felt it was cruel to deprive them of my company."

I was still marveling over the man's willingness to talk to a stranger—as well as his overblown impression of himself—when he added, "So what can I do for you? That is, assuming you're not selling anything. In which case I'm not buying."

"No, I'm not selling anything," I assured him. "Actually, I'm doing research on the benefits of independent adoptions, as opposed to state adoptions," I said. "And from what I've learned in my research so far, it seems that you're one of the nation's most prominent experts."

If there's one thing I'd learned along the way, it was that flattery could indeed get you almost anywhere, just as the old saying claimed. Especially when dealing with someone like Terrance Shelton, who clearly had an ego that was almost as big as the state of Minnesota.

"You definitely have the right guy," he informed me. "What would you like to know?"

It was time to do some quick thinking.

"Maybe we can start with you explaining the difference between state and independent adoptions," I began. "I mean, I think I already know the basics, but since you're the expert, it would be really helpful for me to hear your take on it."

He expounded on that topic for at least five minutes. I kept saying, "Uh-huh" and "I see" and "Really!" even though he was pretty much telling me things I already knew. When we'd exhausted that subject, I went on to ask him a few more general questions, calling upon what Emma had told me. Once I'd gotten him talking—and it turned out that he was quite a talker—I decided it was time to get more specific.

"What you've given me so far is great," I told him, resorting to a little more buttering up. "But I'm also interested in a few specific cases. Cases that demonstrate, well, some of the possible negatives of each method, as well as those that illuminate all the positives."

I was pretty sure I could feel a shift in the vibe between us.

"Like what?" he asked. For the first time during our conversation, he sounded hesitant.

I took a deep breath. "I was reading about a case that dates back a really long time ago, like forty years . . ."

Even though the man was fifteen hundred miles away, I could sense his growing discomfort. "Yes? What case was that?"

"It involved a woman named Merle Moody, who I believe may have worked for you," I said. I was half expecting him to hang up on me, especially when I added, "From what I read online, it sounds as if she was accused of kidnapping one of the babies who was up for adoption. I was just curious about—"

"It wasn't what I'd consider kidnapping," he interrupted. He sounded defensive, but at least he hadn't hung up on me. "It was more like placing a baby in the home that would serve the child best."

"It's true that Mrs. Moody was never actually convicted of a crime," I noted. "So the courts certainly agreed with you on that point."

"Merle meant well, I can assure you," Mr. Shelton insisted. "Maybe she's not the warmest person in the world, but the woman has a good heart. And she's very responsible. I have no doubt that she was an excellent mother. She adored that little boy from the very first time she saw him."

GAME OF CONES   197

"And Mr. Moody?" I asked. "Was he excited about becoming a parent, too?"

Mr. Shelton was silent for what seemed like a long time. "There never was a Mr. Moody," he finally said. "Merle was Miss Moody back when she worked for me. But once she was a mother, she decided that there would be fewer raised eyebrows if she just called herself Mrs."

"So it sounds as if the story had a happy ending," I commented. "Mrs. Moody got the baby she wanted and her son got a doting mother."

"It was just one more success story in a long line," Mr. Shelton replied. He was back to boasting. "Believe me, we arranged for plenty of placements that were much better for the kids than anything the state would have been able to pull off."

"Can you give me another example?" I asked idly.

To be perfectly honest, I was just being polite. Making conversation. I was thinking more about how to find out additional information about Mrs. Moody than the new topic of conversation that we were moving on to.

So I nearly jumped out of the phone booth when he added, "Like the La Montaine placement. That's another great example."

I had had no idea that I was about to stumble upon such a treasure trove of information. My entire body had already been shot through with so much adrenaline that I would have been capable of completing a triathlon. And winning.

"I'm not familiar with that case," I commented, doing a truly amazing job of keeping my voice calm.

"Oh, it was a biggie," Mr. Shelton told me. "The birth mother was Gloria La Montaine, who later on became the founder of the huge, successful cosmetics company with the same name. I'm sure you're familiar with it. Of course, back then she had a different name, since it all happened way before she got married and took her husband's last name. I understand that the marriage didn't last long, but that's another story. Back then, when she unexpectedly found herself pregnant, she was still a kid herself. I seem to recall that the unfortunate girl was barely seventeen years old.

"She came to us on her own, too," he went on. "It wasn't as if she had her parents helping her out. Or anybody else, for that matter. She was just a poor kid from somewhere in the Midwest—Iowa, I think. Or maybe Illinois. Anyway, she'd come to Minneapolis, pregnant and penniless and all by herself, with nowhere to turn. She talked a lot about how important it was to keep everything about her pregnancy secret. I guess her parents weren't exactly supportive. Anyway, she was looking for a young couple who wanted to adopt, but she also needed prospective parents who were willing to help her get through the pregnancy. Financially, mostly, but in terms of moral support, too. Like I said, the girl seemed to be pretty much on her own.

"And that was the kind of thing I was great at, back in those days," Mr. Shelton continued. "Finding couples who were so desperate to adopt a kid that they were willing to put all kinds of money into making it happen. The couple I found really, really wanted to adopt. I remember them saying that all they wanted in life was a child who was all their own, that instead of being just a couple that they would finally become a real family. They also mentioned that they'd just come into a little bit of money. Maybe they'd inherited it or maybe they'd even won some money in the lottery, but whatever it was, it was definitely a one-time thing. They were determined to use that money to make their dream of becoming parents come true."

"I'm just curious," I said, trying to sound emotionally uninvolved, "but was Mrs. Moody—Merle Moody—involved in that case, as well?"

"Definitely," Mr. Shelton replied without a moment's hesitation. "She was very involved. I remember that she took it upon herself to find the best home possible for Gloria's baby. She interviewed each and every couple who was interested in adopting her." He paused, then added, "In fact, I remember that at the time, I wondered if somehow Merle identified with Gloria in some way. Or at least felt a special sympathy for her situation. Merle was completely dedicated to finding the best home possible."

He paused to take a breath, then asked, "But I'm doing most of the talking here, without giving you a chance to say a word. What did you say this research is for?"

I made up a vague story about working on a master's degree in social work. Then I got off the phone as quickly as I could. I didn't want him asking me any more tricky questions. Besides, I'd already learned what I'd hoped to learn. In fact, I'd gotten a whole lot more information than I'd ever dreamed I'd get.

So Gloria La Montaine had given birth out of wedlock, back when she was still a teenager. And keeping it a secret had been a top priority. I suspected that her family had found the incident shameful, since they hadn't even accompanied the seventeen-year-old girl in her search to find adoptive parents for the baby.

I suspected that the entire episode was a piece of Gloria La Montaine's life that she had done her best to keep secret for the rest of her life.

And Merle Moody, it turned out, was one of the few people who knew that secret.

This chapter from the past tied Mrs. Moody to Gloria La Montaine in a way I never would have suspected. And, by association, it tied Mrs. Moody to Bethany.

But what did it all mean? I wondered, thinking so hard that my brain practically hurt. One obvious possibility was that Mrs. Moody had been blackmailing Gloria La Montaine. And if she had been, could Bethany have found out about it?

Or was something else going on that involved the three of them?

And of course there was another important question, one underlying all the others that were floating around in my head. And that was whether Bethany's murder had somehow been related to Merle Moody's involvement in what had been a family scandal nearly half a century earlier.

Chapter 14

In Victorian times, the fashion was to present ice cream in elaborate shapes made from pewter molds. Molded ice cream, or Fancy Forms, remained popular through the mid-1930s, but they fell out of favor in 1965 when the U.S. government prohibited their use because of fears of lead poisoning.

—Everybody Loves Ice Cream: The Whole Scoop on America's Favorite Treat, by Shannon Jackson Arnold

I sat in the phone booth long after I'd hung up, trying to process what I'd just learned.

I was so absorbed in my thoughts that I was only vaguely aware of some low-level noise in the background. Gradually I became aware that it was the sound of a muffled voice and that it was coming from right behind me. It wasn't until I began to find it irritating—mainly because it was starting to become distracting—that I turned to see what was going on.

The voice, coming from the phone booth that was next to mine, belonged to Gordon. And even though there was a wall between us, he was speaking loudly enough that if I leaned back a bit and focused, I could hear him perfectly well.

Which is exactly what I proceeded to do.

I could tell from his tone that he was trying to sound tough. Angry, too. Yet even through that wall I could hear that his voice was tinged with desperation.

"Right," he said, that single word dripping with sarcasm. "Of course," he added. Then, "Uh-huh. I see."

There was a long pause before I heard him demand, "So now you're *blackmailing* me?"

His use of the word "blackmail" made my ears prick up. In short, I was reacting the same way I'd see Digger, Grams's terrier mix, respond to an unusual sound.

"I just don't have that much money," I heard Gordon say. By this point, his tone sounded pleading. "I—I've pretty much given you everything I have."

Another long pause.

"I already did that," he said, his voice still desperate. "Look, I even put my summer house on the market. It's a sweet little three-bedroom cottage overlooking a lake, about an hour's drive from New York. But it's going to take some time to sell it. This time of year isn't exactly prime season for unloading real estate. Even a waterside bungalow like mine doesn't show that well when the lake is frozen solid and there are no leaves on the trees."

There was another long pause. This one was even longer than the others.

When Gordon started speaking again, the tone of his voice had changed. He now sounded angry. Bitter, even. "You know that this really is blackmail, right? You can call it anything you want, but when you come right down to it, that's exactly what it is. Which happens to be a serious crime—"

Whatever the person at the other end of the line had just said caused him to break off mid-sentence. He made a few gasping sounds that sounded almost like sobs.

And then, his voice choking, he said, "Yes, I know that's a crime, too. But I never meant to hurt Bethany or Gloria or anyone else in the company. I just needed the money! I was so sure that the real estate deal was going to put me on easy street for the rest of my life . . ."

I was finally able to put all the pieces together so that they made sense. Apparently Gordon had wanted to get his hands on a large sum of money so he could get in on a real estate investment that he was sure was guaranteed to make him a wealthy man. So wealthy, in fact, that he might have been set for the rest of his life. And in order to get ahold of that much cash in a hurry, he had done something risky, something that was likely to hurt La Montaine Cosmetics.

Selling corporate secrets, I suspected.

But from the way it sounded, his plan had backfired in two different ways. First of all, the real estate deal hadn't panned out the way he'd expected. But what was even worse was that the person he'd been selling La Montaine's secrets to had started blackmailing him.

In other words, Gordon was on the verge of ruin.

And it stood to reason that the person who was most likely to go after him for what he had done was Bethany.

As I crept out of the phone booth, taking care that Gordon wouldn't see that I'd been close enough to him to listen in on his conversation, my head was buzzing.

The new information I'd discovered about him only served to increase my curiosity about everyone else's relationship to the victim—and whether or not it had motivated them to kill her.

When I'd first gotten to Mohawk I'd naively assumed that it was the guests' love of ice cream that had brought them all here. That, and their interest in learning everything about it they could from *moi*, the Diva of the Double Dip. Yet it turned out that every single one of them could have come here expressly to murder Bethany.

Which motivated me to see if I could find out more about one of the other suspects, someone who became more and more intriguing the more I learned about her. So once again I strolled over to Mrs. Moody's office, this time not acting the least bit secretive. As I did, I mentally reviewed what I planned to say, hoping I could steer our conversation in the direction I wanted it to go.

As I got close, I saw that the door to her office was ajar and a light was on inside.

"Mrs. Moody?" I said, knocking lightly on the open door. The knocking part was pretty much unnecessary, since by that point I was already standing right in front of her.

Mrs. Moody glanced up from her computer screen and frowned.

"It's most unusual for one of the guests to come into the employees-only area," she said crisply. "Especially without having been invited."

"I realize that," I replied. "But I wanted to talk to you." I swallowed, then added, "Alone."

She immediately stiffened.

"Is there a problem?" she asked, her voice growing tight.

Only if you consider a history of kidnapping, along with the possibility of having committed murder, a problem, I thought.

But aloud, I said, "Not exactly. It's more like there's something I was hoping you could clear up for me."

"If I can," she said, still guarded.

"I'm curious about Tarleton," I said. I was speaking slowly, mainly because I was choosing my words carefully. I took a deep breath, then asked, "Is he your son?"

Mrs. Moody's eyebrows shot up to the ceiling. "What business is it of yours?"

"None," I replied. "I was just wondering. The two of you seem . . . close."

She stared at me for what felt like an awfully long time. And then, finally, her expression changed. "It's complicated," she said. "But, yes, Tarleton is my son. I adopted him when he was just a baby."

"I see," I said. I was surprised by her willingness to be straightforward with me. But her openness also emboldened me.

"I have a confession to make," I told her. I was suddenly having trouble looking her in the eye. Instead, I fixed my gaze on a stack of papers on her desk. "I did a bit of research on you—and everyone else who's involved with this weekend. I came across something surprising about the circumstances surrounding the adoption."

Her eyes narrowed. "I know what they said," she said, her voice so low and hard it was practically a growl. "All those crazy accusations that I stole him. But it wasn't kidnapping! It wasn't anything *like* kidnapping! I just wanted to give that lovely baby boy the best home possible!

"Those people who were supposed to adopt him were horrible," she continued. "I could tell simply from meeting them a few times that they were totally wrong for him. They were shallow. Materialistic. They were the kind of people who only care about appearances. People with no heart, no feeling.

"The man who was trying to adopt him was one of those hotshot corporate types, executive vice president of something or other," Mrs. Moody went on. She was becoming more animated—more *passionate*—than I'd ever seen her before. "And the woman who wanted to become Tarleton's mother was an empty-headed former beauty queen who spent her days getting her nails done and shopping for designer purses. I knew perfectly well that once they realized what I had realized, that Tarleton wasn't destined to grow up to become another—another *accessory* they could show off, some whiz kid who was destined to become a brain surgeon or something else that would impress their friends—they would reject him.

"I, on the other hand, felt drawn to him from the start," she told me. "He was someone who needed me. Someone I could love with all my heart, and someone who I knew would love me back. Tarleton and I were a much better match for each other than those awful people would ever have been."

Even though she sounded bitter, I could feel my heart melting. Merle Moody had been sincere in her determination to provide a warm, nurturing, loving home to the baby boy she had fallen in love with all those years before. She really had been thinking only about what was best for him.

Still, what she had done was pretty extreme. Extreme enough that I could imagine her committing another drastic act if she believed that her actions were justified.

The question was, what would her motivation have been?

"In that case," I said, "it sounds as if you did the right thing. In fact, I suspect that your main concern was finding the best possible family for each one of the babies whose adoptions you were involved in."

"It's true," she said. Now she was the one who was avoiding eye contact with me. But the reason didn't seem to be guardedness or self-consciousness or anything else along those lines. Instead, from the way she was staring off into the distance, I had the feeling she was looking far back into the past.

"I did feel that same sense of duty when it came to all those other babies," Mrs. Moody said thoughtfully. "I was truly committed to finding the best homes for them I could."

"Then I imagine you must have felt that way about Gloria La Montaine's baby," I prompted, speaking in a soft, gentle voice.

"Of course I did!" she shot back without stopping to think about what I'd just said. "I felt terrible for poor Gloria. She was so young. And so alone! She didn't have anyone else. I owed it to her to find the best possible parents for her baby. Their financial status wasn't important. A lot of people who lived in that part of Minnesota were poor. But what mattered was that they were good people and they desperately wanted a child. I knew just from meeting with them that they would give Gloria's baby a warm, loving home . . ."

All of a sudden, a light bulb went on in my head.

Gloria La Montaine's baby . . . Minnesota . . . a couple without much money who badly wanted to adopt a little girl . . . the handwritten envelope with a personal invitation in the form of a custom-made brochure . . .

Oh my, I thought, feeling all the blood rush out of my brain. Gloria La Montaine wasn't only Bethany's mother; she was also Franny's birth mother!

In other words, Franny and Bethany were sisters!

Chapter 15

Texas has more Dairy Queen locations than
any other state—more than 600.

—*https://www.thedailymeal.com/eat/10-things-you-
didn-t-know-about-dairy-queen-0/slide-8*

Half sisters, I corrected myself. Franny and Bethany were
half sisters.

Still, the two women were connected in the deepest way
possible, even though it seemed highly likely that neither one
of them had known it.

In fact, it was very possible that the only person here at
Mohawk who *did* know it was Merle Moody.

In a surprisingly calm voice, I managed to ask, "Mrs.
Moody, is it possible that Franny is actually Gloria La Montaine's daughter?"

She looked startled. "How did you know that? No one is
supposed to know that!"

And then her expression changed. Her entire posture, as
well. The way she crumbled reminded me of all the times I'd
broken up Oreo cookies so I could use them as a topping on
ice cream sundaes. "Yes, Franny is Gloria's daughter. Which
means that Bethany is—she *was*—her sister."

"Is that why you personally invited Franny to this ice
cream weekend?" I asked, still speaking in a calm, low voice

that was practically a whisper. "Is that why you put together that brochure about it, as a way of trying to make sure she'd be here at Mohawk at the same time as Bethany?"

"That's exactly what I did," she replied, nodding. "I wanted to bring the two girls together. I felt that it was time for them to meet."

"It sounds as if you've kept track of Gloria La Montaine over the years," I observed.

"It would have been impossible not to," Mrs. Moody replied. "Of course I knew all about Gloria La Montaine and her success in business. Who hadn't heard all about the cosmetics empire she built? The woman was in the news constantly. Even without making a point of keeping track of her, I kept spotting her in the headlines or on *Oprah* or in a million other places.

"But even though everyone knew all about Gloria La Montaine, hardly anyone knew about her giving up her first baby for adoption when she was so young," she added. "I held on to that secret for decades. I never wanted to hurt Gloria. And I certainly didn't want to cause either of her daughters any pain.

"All my life, I've felt terrible about the fact that those two sisters—two half sisters—had been kept apart," Mrs. Moody went on. "They grew up so far away from each other and I'm positive that neither one had a clue about her sister's existence. And they lived such different lives! Bethany grew up in New York City with her birth mother, of course. But she also had the best of everything handed to her from the very start. Talk about being born with a silver spoon in your mouth! She went to the finest schools, she traveled all over the world, and she ended up with a fabulous job at the big, successful cosmetics company her mother founded.

"Then there's Franny." She let out a deep sigh. "Her life turned out to be so different—although, to be honest, I think the life Franny lived was just as wonderful. Maybe even better."

"Why is that?" I asked. I was surprised, given Franny's reports of how limited she had always felt by her family's modest financial status.

"Because Franny's adoptive parents were such warm, loving people," Mrs. Moody replied. "They may not have had the material wealth that Gloria La Montaine had, but the Schneffers adored their daughter. Because I'd been involved in that case, I visited their house several times when Franny was still young. So young that she's no doubt forgotten all about me arriving on their doorstep every few months without any warning. But I wanted to see for myself that they were raising her in a loving household.

"And they were," she noted happily. "They doted on her. Maybe they couldn't afford to buy her expensive toys and clothes when she was growing up, but they spent lots of time with her every single day. I remember Franny's mother telling me all about their routine of sitting back down at the dining room table after clearing away the dinner dishes to play board games every night, just the three of them. And afterwards they'd gather together in front of the fireplace, taking turns reading aloud to each other. Every Saturday, the three of them would do something as a family. They would visit a local park with a playground, go on a picnic, take a trip to a children's museum . . .

"Even after I'd stopped making my surprise visits, they continued to be a close-knit family," she went on. "Mr. and Mrs. Schneffer sent me a Christmas card every year, along with one of those letters that talks about what the family has been doing all year. They always expressed such pride in every one of Franny's accomplishments, no matter how minor it was. I remember one letter that boasted about her papier-mâché puppet being picked to be put on display at

Parents' Night at her elementary school. You would have thought she was van Gogh! The Schneffers acted as if their daughter was the most wonderful creature who had ever lived. They seemed positively grateful that she had come into their lives."

Her eyes were shiny with tears. "Do you know how rare that is? Of course, I've tried to do the same for Tarleton. Which is one of the reasons I'm so appreciative of how much Franny's parents did for her."

"And you decided that it was finally time to bring the two women together so they could meet?" I asked, hoping to guide the conversation in a different direction.

"Yes," she replied. "It was something I'd thought about doing for years. Decades, actually. But I never knew how Gloria would feel about it."

"Did Gloria keep track of Franny?" I asked. "Where she was living, how she was doing?"

"Not that I know of," she said. She shook her head sadly. "My impression of Gloria La Montaine is that she was someone who preferred to leave that piece of her history in the past. Besides, if Gloria had made an effort to keep in touch with her, Franny would have known that Bethany was her sister. And you saw for yourself that the two women acted like complete strangers from the moment they both arrived here."

Mrs. Moody paused to take a deep breath. "Which is why I decided to take matters into my own hands. "My plan was to bring them both to Mohawk and let them get to know each other in a comfortable setting. Then, when I saw that the right moment had arrived, I was going to let them both know about their connection to each other."

Her eyes filled with tears as she added, "Sadly, that moment never came."

* * *

As I crossed the lobby, I was glad that I spotted Jake lounging in one of the comfortable upholstered chairs in the Lakeside Room. A fire was roaring in the fireplace, emitting a cozy smoky smell that was one of my favorite scents. But it wasn't the inviting setting that drew me into the room. It was the chance to talk to Jake.

"Just the person I've been looking for," I told him as I plopped down into the big overstuffed chair beside his.

"That's good to hear," he replied. "And why is that, exactly? Is it my charm? My good looks? My devilish love of life?" He frowned dramatically. "Don't tell me it's my fancy car. Ever since I bought that racy red Miata, I've worried about attracting the wrong kind of woman."

I laughed. "Actually, it's all those things. Aside from the car, that is. But even more, it's your levelheadedness, your ability to think clearly, your excellent listening skills—"

"Great," he interrupted, feigning exasperation. "That's exactly what every guy wants to hear."

Then he grew serious. "What's up?"

I let out a long, deep sigh. "I'm still trying to figure out who killed Bethany La Montaine. That's what's up."

"Are you making any headway?" he asked.

"I am, but that's part of the problem," I replied. "The more I learn, the more confused I become. And I'm learning plenty. Not only about Bethany, but also about the people around her. Many of whom have ended up here at Mohawk this weekend. *Probably* not by coincidence."

"It's true that everybody in the universe knew she'd be here this weekend for your ice cream workshops," Jake observed. "When you're addicted to social media, the upside is the same as the downside, and that's that anybody who's the least bit interested can find out everything there is to know about you."

"But I'm still trying to digest the whammy I just stumbled

upon," I told him. "You're absolutely not going to believe this."

"Try me," Jake said. "I actually have a much better imagination than you might think."

I leaned forward and looked him in the eye. "Bethany and Franny are half sisters," I announced.

Jake's jaw dropped so far I was afraid he'd get lint from the carpet stuck in his early-afternoon chin stubble.

"Get outta here!" he replied once he'd regained the ability to speak. "You're kidding, right?"

I shook my head. "It's the truth," I insisted. "At least, according to Mrs. Moody."

His expression changed to a look of skepticism. "Since when do we believe everything Mrs. Moody tells us?"

That was a perfectly valid question. Why *should* I have believed her?

The answer to that question came to me immediately. "Because I feel it in my gut," I told him. "Besides, the story that Mrs. Moody told me was pretty convincing. And it was backed up by a telephone call I made to the lawyer she used to work for in Minnesota forty years ago . . ."

"Wait, I think I missed something," Jake said, holding up both hands. "Let's go back a minute."

I leaned back in my chair again. Staring into the fire, I told him everything that had happened since I'd last filled him in.

When I'd finished, Jake was silent for a few seconds, just thinking. And then he said, "I guess all this information you've uncovered shines an entirely different light on Bethany La Montaine's murder."

I nodded. "I'm still reeling from this bizarre revelation. But as shocking as it is, it hasn't helped me figure out the identity of the killer."

"Here's an idea," Jake said, his tone becoming light. "How about forgetting about all this for a while? Let's just close the book on *The Case of the Missing Heiress.* Or maybe a better title would be *The Case of the* Doomed *Heiress.*

"And instead of doing the Nancy Drew thing, what do you say you and I tiptoe over to my room—or your room, if you prefer—for a little downtime? Of course, we have to be careful that Mrs. Moody doesn't notice us, or she's likely to whip us up some more of her vile hot chocolate—"

"Actually," I said, "I was thinking that this might be a good time for me to talk to Franny."

Jake's posture suddenly became rigid. "Even Nancy Drew made time for her boyfriend," he said dryly.

"Ned Nickerson," I said automatically. "His car was always referred to as a 'roadster,' which I thought was hilarious. It's funny the things you remember—"

"You're changing the subject!" Jake cried. The anger in his voice startled me. When I glanced over at him, I saw that his eyes were blazing.

I blinked. "What exactly *is* the subject?" I asked, sincerely confused.

"How about the possibility that the reason you've gotten so involved in investigating the murder of someone you don't even *know*, someone you never even *heard* of until thirty-six hours ago, is because in your mind it provides the perfect distraction from spending time with me?" Throwing out his hands in despair, he added, "Which I thought was the main reason we came here in the first place!"

"I didn't—I wasn't—"

"No?" Jake countered. "This weekend was supposed to be a chance for us to spend some 'quality time,' as it's popularly known, with each other. Instead, you've been so busy investigating Bethany La Montaine's murder, doing the whole amateur detective thing, that I've hardly had a chance to sit in the same room as you!"

"That's not true!" I protested. "First of all, I've been pretty busy with the ice cream workshops, in case you haven't noticed. I've led three of them since we got here, and in between Mrs. Moody has made it clear that I'm expected to interact with the guests. But even so, you and I have managed to spend plenty of time together!"

"Right," Jake replied bitterly. "With most of it consisting of you agonizing over whether—whether Naveen is as nice a guy as he appears and whether Gordon's general nastiness is rooted in some deep hatred of the woman who's supposed to be his girlfriend and whether Mrs. Moody's general creepiness is bad enough to make her a murderer."

He paused to take a deep breath. "To be perfectly honest, it's hard for me *not* to conclude that you've been throwing yourself into this murder investigation as a way of avoiding me."

His comment startled me. Was he right? Was that what I'd been doing—using my impulse to stick my nose into places where it might not necessarily belong as an excuse to avoid being with Jake?

Before I had a chance to tell him that there might actually be some truth behind his accusation, he said, "Speaking of which, what *about* us? How are you feeling about us?" He was suddenly speaking in a calm, controlled voice. Somehow, I found that even more upsetting than when he had sounded angry.

And I suddenly felt as if I was in the proverbial hot seat. I could practically feel the heat of a high-wattage light bulb shining down on me.

"I'm feeling good about us," I said. But my words sounded meek. Unconvincing, even to me. So I added, "I've really enjoyed the time we've spent together here at Mohawk. I always like spending time with you, Jake."

I didn't think that part sounded much better.

I guess Jake didn't either, because he stood up abruptly. "Okay, fine," he said. "I think I get it."

And with that, he stalked off.

I waited a few more minutes, hoping that Jake would come back. When that didn't happen, I finally got up and, feeling dazed, headed back to my room.

The idea of being by myself was suddenly feeling very attractive.

As I crossed the lobby, my head filled with a fog that was at least as thick as what was hovering outside the windows, I thought I noticed a shadow off in the distance. But as soon as I turned my head, it seemed to vanish.

Probably just Mrs. Moody, I told myself. I swear, spying on people must be part of her job description.

As I made my way along the long corridors that led to my room, the hallways were as dark as always. And as quiet.

Actually, they felt even darker and quieter than usual. But I figured that was simply because of my dark, quiet mood.

Still, somehow the corridors managed to feel even more ominous than usual.

And then I realized that that was because there was even more going on than the usual dim lighting and thick carpets. I had that creepy feeling I wasn't alone.

"Who's there?" I called, quickening my pace. I was already scrounging around in my pocket, pulling out the big old-fashioned metal key that would open my door.

There was only silence.

At least, it sounded like silence at first. But a second or two later, thanks to the adrenaline rushing through every vein in my body and the hyperawareness it gave me, I was pretty sure I could hear a sound so soft it was barely audible.

I immediately knew what it was. It was the sound of someone breathing.

Someone close.

"Hello?" I called out again. By this point, I was certain somebody else was there. Either that or the walls had come to life.

No response.

"I know there's someone here," I said. "Mrs. Moody? Is that you?"

She, after all, was the number-one lurker around here. If anyone was an expert at sneaking up on people, it was her.

Again, no one spoke. And the sound of breathing seemed to have stopped.

At least until I suddenly heard what sounded like a gasp for breath.

It was right behind me.

Instinctively I whirled around. But before I had a chance to see who was standing behind me, I felt a whoosh of air.

Suddenly, everything went dark. Despite my shock, I quickly realized that something else was going on. I couldn't breathe.

Someone was trying to smother me.

Chapter 16

Blue Bunny Ice Cream dates back to 1913, when
Fred H. Wells of Iowa bought a horse-drawn
wagon and an existing milk delivery route for
$250. Around 1925, he and his sons started
manufacturing ice cream and selling it locally.
While Fairmont Ice Cream bought the distribution
system and the Wells name in 1925, a decade later
the Wells family decided to sell ice cream again.
Since they couldn't use the name "Wells," they
held a "Name That Ice Cream" contest in the
Sioux City Journal. "Blue Bunny" won, submitted
by a man who had noticed how much his son
liked the blue bunnies in a department store's
Easter display window.

—*https://en.wikipedia.org/wiki/Wells_Enterprises*

Frantically I pawed at my face, trying not to panic. I was so
shocked by what had just happened, and so totally disoriented, that I was only vaguely aware of a noise behind me:
the creaking of the ancient wooden floor that was beneath
the thick carpeting, the kind of sound made by footsteps.

Fortunately, the footsteps were going in the opposite direction, growing softer and softer—a sign that whoever was
making them was moving farther and farther away.

But at the moment, I was much more focused on being able to breathe. Even though only a few seconds had passed since I had been attacked from behind, I was starting to panic. Suddenly having no access to oxygen is one of those things that instantly takes away someone's ability to think fast. And the advice that my best friend and yoga aficionado Willow was always giving me during times of great stress, which was to take deep cleansing breaths, wasn't doing me much good at the moment.

As I tore at whatever was covering my face, I could feel my fingertips making contact with what felt like smooth fabric. Unyielding fabric. I pulled at it, yanking it from side to side, but I couldn't manage to tear it.

Don't panic, I told myself. Still, I was having more and more difficulty following my own advice.

I kept pulling, trying to wrench off whatever was covering my face. By that point, I was definitely in panic mode. Which meant I wasn't even close to thinking straight.

And then, totally by chance, my fingers brushed against what I immediately realized was the bottom edge of whatever it was that had been enveloping my entire head.

The culprit was shaped like a bag, something I instantly understood that I should have known from the very start. Otherwise, how else would someone have been able to jam it over my head?

In the end, pulling the thing off was simple. As soon as I did, I spent a few seconds gasping for breath. I realized that only a moment or two had passed since I'd been sneaked up on from behind. Even so, I couldn't remember the last time the simple act of breathing had felt so good.

I held the bag in my hands, staring at it in the dim light. I immediately knew what it was: one of the laundry bags that Mohawk supplied its guests with. I remembered Mrs. Moody pointing it out to me after she'd shown me to my room and telling me about the resort's laundry service. Now that I was studying it up close, I saw that it was a dark blue bag made of something that looked like cloth but was lined with some kind of plastic.

When I'd first encountered it, I'd barely given it a glance. It hadn't occurred to me that anyone might find it a handy tool for scaring the pants off somebody. Yet that was exactly how it had just been used: to send me a warning.

And there was no doubt in my mind who that had been: the person who had killed Bethany La Montaine.

Someone must have been listening in a few minutes ago when I was talking to Jake about everyone on my list of suspects, I thought. Or maybe that person was listening in on one of the other conversations I'd had with Jake about Bethany and her possible killers. Or perhaps that someone had been hovering outside the phone booth when I'd been on the phone with Emma, taking in every word I said.

Here I've been comparing this resort with the mansion in that scary movie The Haunting, *I thought.* In the movie, the walls had eyes. But here at Mohawk, it turns out that the walls have *ears.*

I let myself into my room, carrying the plastic-lined bag with me. As soon as I got inside, I slammed the door shut and quickly locked it. A great sense of relief washed over me. But at the same time, I couldn't ignore the fact that the murderer, whoever it was, was well aware that I was doing everything I could to figuring out his or her identity.

I dropped the offending laundry bag onto the floor and sprawled across the bed on my back. Then I threw my arm over my face melodramatically like the heroine in a silent movie.

Think! I ordered myself. *Who might have been following me when I crossed the lobby after my argument with Jake?*

At the time I thought I sensed someone's presence, but I'd

been too distracted to give it much thought. Now, I realized that I should have paid closer attention.

I was still desperately trying to do a mental reenactment of every single moment that had passed since Jake and I had parted ways, when I gradually became aware of something strange in the room. It wasn't a noise. It wasn't anything visual, like a shadow, either.

Instead, it was a smell.

A faint smell. But a very distinctive smell.

A smell so subtle that most people probably wouldn't even have noticed it.

But *I* noticed it.

I bolted upright, my heart pounding wildly. Reaching down, I grabbed the laundry bag off the floor, stuck it directly under my nose, and inhaled deeply.

A revelation shot through me like a bolt of lightning. Just like that, I knew who had killed Bethany La Montaine.

What now? I wondered.

I had been in this situation before. On a few other occasions, I had managed to figure out who the culprit had been in a murder even before the homicide detective who was working on the case had. That was what could happen when a determined person like me started poking around and asking questions and struggling to make connections. And based on my past experience, I knew that one of the most useful things I could do was get the killer to confess while secretly recording our conversation on my cell phone.

But I also knew that accomplishing that would involve confronting the murderer and revealing that I had figured out, well, whodunnit.

There was another option, of course. And that was to do nothing at all. At least, not until the access road to Mohawk had become accessible once again and the police were able to arrive on the scene. Then, I could tell them what I'd learned.

That's definitely the safer path to follow, I thought. *Especially since we're all still trapped up here in the middle of nowhere with no way out and no idea how much longer it will be before we can regain contact with the outside world.*

Yet the idea of having to pretend that I didn't know what I now knew, finding a way to interact with everyone the same way as before, was nearly impossible to imagine. On top of that was my strong sense of justice. It was gnawing away at me, deep in the pit of my stomach, that difficult-to-shake idea that the person who had committed this horrific crime deserved to have their identity revealed—the sooner, the better.

I was still trying to decide what to do with my sudden revelation when I heard a strange sound. Glancing over in the direction from which it had come, I saw that it was exactly what I had thought it was: the sound of someone slipping something under my door.

A piece of white paper.

I jumped off the bed and dashed toward the door. Pausing only a moment to consider whether what I was about to do was foolhardy, I quickly unlocked it and opened it, just a little.

From what I could see, there was nobody outside in the hallway. No sound of footsteps, either.

I took a deep breath, then flung open the door to get a better look.

No one.

Whoever had pushed this piece of paper under my door was a master at disappearing.

So I immediately slammed the door shut, locked it up tight, and picked up the paper.

A note? I thought, crossing the room and dropping into

the rocking chair. *Or maybe Mrs. Moody slipped the bill under the door, the way they sometimes do in hotels . . . ?*

Then I remembered that I wouldn't be getting a bill. After all, part of the deal had been getting free room and board the whole time I was at Mohawk.

By that point, I had picked up the piece of paper and begun studying it. I immediately saw that it was a note from Jake.

Sorry about the way things ended before, was written across the page in big, boxy letters. *I want to make it up to you. Meet me at the maze as soon as you can.*

It took me a few seconds to realize that I was wearing a big smile. Jake had shown this romantic side of himself before and, as always, I was tickled. Bethany La Montaine's murder was going to have to wait.

And that's probably just as well, I decided. *Not doing anything until the police can get here really is the best way to proceed, given the situation. After all, confronting the killer on my own is bound to be bad for my health.*

Besides, joining Jake on a surprise adventure sounded like much more fun than dealing with a murderer.

I stepped into the bathroom, where I gave my hair a few quick swipes with my hairbrush and checked my teeth for any unwelcome intruders. Then I headed out, taking care to grab my warm coat and my umbrella.

As I embarked on my impromptu romantic rendezvous, my heart felt all fluttery. I was happier than I would have expected about Jake's anxiousness to smooth things over.

And yet . . .

There was something about the way this had all played out that I couldn't ignore. Something that made me . . . well, suspicious.

So I decided that before hurrying out, I would take a minute or two to do one more thing.

* * *

I'd been thinking that meeting Jake at the maze would be romantic. I could pretend I was an English duchess, or maybe a baroness, sneaking off to a secret assignation with a count. Preferably one who looked great in a white wig and a pair of tight satin pants.

Instead, I was miserable as I stood outside in the gray drizzle that had unfortunately returned, huddled under an umbrella that undoubtedly meant well but still wasn't doing a particularly impressive job of keeping me dry. I was shivering and my feet were damp. Even Mrs. Moody's hot chocolate was starting to sound good.

And Jake was nowhere in sight. I peered through the fog, wishing his note had been a little more specific about exactly where we were supposed to meet.

"Jake?" I called.

My voice was sucked into the raw air. Even I could barely hear myself. I realized that I was going to have to be a bit more proactive. So I pulled the collar of my coat up a little higher, stepped around a giant puddle, and headed into the maze.

How hard can this be? I thought as I took a few steps along a fairly wide walkway. I was immediately swallowed up by tall hedges on both sides. At first, they seemed pretty. But before long, I started to feel just a tad claustrophobic.

That feeling was intensified when I reached a decision point. The initial path suddenly divided, offering me a left turn option and a right turn option. Having no idea which way to go, I chose to go right.

I took a few more steps, not exactly moving with anything that could be considered confidence. I was still hoping to stumble upon Jake. Who would hopefully be carrying a flask of hot chocolate. Or maybe something that actually tasted good.

Was it my imagination or was the path actually getting narrower and narrower?

"Jake?" I called again. This time, the hedges seemed diabolically delighted to swallow up the sound of my voice.

Okay, forget about the flask, I thought grimly. *He can even jump out from behind a gigantic bush and yell, "Boo!" and I'd be fine with that.*

By that point, I'd reached another decision point. Right or left. It sounded simple enough, but making a choice suddenly seemed monumental. This time, I picked left.

I was nearly positive that the pathway was getting narrower. Either that or my shoulders were inexplicably growing larger, for some bizarre reason jutting out like a football player's—or like someone wearing the jacket from one of those power suits from the 1980s.

"Jake, this isn't funny!" I called. I could hear the desperation in my voice. Unfortunately, it didn't seem as if anyone else was around to hear anything at all.

The fact that the rain was becoming more intense didn't help matters. Instead of an annoying drizzle, it was moving into torrential territory. Or at least sheeting. My feet were no longer merely damp. By this point, they were what is popularly known as soaking wet.

I reached another decision point and just for the heck of it turned left. It wasn't long before I came across another decision point, then another. By that point, I'd stopped keeping track of which way I chose to go.

I was starting to wonder if it was time to forget all about meeting up with Jake and instead simply go back inside, when a gust of wind suddenly came from out of nowhere. Before you could say "Mary Poppins," it turned my umbrella inside out, snapping one of the thin metal spines. That meant that once I pulled it back into its correct shape, one of the panels flapped downward.

The rain couldn't have been happier. It now had a much better shot at completely saturating its target.

It was definitely time to give up.

But at that moment, I suddenly caught sight of what was ahead.

A clearing.

The hedges seemed to magically part, opening up into a space that was large enough for a small table and two chairs. Not that those things were actually there, but that was fine given the fact that this wasn't exactly picnic weather. Still, the openness of the clearing struck me as a welcome relief from the ever-narrowing path and the constant turn-right-turn-left decisions and the oppressive hedges that were getting more and more comfortable with the idea of pressing themselves into me so they could slather me with cold wet rain from their evil leaves.

So I walked a few more steps, heading directly into the clearing.

I'd barely stepped inside it when I heard the rustling of leaves behind me. And then, before I had a chance to turn around, I felt someone grab me from behind in a chokehold.

But my assailant only used one arm to grasp me around the neck. The other one was used to clasp a knife. A sharp knife.

A knife that was held against my throat so tightly that I could feel it cutting into my skin.

Chapter 17

"The Baskin-Robbins ice cream parlors started as separate ventures of Burt Baskin and Irv Robbins, who owned Burton's Ice Cream Shop (opened in 1946) and Snowbird Ice Cream (opened in 1945), respectively. Snowbird Ice Cream offered 21 flavors, a novel concept at that time. When the separate companies merged in 1948, the number of flavors was expanded to 31 flavors."

—*https://en.wikipedia.org/wiki/Baskin-Robbins*

Sneak up on me from behind once, shame on you. Sneak up on me from behind twice, shame on—well, you know how that saying goes.

So did I. Which is why I felt like a fool as I stood there lost in the middle of a maze with Bethany La Montaine's murderer, a very sharp knife, and a dribble of blood running down my neck.

Here I'd been trying to figure out how to trap Bethany's killer. Instead, she had trapped me.

But at the moment I was feeling a lot more than foolish. Like *terrified*, for example.

"Don't move," I heard Franny hiss in my ear, her breath hot against my skin.

As if I had any intention of doing that, given the situation, I thought.

I realized then that she was still immersed in a cloud of bad-smelling perfume, the fallout from Yoko's disastrous new line of beauty products. It was the same smell I'd noticed on the laundry bag that had been used to smother me, or at least to scare me.

So I was right, I thought, giving myself ten points for my superlative investigative skills. *It is Franny who killed Bethany!* But almost immediately I realized that I had to take away a few points for walking straight into the trap she had set for me.

I stood frozen to the spot, my eyes cast downward so I could keep an eye on the knife in her hand. The one that was digging into my flesh. In a particularly vulnerable spot, no less.

While most of the handle was covered by Franny's hand, I could see enough of the thing to get a good look at it. Even though it looked familiar, it took me a few seconds to place it.

The last time I'd seen that knife, it had been in the hand of the mannequin depicting a Lenape warrior in Mohawk's lobby. I immediately surmised that it was also the knife that had been used to kill Bethany.

Which meant that despite her image as a woman who was somewhat lost, someone uncertain, and somewhat *nice*, Franny Schneffer was someone who wasn't afraid to use a sharp object in a most undesirable way.

"I was expecting Jake, not you," I said. I was attempting to normalize this bizarre situation by making conversation, the best way I knew of reminding her that I was an actual person. Not surprisingly, my words came out as gasps. Which meant I wasn't sounding even close to normal.

"Jake isn't here," she said. She seemed to be having no trouble at all speaking in a normal voice, which given how close her mouth was to my ear, sounded like a shout. "He isn't coming, either. He doesn't know anything about you and me meeting up here. No one does."

This wasn't exactly what I'd call a meeting, but I wasn't about to argue. Instead, I just nodded. As I did, I could feel the blade press more closely against my flesh.

"So I guess he's not the one who actually wrote that note," I said. "I suppose you know that he and I had kind of an argument, and I really believed that—"

"You knew that I killed Bethany, didn't you?" she said accusingly. Her voice was back to sounding like a snake's. "You figured it all out."

"No!" I lied. "It's true that I was trying to solve the mystery of who killed Bethany La Montaine. But that doesn't mean I actually managed to accomplish that."

She tightened her grip, causing me to lurch backward. "But you knew all about my connection to her," she insisted. "You found out that Gloria La Montaine was my birth mother, which means that Bethany and I were half sisters. I'm sure the fact that I had stronger ties to her than anyone else here put me high on your list of suspects in this nosy little investigation of yours."

"I did know that you and Bethany were half-sisters," I admitted. After all, she clearly knew that I knew, so I figured there was no point in lying. At least not about that. "But how did *you* know?"

Franny laughed coldly. "Merle Moody is such a know-it-all. She thought the story behind my adoption was such a big secret. But what she *didn't* know was that my adoptive parents told me who my birth mother was on my twenty-first birthday. They'd decided that I was old enough to know the truth. They wanted me to know about my mother's identity because she had turned out to be such a huge success. They thought it would give me more confidence. Make me feel more important.

"And it's true that at first, I was fascinated. I began following Gloria La Montaine's career from that point on, admiring her and cheering her on from the sidelines. But at some point, the story of my past started to make me angry. Gloria and her daughter Bethany were having such a wonderful life. And mine was so, well, *ordinary.*"

"I'm sure that was difficult for you," I said as calmly as I could, "and I'd really like to hear more about it. So why don't you put down the knife so we can talk about all this without—"

"Don't you understand?" Franny cried. "Bethany La Montaine ended up leading the life that *I* was supposed to lead! *I* was supposed to be her. *I'm* the one who should have grown up in a Park Avenue apartment, going to fancy schools, traveling and eating in expensive restaurants, wearing fancy designer clothes . . . *I* should have had a life of being rich and spoiled and happy!"

Her tone was rancid with bitterness as she added, "Bethany was born with a silver spoon in her mouth while I was born with no spoon at all. My adoptive parents are great people, and of course I love them. But I had to struggle for everything I had. She, meanwhile, had every single thing handed to her. I worked one or two jobs the whole time I was in school. I bought my clothes at thrift stores. My idea of fine dining was splurging on dessert at Applebee's. As for travel, the farthest away I've ever been is Disney World, a special trip my family took to celebrate my eighth birthday."

"It's true that Bethany had a pretty nice life," I agreed, doing my best to sound as if I was on Franny's side. "But you're grown up now. You can live anywhere and any way you want. You said yourself that you're going to move to New York and start a whole new chapter of your life. What difference will it make that she's gone?"

As soon as the words came out of my mouth, I understood. That had been Franny's plan all along. In her mind, she wasn't going to simply show up in New York City and create a new life for herself. She was going to announce herself to Gloria and move into the life that used to be Bethany's. She was going to become the *substitute* Bethany.

Apparently I was right.

"Because now, finally, it's my turn," Franny replied. "Now that Bethany is gone, Gloria—the woman who's *my* mother as well as Bethany's—can start treating *me* like a daughter. It's *me* she'll hand her cosmetics empire over to. It's *me* she'll mentor, teaching me everything she knows. It's *me* who will eventually inherit everything she owns: her posh apartment, her Rolls-Royce, and all the other wonderful things she's acquired."

I didn't remember anyone saying anything about a Rolls-Royce, but I wasn't about to quibble.

"But there's something even more important," Franny went on. "I'll finally *be* somebody. Instead of drab, boring, mousy Frances Schneffer, I'll become Francesca La Montaine. I think Francesca is a much more appropriate name for someone who presides over a glamorous cosmetics company, don't you? I'll be someone who sits at the head of the conference table at board meetings and tells everybody around me what to do. I'll be somebody who goes to the Met Gala in a gorgeous evening gown and sits in a box at the opera and the ballet. I'll do everything I've ever dreamed of, from traveling to eating in fabulous restaurants to shopping at designer boutiques . . . not only in New York but all over the world!"

Her voice became dreamy as she said, "I've got it all planned out. I've pictured the entire scene in my mind a million times. I'll show up at Gloria's apartment, dressed up in some wonderful outfit I bought at a Madison Avenue boutique, with my hair just cut and blow-dried and a professional makeup job. And I'll tell her, 'I'm so sorry for your loss. I know you loved Bethany. But there's a silver lining. I'm your other daughter! I'm here to replace her!' "

Franny's use of the word "replace" made me cringe. As if one person could replace another! And of course the fact that Franny had murdered Bethany, causing their mother untold grief, only made the ridiculous situation she was imagining that much more ghoulish.

But I wasn't about to argue with her. Not when she was still holding that knife against my throat.

"It sounds like a very solid plan," I told her, doing my best to keep my voice from wavering. "And I promise that I won't say a word to anyone—"

"Not so fast," Franny interrupted. "First I have to complete the other part of my plan. Which is getting rid of the one person who was smart enough to figure out that it was me who killed Bethany."

"But aren't you forgetting about the police and the investigation they'll carry out as soon as the road clears?" My mind raced as I desperately tried to come up with viable arguments for her not killing me. "I mean, you clearly managed to pull off the perfect crime when you killed Bethany. You could probably get away with it. But if you killed me, too, there's a good chance the police would figure out that you committed both murders, Bethany's *and* mine!"

I could hardly believe that I was calmly discussing my own murder with the person who was holding a knife at my throat.

"Ah, but that's the beauty of being at a place like Mohawk," Franny announced triumphantly. "There are millions of cliffs and ravines and all kinds of treacherous spots all around this huge mountainous preserve."

"That's true," I said. But at this point, I had realized that I really had to start focusing on stalling for time. "But what does that have to do with me?"

"I think you're clever enough to know that jumping to

your death is better than the alternative," she replied. "It's much less painful. So you and I are about to take a little hike. You and me and this wonderful antique knife, which is my insurance policy that you'll go along with my plan. Then, once we've found the perfect spot, you'll 'accidentally' fall. Later on, at dinner or tea or whatever, when you fail to turn up, I'll tell everyone that I spotted you earlier today going out for a hike in this horrible fog." With a little shrug, she added, "Chances are that your body will never be found. That is, whatever is still left of you after you've fallen a few hundred feet!"

I shuddered. The scenario that Franny had laid out for my impending demise was horrific enough to chill anyone to the bone. Especially the person who was playing the lead role in it.

"Franny, none of this is going to work," I said. By this point, I was *really* stalling for time. After all, I'd come up with a plan of my own. And so far, it wasn't going nearly as well as hers seemed to be going.

Which was why a tremendous wave of relief rushed over me as soon as I heard a voice not far in the distance.

"Ms. McKay?" Tarleton called. "Are you lost? I know this place can be kind of tricky, even though I know every single inch of it. I've spent hours and hours in this maze. I'm ready to give you that tour, if you'll just say something to let me know where you are."

I didn't have to. A second or two later, Tarleton burst into the clearing. He was dressed in a black rain slicker, covered from head to ankles, carrying two umbrellas. He held one of them over his head, while the second one was in his hand.

I couldn't remember the last time I'd been so happy to see someone.

"There you are!" he cried. "Look, I brought you an extra umbrella, since—" He stopped, frowning. Then he demanded,

"What's going on here? Why do you have a big knife, Franny? And why are you holding it against Kate's neck like that? You could really hurt her! And isn't that the knife from the history exhibit in the lobby?" His expression was stern as he concluded, "It looks to me like something really bad is happening here."

"There's nothing bad happening," Franny replied. She had already let go of me, stepping over to my side and dropping her arm so she could put the knife behind her back in an attempt at hiding it. "Nothing at all, Tarleton. Aside from Kate and me playing a little game, that is."

Tarleton looked confused. "A game with a knife? That sounds like a pretty scary game. I think I better tell my mom—I mean, Mrs. Moody—about this. She won't like it that you took that knife, either, Franny. It's very old and very important."

"I think you should tell your mother, Tarleton," I said. "I think you should tell everyone you can about what you saw here."

He nodded gravely. "I will," he said. "And I don't think Franny should come on the tour with us."

"The tour?" Franny repeated. "What is this tour you keep talking about?" She was back to sounding like her old self. The shy, uncertain self I had seen before the demonic side of her had come out.

"Kate left me a note on the desk in the office, saying she wanted me to take her on a special tour, just like I offered," Tarleton said. "She told me to meet her here in the maze as soon as I could."

He thought for a second, then added, "And in exchange for me giving you a tour, you promised to tell me a special secret about ice cream, right? Something that nobody else knows but you?"

"It's a fabulous secret," I told him. But I took advantage of

Franny's moment of distractedness by grabbing her arm and squeezing it as tightly as I could. Just as I'd hoped, she reacted by dropping the knife.

"That knife is too valuable to be on the ground like that!" Tarleton cried, stepping over to pick it up.

But I was faster. "We'll need this just as it is," I said as I grabbed it, "without any additional fingerprints on it." I retrieved a crumpled tissue from my pocket and used it to hold the knife at one end. I knew it was going to play a big role in helping convict Frances Schneffer of Murder One.

I was still holding the knife gingerly when another voice suddenly cut through the raw gray air. "Tarleton? What are you doing out here? For heaven's sake, you're going to catch your death of cold—"

Suddenly Mrs. Moody appeared in the clearing, looking distraught. She had thrown a raincoat over her shoulders, but otherwise looked totally unprepared for the rain that was doing such a fine job of drenching all four of us.

"Tarleton!" she cried, sounding as commanding as—well, as commanding as a mother who had just caught her son doing something he shouldn't have been doing. "Why are you out here with these two? In the pouring rain, no less! And what on earth is that knife doing here? Isn't that the one from the Lenape statue?"

"Franny was doing bad things with it," Tarleton replied before I had a chance to say a word. "She was holding it right up against Kate's neck. She said it was a game, but I thought it looked like she could hurt her. That maybe she even *wanted* to hurt her."

"Tarleton is right," I said. "That was no game. In fact, Franny confessed to killing Bethany La Montaine."

All three of us looked over at Franny. She looked like a rag doll that had been left outside on the lawn overnight and was going to need a long stint in a clothes dryer to get back to looking even close to its old self.

"Not Franny!" Mrs. Moody cried. "But that's impossible! It couldn't have been Franny! Surely there's been a mistake!"

Her words had the effect of energizing Franny. "Why not?" she demanded. "Because you don't think I'm strong enough to take matters into my own hands? Because I'm not clever enough? Not *daring* enough?"

Sticking her chin high up in the air, she announced, "There's no mistake. I *did* kill Bethany. And I have no regrets. It was time for me to stop being such a wimp, to take control of my own life—"

"Besides, Kate never makes a mistake," boomed a male voice.

Someone else had just come into the clearing, edging his way into the small space. It was starting to feel very crowded in there.

"Jake!" I cried. "You're just in time. We were all about to escort Franny back into the building."

"Good idea," he replied. "I don't know if any of you have noticed, but it's raining."

"We noticed," I said. "But it was worth getting wet since we also learned that Franny killed Bethany."

"I know," Jake said. "I heard her confess."

"And here's the knife she used to do it," I added. "She planned to use it one more time, too, which is why she lured me out here."

Jake wasted no time in going over to Franny and taking hold of her arm. "Let's go inside," he said. "Mrs. Moody, is there a place where we can keep Franny under lock and key until we can get the police up here?"

"There certainly is," Mrs. Moody replied. She still looked a bit shocked by everything that had happened. Frankly, I didn't blame her. "I know the perfect spot."

I wasn't surprised. In fact, I wouldn't have been surprised if it turned out to be something along the lines of a dungeon.

By this point, I was more than ready to go inside. Bethany's murder had been solved and the criminal had been caught. A sense of peace had washed over me, as palpable as the cold rain that by this point had soaked every item of clothing I was wearing. The top three or four layers of my skin, too.

Still holding on to Franny tightly, Jake glanced around.

"Now that we're all in here in the middle of this crazy maze," he asked, "is anybody clever enough to know how to get us *out*?"

That was when Tarleton stepped forward, wearing a big grin that was so bright that it shined like a beacon through the dreary wetness all around us.

Chapter 18

The Blizzard, soft-serve ice cream blended with other ingredients, was first introduced by Dairy Queen in 1985. More than 100 million Blizzards were sold that year. Popular flavors include Oreo cookies, chocolate chip cookie dough, and Butterfinger, known as Crispy Crunch in Canada. Dairy Queen also offers such seasonal flavors as pumpkin pie in October and cotton candy in June.

—https://en.wikipedia.org/wiki/Dairy_Queen

As soon as our scraggly, sopping wet troupe tromped into the lobby, my heart nearly exploded with joy. Standing near the front door, chatting with Naveen, were two men in work boots and puffy orange vests.

"We've been freed!" I cried, rushing over.

"Yes, ma'am," one of the workmen replied. "It took us a pretty long time to cut up that tree, but the access road is finally passable."

I was about to thank them profusely when the front door opened behind them. My reaction to the arrival of two more men was even more gleeful.

"We're responding to a nine-one-one call we received," one of the police officers announced.

"Just in time," Mrs. Moody replied. But instead of sounding triumphant, or even relieved, she sounded sad.

It was only now, with the ordeal that we had all just gone through finally over, that I was able to think about the implications for Mrs. Moody. Here she had been trying to do a good deed by bringing two long-separated half sisters together. Yet the consequences had been devastating. Deadly, in fact.

That old saying about no good deed going unpunished had never rung more true.

As Jake brought the forlorn-looking Franny over to the two police officers, Mrs. Moody led Tarleton away. I was glad they had each other to lean on.

Meanwhile, Naveen came right over to me, his eyebrows knit in concern.

"Is it true that Franny is the person who killed Bethany?" he asked me, his voice filled with disbelief.

"That's right," I told him. I decided not to tell him that she had had plans to do the same to me. At least, not right now.

"It is difficult to believe she was capable of such a terrible thing," Naveen said, shaking his head slowly.

"That's because you're one of those people who sees the best in everyone," I replied. Smiling warmly, I added, "One of your best traits, I might add."

"I do try to do that," Naveen agreed. He sighed, then added, "This explains why Franny was the first person at the scene of the crime," he commented. "Here I had been feeling sorry for her that she was so traumatized. Yet it turns out that she was the *reason* there was a scene of the crime in the first place."

He was silent for a few moments, then in a soft voice said, "I was involved in something like this once before. It was a truly traumatizing experience. It left such a scar on me that I actually changed my name legally, just to escape from the bad feelings that lingered from the incident. To keep myself out of the public eye, as well."

Before I had a chance to comment, movement near the front door caught my attention. I glanced over just in time to see the two police officers leading Franny away. In handcuffs. The sight was jolting.

But it also drove home the point that this horrific weekend had finally come to an end.

"Okay, folks," one of the workmen announced. "The road is now officially open. It's safe to leave whenever you want."

Naveen turned to me. "If you will excuse me, I think I will return to my room and pack up my things. I would like nothing more than to leave this place."

"I think we all feel that way," I replied.

"I know I do," Jake said as he came over. "I'll get my things and we can meet back here in about ten minutes so we can get on the road."

"Okay," I agreed. But as he started to leave, I said, "Jake, we need to talk." I took a deep breath. "You're right. I do have reservations about being in a relationship."

In an attempt at softening my words, I added, "And it's not about you. It's about being in a relationship with anyone. So much in my life is in upheaval right now. In the past nine months, I've given up the life I'd been totally happy with for years. I left the city I lived in and loved, having my very own apartment, my demanding but exhilarating job . . . I'm a completely different person than I was a year ago! Or at least the same person in an entirely different life. And now, the idea of adding someone into my life, and not just anyone but someone who has the potential to put me smack in the middle of a serious relationship . . ."

"I get it," Jake said softly. "I do. And I realize I have to be more patient."

"It's a lot to ask," I said.

"It is," he agreed. "But the stakes are high. I want you in my life, Kate. I'm not about to walk away from the chance to have what at this point seems like the most important thing."

Just then the front door opened again. Actually, this time, it was more like it *burst* open.

The sight of these two arrivals set off fireworks of joy in my heart.

"Aunt Kate!" Emma cried as she rushed over, her mass of curly black hair streaked with blue streaming behind her like a cape.

"There you are, Katydid!" exclaimed Grams, who was right behind her.

As I returned Emma's big hug, I said, "What are you two doing here? How did you know the road was open again?"

"I've been checking this great website I found that has updates on all kinds of local news," Emma explained. "And as soon as I saw that they were working on clearing that fallen tree away, I said to Grams, 'Let's get in the car and drive up to Mohawk, just for the fun of it!'"

Her eyes were shining as she asked, "How has the weekend been? Fabulous, I hope!"

"It's been ... memorable," I replied. Glancing over at Jake, I added, "In lots of ways."

"I'll say," Jake agreed. "You're not going to believe what went on here. Kate got involved in—"

"In so many fun things!" I interrupted. "I taught the group how to make ice cream without a special ice cream maker and—and how to make that thin chocolate shell that you can put on top of ice cream, and how to make amazing ice cream–based desserts that none of them had ever heard of."

"That's right," Jake agreed. "She did all those things. It was a totally relaxing and enjoyable weekend from start to finish." I was pretty sure that no one else but me noticed the twinkle in his eye.

I would tell Grams and Emma about what had really gone on this weekend. Eventually. But not right now. At the moment, I was too busy simply savoring the moment.

Lemon Ice Cream

(Made Without an Ice Cream Maker)

Just as Kate says in her workshop, it's possible (and easy!) to make ice cream without an "official" ice cream maker. While in this recipe bottled lemon juice will work just fine, using fresh juice and real lemon zest really gives this ice cream a punch.

1 cup heavy cream
1 cup milk
⅞ cup sugar (add more or less, to taste)
Juice from 2 lemons (about ¼ cup)
1 Tablespoon of grated lemon zest
Touch of salt

Using a whisk, mix the sugar, salt, lemon juice, and lemon zest in a large bowl. In a separate bowl, combine the cream and milk, then slowly whisk into the lemon mixture. Keep whisking for about two minutes until the mixture is smooth and the sugar has completely dissolved.

Pour into an 8-inch metal baking pan and cover with aluminum foil. Freeze for two to three hours until it is firm around the edges but still soft in the middle. Give it a good stir, cover the pan with the foil again, and return it to the freezer for another hour. Once the entire mixture is firm, enjoy!

Serving tip: Lemon ice cream is divine when topped with a splash of raspberry-flavored balsamic vinegar. Yum!

Kulfi

Kulfi is the Indian version of ice cream. It dates back to the Mughal Empire, which was founded on the Indian subcontinent in the early 1500s. Kulfi is different from more traditional ice creams in that it isn't churned during preparation.

This basic yet tasty recipe takes under a half hour to prepare (not including freezing). It yields about a dozen servings. The hint of cardamom gives this refreshing treat a slightly exotic flavor, making it a delightfully surprising finale for any meal.

4 cups whole milk
1½ cups dried milk powder
1 14-ounce can of sweetened condensed milk
Additional sugar (optional, to taste)
½ to 1 teaspoon cardamom (to taste)
Pinch of saffron (optional)
1½ Tablespoons cornstarch (optional)
½ cup chopped pistachio or cashew nuts

In a saucepan, heat the whole milk. While stirring, add the condensed milk, then the dry milk powder. Heat the mixture to a boil. Add the cardamom and saffron and additional sugar, if desired. Lower the heat and continue stirring for another ten to twenty minutes until the mixture thickens. (The cornstarch can be added to help with thickening.)

Remove the mixture from heat and let it cool completely. Once it is cool, stir in the nuts. Pour the mixture into small cups. (Paper cups are ideal, especially with a wooden popsicle stick stuck in the middle. Another idea is pouring the mixture into a cupcake tin lined with cupcake papers.) Cover with aluminum foil and freeze. Enjoy!

Variations: For Mango Kulfi, stir about two cups of pureed mango into the basic mixture once it has cooled. Strawberries also work well. Fresh fruit is preferable but frozen fruit, thawed at least enough to be pureed, works just as well.

Frozen Zabaglione

Zabaglione is a custard made with egg yolks, sugar, and a sweet dessert wine—traditionally, marsala. It is also known as zabayon or sabayon. It is believed to date back to the court of the Medici in Florence, Italy, in the sixteenth century.

While zabaglione is usually served warm, it can also be frozen. Because the alcohol doesn't freeze, this luxurious dessert has a wonderful silky texture. Instead of marsala wine, sweet sherry can be used. Another option is a bubbly wine like prosecco, cava, or champagne.

Try topping the zabaglione with fresh fruit, such as strawberries, raspberries, peaches, or poached pears. Nuts, especially toasted almonds, give it a bit of crunch. This recipe makes about 6 servings.

6 egg yolks
⅓ to ½ cup sugar
¾ cup sweet dessert wine, sherry, or prosecco
1 teaspoon vanilla extract
A few drops of lemon juice
1 cup heavy cream, whipped
Fruit or nuts for topping

Create an ice bath by half filling a large bowl with ice and a bit of cold water.

In another bowl that's heatproof, whisk together the wine, egg yolks, sugar, and vanilla. Put the bowl over a pan of water that's boiling gently. Whisk the mixture until it becomes thick.

Once it has thickened, remove the bowl from the

stove and put it into the ice bath. Allow the mixture to cool, stirring gently from time to time. Once it has reached room temperature, add the lemon juice and fold in the whipped cream. Put the entire mixture into a covered container and freeze for a minimum of eight hours.

To serve, top the zabaglione with fruit, nuts, or both. *Delizioso!*